THE CHARMSTONE

THE CHARMSTONE

C. C. HARRISON

FIVE STAR

An imprint of Thomson Gale, a part of The Thomson Corporation

THOMSON

GALE™

Detroit • New York • San Francisco • New Haven, Conn. • Waterville, Maine • London

THOMSON

GALE

LIBRARY OF CONGRESS CATALOGING-IN-PUBLICATION DATA

Harrison, C. C.
    The charmstone / C.C. Harrison. — 1st ed.
        p. cm.
    ISBN-13: 978-1-59414-579-7 (alk. paper)
    ISBN-10: 1-59414-579-2 (alk. paper)
    1. Monument Valley (Ariz. and Utah)—Fiction. I. Title.
PS3608.A7833C47 2007
813'.6—dc22   2006038240

First Edition. First Printing: April 2007.

Published in 2007 in conjunction with Tekno Books.

Printed in the United States of America on permanent paper
10 9 8 7 6 5 4 3 2 1

For my VISTA mates Amanda, Tricia and Melissa who shared with me an experience of a lifetime.
To my dear friend Don Mose whose passion for his culture burns with a white-hot flame.
Thank you for all you do.
To the spirit of Monument Valley, and to everyone who lives there, including the *wannabes*.

CHAPTER ONE

Amanda Bell slammed her bedroom door behind her. She'd made up her mind and nothing—*and no one*—was going to change it.

Francina Bell Broadmoor, still beautiful enough to turn a man's glance into a stare, swung the door open and swooped in, continuing the protest the slam had cut off in mid-sentence. Elliott Sheffield, his brow furrowed in a perpetual frown, strode in behind Francina. *Both barrels,* thought Amanda—her fiancé and her mother. She mentally firmed her resolve. She was leaving.

"Amanda, you can't possibly do this. You can't go there."

"Why not, Mother?" Amanda opened the suitcases she'd hauled down from the dressing room shelf.

"Well, really, Amanda. You don't want to go to that godforsaken desolate place in the middle of the desert on an Indian reservation!"

"But, Mother, I do."

"Look, Amanda," Elliott piped, his voice commanding but reasonable. Elliott was always reasonable. *Always.* "It isn't what you think. It's not what you're used to. There's no place to live. There's nothing there but—"

"Indians," Amanda finished for him. "Yes, I know. I want to do it." She slipped a couple of pairs of jeans off hangers, then opened a drawer, took out some T-shirts and shorts, and tossed it all on the bed next to the suitcases.

Francina's loud sigh ended with her lips drawn in a narrow

line of disapproval. "I don't understand why your father would even consider asking you to do such a thing," she said half to herself. "He must have been out of his mind."

Amanda spun from the closet and faced her mother, who looked up at her in surprise.

"But I *want* to do this, Mother." Because she was angry, she couldn't stop her words from breaking on the emotion, and to compensate raised her voice to a shout. "Lord knows it's not like we ever did anything for him while he was alive!"

The room fell silent as her mother and Elliott stared at each other and then at her, astonished by her outburst. Amanda rarely raised her voice. For the most part, she went along to get along, sidestepping confrontation to avoid hurting the feelings of those closest to her. But she was raising it now, and her reaction surprised everyone in the room, including Amanda herself.

She returned to her packing, but not before catching the conspiratorial glance that passed between Elliott and her mother. Next, they would try to stall her. She knew the routine; Elliott and Francina had joined forces in it often enough. Amanda paused in her packing, lifted her eyes to the ceiling, waiting. Three beats passed, and right on cue, her mother spoke.

"Amanda, dear," she said as if placating a bad-tempered two-year-old. "Maybe we should take some time to talk about this."

"You mean talk me out of it, don't you?" In her lavish bathroom, Amanda collected bottles and jars of moisturizers and lotions. They clinked together as she hurriedly placed them in a quilted satin cosmetic traveling case.

"Surely this can wait a few more weeks."

"No, Mother, it can't. The lawyer said Dad's office has already been cleaned out. I have to drive up to the University of Colorado to pick up his things."

Elliott, brow creased with frown lines made permanent by

frequent repetition, hadn't said anything for a long time. He was serious and scholarly looking with blue-gray eyes set in a broad suntanned face. Students filled lecture rooms to standing room only when he presented his seminars on the ethical issues surrounding Native American excavation at UCLA where he was a visiting professor. All the freshman girls fell in love with him. He was interesting and intelligent, and he liked it when she consulted him on things, thereby affirming his superior wisdom. Only this time she hadn't done that, and she knew in his silence he was formulating an argument against her decision.

"Since we are engaged to be married, I think I have a right to say what's on my mind, and you can't—"

"Be quiet, Elliott," she cut him off, exasperated.

He snapped his mouth shut, but he obviously wasn't happy about it, and Amanda ducked her head to avoid his soul-shriveling frown.

"The wedding's next week," her mother put in. "You can't just leave now."

Abruptly, Amanda turned to face them head on, fists to hips, lips pressed tight. Taller than her mother by nearly a foot, and even an inch taller than Elliott, she was a grown-up adult woman with two college degrees and a condo. What made these people think they could control her life as if she were a child? Even in her own home.

"Will you two please stop telling me what I can and cannot do? I'm twenty-seven years old, and it's time I started doing what *I* want to do. And I want to fulfill my father's last request. It's the least I can do!"

In the silence, Elliott cleared his throat, the sound a familiar precursor to the sanctimonious lift of his chin.

"Technically, Amanda, this cannot be considered your father's last request. He hasn't been declared dead. His body hasn't been found. He's missing and *presumed* dead."

This was too much even from Elliott Sheffield, and suddenly she had enough of his smug pomposity. With a quick movement, she slipped the diamond ring off the third finger of her left hand and placed it in his palm, closing his fingers over it.

"Well, *technically,* we're not engaged, so you have nothing to say."

Her mother's eyebrows shot up in surprise, but a look Amanda couldn't read crossed Elliott's face and those blue-gray eyes grew still. Then suddenly they were both talking at once, their voices climbing, one louder than the other, demeaning Amanda's decision, trying to intimidate her into changing her mind.

"Now, look here," Elliott began, self-righteous superiority clipping off the ends of his words.

"You're throwing away your future," Francina implored in her impeccably modulated voice. "You have a prestigious position at the historical museum—"

"I quit yesterday. I forgot to mention it."

"—and a fabulous wedding planned to a wonderful man. Why would you want to go to an Indian reservation in the middle of the desert?"

"It's a ridiculous idea . . ." This from Elliott.

"It's absurd . . ." Mother again.

"It's insane . . ." A mutual opinion.

When they saw Amanda wouldn't be moved by badgering, they appealed to her sense of place in trendy Beverly Hills society, just as she knew they would. It was an argument that might have worked on someone who felt she belonged in that rarified upscale atmosphere, someone who felt she measured up. But Amanda *didn't* belong there.

Hard as she had tried, hard as her mother had tried to force it, Amanda had never fit in with the girls in her crowd—beautiful, petite young women with slender hips and delicate features, expensive boob jobs, and fine silky hair. No one had to tell her that her nose was too long and her mouth too wide, that her lips were too full and her brow too broad. Her thick mane of hair, despite the best efforts of her mother's favorite hairdresser, was unruly much of the time, bunched carelessly in a messy bun on top of her head. And though she wasn't what one would call flat-chested, she was most certainly cleavage deficient. She was a misfit and she knew it.

"What about my friends?" Elliott implored, interrupting the dose of reality in her thoughts. "And my associates at the university? What will I tell them?" He hesitated, then threw in what he apparently thought would be the clincher. "What about your stepfather? Daniel is paying for the wedding. What will he and all *his* friends say?"

Amanda gathered up all six feet of herself, ready to tell Elliott exactly what she thought about all of them, but before she could reply, her mother took on a forlorn expression, and lapsed into the pettish, put-upon voice she always used when she didn't get her own way.

"But, Amanda, what about the caterer?"

Amanda, barely able to suppress a laugh at her mother's transparent ploy, deflated like a balloon that had sprung a leak.

"Bring him on," she said, with a smile, reaching out to give her mother an indulgent hug, "—and have yourselves one hell of a party, because I'm going to the Navajo Reservation in Monument Valley, Utah."

When Amanda crossed the San Juan River into Navajoland, she was stunned speechless. Except for the brilliant blue sky, everywhere she looked was red—the sand, the craggy summits, the steeply inclined rocks leading to sharp-crested ridges, even the water and the river rafts gliding under the bridge.

"How magnificent," she breathed.

Huge vermilion buttes and hobgoblin spires reached toward the heavens like monstrous sentries guarding a sacred place. Charcoal-colored prehistoric volcanic formations punctuated the vista, spiking skyward from the russet flat-topped tableland.

She couldn't keep her eyes on the road, drawn as they were to the surreal desertscape. She veered off the blacktop, set the brake, got out, and walked a little way into the desert.

At the edge of a promontory, she lowered herself onto a slab of rock overlooking a maze of canyons that meandered into the distance. Far away to her left, a rocky, ragged horizon peaked sharply into a cerulean sky. In between was nothing but blinding sun, sagebrush, and an endless expanse of red rock and sand—the utter perfection of absolute nothingness; broad, barren, a little eerie.

The total and complete silence produced a sensation that was new to her, a balm of soothing languor that seeped into her body and mind. Invisible voices carried on the desert breeze seemed to speak to her, and she could almost feel the presence of ancient inhabitants. She began to understand what it was her father had loved about this land and the people who lived here, now as well as those who came before. Swallowing back a hard lump forming in her throat, she resolved to make this trip a lasting legacy to him, a tribute to his memory.

She stood, brushed dust from the seat of her pants, and got back in the Jeep.

Before pulling onto the highway, she checked for oncoming traffic, and waited as an aging flower power van slowed to make the steep incline toward Mexican Hat, a small, sparse desert outpost. The equally aging hippie behind the wheel gave her the peace sign as he went by, and she smiled before driving on in the opposite direction.

Just when she was sure she must have crossed over the Utah

state line into Arizona, she saw it. There, off the highway on the right, tucked into the shadow of a soaring red butte, a low-sprawling building nestled so neatly into the landscape she might have missed it if she hadn't been looking for it.

She turned right, then left over a cattle guard onto a surprisingly modern high school campus that resembled a small community college. What looked like single-story apartments terraced up an incline, rising in measured steps toward a stately red monument.

Guess that's where I'll be living, she thought. Since there's nothing else around.

Lined up front-to-rear along the eastern perimeter of the parking lot, was a row of doublewides, some of which she guessed were portable classrooms. She parked in front of the trailer displaying a sign identifying it as the Navajo Cultural Center, and walked up the steps of a small wooden porch badly in need of paint. The door hung open, so she went inside.

The interior was in chaos. Broken pottery, stone carvings, dusty ceremonial objects, jewelry, and all manner of Native American artifacts were jammed on top, inside, and under display cases. Bows and arrows along with crudely carved flutes were propped in the corner. Pipes, drums, and brightly beaded belts and moccasins spilled out of cabinets and open cardboard boxes.

A man was working on a computer, absorbed. Long jeans-clad legs that didn't fit under the desk stretched out to the side and crossed at the ankles. Tawny, cowhide cowboy boots were molded to his feet.

He looked up when she came in, and stopped his two-fingered typing, but his hands stayed on the keyboard. His shirtsleeves were rolled back over forearms the color of burnished copper. A wide silver watchband studded with chunky turquoise stones circled his wrist.

13

"Can I help you?" he asked. His dark Native eyes set deep in a bronze face flickered inquisitively as they moved over her.

"My name is Amanda Bell," she said. "I'm looking for Durango Yazzie."

He didn't reply but continued to look at her with a penetrating gaze she could almost feel on her skin. Handsome of face, lean of body, but his profound intensity made her uncomfortable.

"My father is . . . was Dr. Maynard Bell. An archaeologist from the University of Colorado," Amanda began under his silent scrutiny. "When he retired, he made an endowment to the Cultural Center, but died before he could bring everything here. So I've been asked to bring it." She couldn't stop herself from lifting her voice at the end of the sentence, like she was making a query instead of stating a fact.

"I'm Durango Yazzie," the man said, and stood.

It surprised her to see that he was taller than her. She usually soared over everyone she met. Their eyes were nearly level. His were black, and so absorbing her thoughts faltered and she stumbled over her words.

"Well, then . . ." Nervously she licked her lips. "You're expecting me then." The bright hopeful tone she tried for trailed off as he continued to watch her.

"No," he said. "I'm not."

He looked over her shoulder through the open door to her Jeep parked out front, the hatchback filled with bulging cartons of books, papers and file folders. She followed his gaze, forcing a smile even as she felt a tiny worry line crease her brow.

"That's the literature collection my father is donating to your Cultural Center," she said, feeling the need to over explain. When he didn't reply, she asked uncertainly, "Didn't Dr. Bell tell you I was coming? He said housing had been arranged for me and workspace would be provided. I'm to stay here and ar-

14

chive the collection."

At that, the expression on Durango's face transformed, going from mild curiosity to utter surprise.

"Here? You mean to stay here?"

Clearly, this was news to him, and she suddenly felt like the worst kind of interloper. A long moment strung out between them during which she was tempted to thrust her father's letter at him to prove she had a right and a reason to be there. Instead, she took it out and read it again to make sure she was at the right place. He was a dark and sullen presence, watching her.

Satisfied, she looked up from the letter. "This is the Navajo Cultural Center, isn't it?"

"Yes, it is."

His voice was a deep, sexy rumble that evoked a fascinating but disconcerting sensation somewhere between her chest and her stomach. It caught her so off guard, she involuntarily averted her gaze and spoke randomly into the air, avoiding his eyes.

"Well, this is where I'm supposed to be," she said, shoving the letter into her shoulder bag. "If you'll just show me to my housing, I'd like to get settled in."

She made an expectant move toward the door, but stopped when he maintained his motionless stance, holding her in an unwavering look. Something was wrong, she could feel it, and her composure slipped. Wiping damp palms on her jeans, she pressed blindly on, hoping to sound assertive rather than desperate.

"If you'll just tell me which one of those apartments is mine and give me a key, I'll stop bothering you and you can get back to work."

"I'm afraid I can't do that," he said.

"Why not?" A vision of her big, comfortable, well-appointed poolside condominium back in Los Angeles flashed to mind, and she felt a vague desire to be there.

"There is no apartment," Durango replied evenly. "The teachers from the high school live in that complex. All the apartments are taken. I'm grateful for your father's donation, but I have no housing for you."

She gaped at him in disbelief and flicked a baleful glance out the window at the endless expanse of rock, sand, and cactus.

"You must have! Where else is there?" In the space of a split second, the beautiful nothingness she'd admired and driven through to get here had taken on a maleficent cast. Then she was struck by another disturbing thought.

"Could you tell me where I'll be working?" she inquired, already dreading his answer.

"No, I can't tell you that, either." Durango's arm swept the interior of the trailer indicating its general state of upheaval. "As you can see, I have no space here."

Exasperated, she lifted her arms and let them fall helplessly at her side. *Well, this is just great! No place to live and no place to work.* She let out a long breath, composing herself before she spoke. There was no point arguing with him.

"Thank you, Mr. Yazzie."

Turning abruptly, she strode out. She had just swung open the Jeep door when Durango called out to her. Squinting against the sun, shielding her eyes from the glare, she turned back.

He'd come outside to stand at the railing of the little wooden porch. His ebony colored hair, sleek and shiny as a crow, lifted gently in the breeze, then settled back to his shoulders.

"If you'll come back tomorrow, I'll see what I can do about arranging workspace for you."

"Thanks," she replied and climbed in her Jeep.

"For nothing," she added sourly as she turned the key in the ignition and punched the accelerator. He didn't say he would have a place for her to work only that he'd see what he could do about finding one. And she still didn't have a place to live.

After Amanda left, Durango hastily pushed around the clutter on his desk, pulling out and examining letters, notes, phone messages. He hadn't received a letter about anyone coming to catalogue a literature collection. Had he?

He frowned and tracked backward in his mind trying to remember, but shook his head, frustrated at the disorder in front of him. If he had any regrets about his UCLA Film School education, it was that it didn't include typing and filing and answering mail.

As he searched the littered desktop, his elbow bumped a three-tiered file tray, jarring loose a pile of papers that slithered off and disappeared into the crack between the desk and the wall. When he pulled the desk out to retrieve them, he saw it wasn't the first time something important had disappeared into that particular black hole. How long had those other letters been down there?

He picked up the wayward items and hurriedly glanced through them—an invitation to speak before the Tribal Council, requests for school field trips, grad students wanting to schedule research time with him, a letter from a production company about filming a commercial in Monument Valley, an unopened letter from his good friend Noah Tucker in Los Angeles. This last he put aside to read later. And, yes, there it was. A letter from Dr. Bell.

He tore open the envelope, pulled out the single sheet of paper and read Dr. Bell's letter requesting that arrangements be made for his daughter's arrival. Durango turned over the envelope and looked at the postmark—a week before Dr. Bell's van crashed and burned in the desert.

He frowned, his thoughts filtering back to the day the wreck was discovered, the memory so clear in his brain, and then not finding a body dead *or* alive. After the owner of the van was identified by the license plate, there had been a vague rumor—quickly squelched—that Dr. Bell had not been driving alone, that there had been a passenger, but no evidence of that ever turned up.

Later, with all the leads played out and nowhere else to look, the overworked Tribal Police had been forced to put the case on the back burner. Further investigation was a low priority.

But as far as Durango was concerned, the investigation had been called off too soon, leaving some important questions unanswered. Not only what happened to Dr. Bell's body, but also what happened to the collection of Native American art and antiquities he was bringing to Monument Valley.

Durango looked back at the letter, read it again, then shrugged in resignation. He couldn't change the fact that housing on the reservation was scarce and besides, he tossed the letter aside, she probably wouldn't be back anyway. He hadn't been any help to her, and preoccupied as he was when she came in, guessed he'd come across as rude. He could tell by the look she gave him when she left that she was mad as hell.

Amanda stopped the Jeep at the edge of the pavement, unsure where to go or which way to turn. First order of business was finding a place to live. She'd stopped for gas at a trading post some twenty miles back and remembered seeing a newspaper office there. Newspapers usually carried classified advertising. Maybe she could find a place to rent that way. Somewhat mollified, she turned left toward Mexican Hat, but as the miles sped by, she began to feel vulnerable and overwhelmed.

Distracted by the scene just played out at the Cultural Center, and by the urgency of finding somewhere to stay before night fell, she didn't see until almost too late a half-dozen cows grazing by the roadside, nor the two that had wandered onto the highway.

When they loomed into view, adrenaline spiraled sharply through her chest, preparing her for the impact as she slammed her foot on the brake. Fueled by momentum, the boxes in the cargo hold flew forward smacking into the back of her seat with a hard thump. The Jeep skidded to a stop just inches from the beefy flank of an animal who didn't flinch, but merely turned its head to gaze at her through the windshield, unperturbed, with huge soulful eyes.

Her racing heart subsided as she waited for the cows to make their unhurried crossing. From then on, she kept her speed down and a close eye out for animals on the open range.

In the dwindling late afternoon light, she noticed the desolation broken by sparse settlements dotting the landscape, trailers and barns and corrals and sheep pens. Most of them were partially hidden—deliberately so, she suspected—behind a roll of land or steep rise of red earth. Well-traveled two-tracks leading from the highway to the desert floor disappeared behind rocks or into canyons. Lights twinkled here and there in the distance, signs of habitation far from the highway.

She made it to the trading post in under thirty minutes, and nosed the Jeep past gas pumps, a mini-mart, a café that didn't look to be open, and a laundromat sagging under the weight of its roof. Off to the side, she spotted the aging flower power hippie van she'd seen on the highway at the Mexican Hat incline. It was parked in front of a door under a wooden signboard that said *Desert Times Weekly*. Lights showed through a dusty plateglass window next to the door.

She parked and went inside. A man sat behind the desk reading a newspaper, but he looked up and smiled when she came in. A nameplate on the desk identified him as Jack Rice, Editor.

"Hi," he said. "How can I help you?"

"Could I buy a newspaper? I need to look at the rental ads."

"Don't think that'll help much." Jack Rice put down the newspaper he was reading, and spoke through a salt-and-pepper beard. "It hasn't been published in over a month. It's a weekly paper, but that doesn't necessarily mean every week, only when I get around to it. Or when an advertiser is able to pay his bill," he quipped.

Disappointed, Amanda's shoulders slumped.

"You new here?" he asked.

She nodded. "Just arrived and I need a place to stay."

"There's a room at the trading post next door," said Jack. "See Bessie inside. She has the key. I'm not sure if it's available or what the rent is, but she'll know."

Amanda hesitated uncertainly. "Are you sure?" she asked. "When I was in there a while ago, the woman behind the counter didn't speak English."

Jack laughed. "Oh, Bessie speaks English," he told her. "She just pretends she doesn't."

Amanda tilted her head at Jack, puzzled. "Why would she do that?"

Her question seemed to amuse him, and he chuckled before answering. "Let's just say the Indians have a natural distrust of authorities. And who can blame them, eh?"

"But I'm not the authorities."

"No, but you're white and an outsider. To some of the Natives, it's the same thing. At least until they get to know you. Don't let Bessie scare you off. Just tell her Jack said it's all right to give you the key."

Amanda thanked him and did as Jack suggested.

Bessie, flashing dark suspicious eyes, said something in a language Amanda didn't understand to a teenaged boy stocking shelves with cans of chili. The boy responded with a few guttural words and a one-shouldered shrug, then went back to his work. Reluctantly, Bessie took a key from a hook on the wall behind her and handed it to Amanda.

"Last door. End of building." She pointed with her chin. "That way. By the laundry. Fifty dollars. In advance."

Amanda gladly paid the first week's rent sight unseen, relieved to have a place, *any* place for the night. Key in hand, she followed Bessie's directions, old boards creaking under her feet, and stopped at a door at the end of the log building. A window in the top half of the door was covered over with what her grandmother used to call oilcloth. The key turned easily in the lock—too easily, she thought—and when the door swung open, she stepped into a darkened room.

A dusty, unused smell drifted to her nostrils, but she was thankful to see a double bed with crisp, clean-looking sheets and fluffy pillows against the far wall. To her left, a card table listed on crooked legs, and in its center was a lopsided lamp, its pleated shade tilted off kilter. Absently, she straightened it.

Two old-fashioned kitchen chairs on either side of the table backed up to the wall. The front window would have looked out on the gas pumps, but it, too, was sealed with the same thick plastic covering. No light entered the room from outside except through the open door.

Leaving it ajar, Amanda flicked on the lamp, walked to the bathroom and peeked in. It smelled faintly of gasoline. A small sink with exposed pipes hung from the wall. Behind the door was a tub with a dingy shower surround, but the white plastic shower curtain was clean and new, the fold lines not yet hung out. Cracks veined the ceiling and there was a spider web in the corner. She dragged a breath and let it out in a rush.

A fifty-dollar-a-week room, no question, but it would have to do until she found something else. She snapped out the light, turned around, and fell back in alarm.

"Oh!" she gasped, and froze.

A man was standing in the open doorway backlit by the bright sunshine streaming in from outside. He stepped over the threshold, his arm raised toward her. Her startled brain didn't understand the significance of the money he held in his hand. Before she could speak or cry out, he spoke.

"Can I pay you for my gas?"

Amanda touched her fingers to her chest, dropped her eyelashes, and heaved a huge sigh of relief. "In the store," she said pointing and forcing a tight, polite smile. "This is a private residence."

"I'm sorry, the door was open . . . I thought . . ." The man backed out, apologizing profusely. She listened to his footsteps recede along the wooden decking. After the screen door leading to the grocery store squeaked open and slammed shut, she quickly closed and latched her own door, knowing it would have to remain so unless she wanted a steady stream of tourists coming in trying to pay for their fill-up.

Okay, so no fresh air or daylight, but at least she had a bed. She sat on the edge of it and looked around gloomily. Elliott was right. This was nothing like what she was used to.

Quickly she squared her shoulders. *This is only a minor setback,* she told herself, and she could handle it. She'd figure something out, because there was no way she was going back. This week would be spent setting up an office and finding another place to live. She'd make it work.

Gamely, she tried to settle in, but as the purple-gray nightfall crept in over the desert, her optimism flagged. The red-hued wilderness she'd found so inviting during the day became infused at night with an ominous inky blackness that cloaked the trading post in muffled, cottony isolation.

After a dinner that consisted of a box of Cheez-Its and a Diet Coke from the grocery store, she undressed for bed. Bone tired and a little chilled, she crawled between fresh-smelling, crisply ironed sheets, and huddled under the warm covers. A clock radio on the decades-old nightstand was tuned to KTNN, a Navajo language station in the middle of a broad band of static. Broadcast fare included country-and-western songs and a mix of traditional and contemporary Native American music, and though she couldn't understand the Navajo-speaking DJs, she enjoyed the music.

It crossed her mind to ask Durango Yazzie to teach her the Navajo language, but she immediately dismissed the idea. He hadn't been overly cooperative so far. Besides living quarters, she had expected a measure of gratitude from him and was disappointed it hadn't been extended. Her mind formed a picture of his face and how his black eyes bored into her, making her feel like an intruder when all she wanted to do was bring a gift.

Sighing, she rolled over, pulling the heavy quilts with her, punching up her pillow into a comfortable headrest, and tried unsuccessfully to erase his image from behind closed eyes. He'd held his head high with pride and sureness, maybe even a touch of arrogance. When he looked at her, his expression had been neither friendly nor hostile, but remote. For some reason, she felt let down by his air of detachment.

No, this hadn't turned out the way she'd expected it would, but she'd give it time, learn the ways of the people, and follow their lead. Only time would tell where that lead would take her.

Amanda woke with a start, all her senses on alert. Her eyes sought the glowing green numerals on the clock beside the bed. Only two-thirty, hours to go before daylight.

Outside, the moon had risen. She could see a silvery skim of light where it slipped in around the edges of the window coverings. She thought she'd heard something and strained to listen, but the silence of the desert was so complete, so absolute, the only discernible sound was the beating of her heart.

When she heard faint scratching at the door, she couldn't tell if it was coming from inside or outside the room. Her heart pounded as she tried to decide which would be the greater peril. Raising herself on one elbow, she held her breath so she could hear better, but silence fell again, pressing like fingers on her eardrums.

Then there was no mistaking it—a scraping at the door. Her heart jumped as a shadow momentarily broke the sliver of moonlight that sliced in along the edge of the oilcloth covering the window. Stricken, she stared at the door.

Swallowing the lump in her throat, she called out, "Who's there?" It came out shrill and frightened, but apparently loud enough to chase whoever it was away.

Footsteps bounded on the decking, then thudded away through soft dirt, fading into the distance. She stared at the door, her body stiff with apprehension as her thoughts flew to her Jeep and the boxes of historic literature locked in the cargo hold.

Each agonizing minute lumbered by one after the other. When no further sounds disturbed the quiet night, she steeled herself, laid back the covers, and trembling, got out of bed and tiptoed to the door. Holding a taut breath, she put her eye to the quarter-inch slit of glass showing along the window sash and tried to pick out objects in the murky darkness. Slowly she turned the doorknob, inching the door open so she could see better. Her car, a shadowy hulk in the moonlight, remained where she had parked it, unmolested.

When she was sure no one was out there, she opened the door wider and stuck her head out. Her heart jerked as a flutter of something white feathered to her feet on the breeze. She bent and picked up a folded piece of paper. Taking one last look around, she stepped back, and closed and locked the door.

In the dark, she bumped her thigh against the table edge as her hand fumbled for the lamp. She turned it on then sat down in the dim light and unfolded the note. A bolt of fright darted through her when she read the hastily scrawled words.

Get out! someone had printed with a broad black marker. *Go back where you belong!*

She shivered, as if a cold draft swept over her skin. The note was meant to scare her and it did, but after the initial fright subsided, curiosity crept in, and she wondered who she'd offended in the few short hours since she'd arrived in Monument Valley.

She instantly eliminated Durango as a possibility. Durango, with his brooding eyes and arrogant manner, was not the type to take clandestine action. She had no doubt he'd make his feelings known more directly.

She sat a long while looking at the note. When anger displaced curiosity, she crumpled it in her hand.

Okay, she thought. *I'll leave. I'll get out. But not yet.*

She had no intention of leaving before she fulfilled her father's wishes.

A wave of remorse washed over her, causing a painful clutch in her heart.

"I'm sorry, Daddy," she whispered, hoping that wherever he was he could hear her now. "I'm so sorry I wasn't a better daughter." Despairingly, she knew she could have been if only she'd tried harder.

When her parents divorced, she and her mother moved to Los Angeles. Soon after, her mother met and married wealthy businessman Daniel Broadmoor, life had taken on its own momentum, an uneasy current that carried her along. Daniel had made a fortune spearheading several locally successful businesses into national prominence. In Francina's view, she'd elevated herself and Amanda from a dusty, dull existence to a gated mansion in Beverly Hills. She saw no need to encourage a relationship from the past into a very comfortable present.

As time passed, overwhelmed by adolescence and the wrenching struggle to fit into a new school and a new way of life, Amanda often failed to return her father's letters and phone calls. By the time she graduated from college, the years had created a chasm that could not be crossed.

Now, driven by the fire of punishing guilt, she was determined to cross that abyss. She'd stood up to her mother, and defied her fiancé to come here. A mean-spirited note from a stranger wasn't going to send her scurrying back home.

CHAPTER TWO

Next morning, the sun was painting the desert its usual red and gold but had not yet chased the chill from the air when Durango unlocked the door to the Cultural Center. Amanda Bell was on his mind.

When she'd walked through this door the day before, his first thought had been—*so this is what they mean by striking!* Strawblond hair, full lips, strong nose, more muscular than willowy, not pretty in the usual sense, but captivating, appealing. The earthy sort of woman some men are drawn to. Not him, but some men.

He'd immediately figured she was just another do-gooder come to the reservation to help—make that exploit—the Navajos, one of a steady stream of Indian *wannabes* who showed up every summer with dubious promises of a better life for those living here. The minute he looked at her, he could tell she wasn't from around there, didn't belong there, and wouldn't last long if she stayed. People drifted into Monument Valley all the time and sooner or later drifted right back out again when eventually the isolation bored them, bothered them, or drove them crazy. Hardly anyone stayed.

He smiled, picturing her lanky walk as she strode back to her car, her hair a golden glissade falling from head to waist, swaying with each leggy step. But he shook the memory away. She probably wouldn't come back, and it was just as well if she didn't. As much as he would have liked the literature collection for his research library, he wasn't sure he wanted Dr. Bell's daughter around. With her tall, fair, good-looking demeanor, she would be a curiosity and a distraction, not to mention a constant reminder to an already superstitious community of the mysterious crash in the desert and the body that was still out there, never properly put to rest.

Yes, it was for the best if she went back home. He had other far more important things to worry about. Like losing his land to Buck Powell.

Durango turned his attention to the rug-weaving loom he was assembling for display.

It had belonged to his grandmother and as a young girl she'd made her first rug on it. She'd used it most of her life, and when it was replaced with a newer, bigger one, he asked for the old one. Now he was trying to figure out how to display it to its best advantage without leaving it exposed and vulnerable to the curious hands of viewers. He was sufficiently engrossed that the unexpected sound of Amanda's voice calling in from outside made him jump.

"Good morning, Mr. Yazzie."

She'd backed her Jeep up to the bottom of the steps outside the open door and when he turned, he had a clear view of her fetching backside as she bent over into the hatchback, gathering and sorting papers that had spilled from boxes split at the seams.

"Well, what do you know," he said under his breath, trying to subdue a curious hitch in his heart. "She came back." He leaned the loom against the wall, and watched her through the window.

She wore a sweatshirt, denim cut-offs, and sneakers, and his eyes wandered the length of her tanned legs. She walked up the porch carrying a box of books, and stood in the doorway, giving him a where-do-I-put-this look. She'd piled her hair on top of her head today. Some of it fell in curling tendrils around her face. *That's sexy.*

"I didn't expect you to come back," he said. "I'm afraid I haven't made arrangements for a place for you to work."

Amanda stood her ground, swung a one-eighty around the room, stopping at the closed door to her left, and tossed a sideways nod.

"What's in there?" she asked sweetly.

"That's an adjoining trailer, but it's used for storage. There's no room for—"

Her voice overrode his deliberately. "It will do just fine, Mr. Yazzie."

He wished she'd stop calling him Mr. Yazzie. Besides the fact that nobody called him that anymore, it especially bothered him that she did, though he couldn't say why.

Amanda braced the box on her hip, opened the door with her free hand, and peered into the dusty gloom.

"It's perfect," she said.

He followed her into the room jammed with boxes, old furniture, and bookcases filled with everything but books. A protest formed on his lips, but again she cut him off.

"Don't worry, Mr. Yazzie." She swung around to face him squarely, the box still in her arms, a brittle smile on her lips. "I'm only staying long enough to finish my father's project. Then rest assured, I'll be leaving. You're not the only one who doesn't want me here."

Amanda plopped the box on a cleared space, raising a cloud of dust, then went back to the Jeep to unload the rest, concentrating on ignoring Durango who stood there scowling, watching her every move. She didn't know what she'd do if he tried to stop her or block her way. For a moment, her confidence slipped again, but she remembered her mother's oft-repeated admonition during their early country club years to act as if she belonged. *Okay, Mother, I'm acting.*

29

Head high and eyes straight ahead, she brushed past him. Without warning, he reached for the box she was carrying. Tightening her grip, she pulled back, but though she was strong, he was stronger and the box was yanked out of her arms into his.

"Hey! What do you think you're doing?" An unattractive snarl lifted her lip as she pushed the words through her teeth. She immediately wished she could take them back when he carried the box into the storage room and set it gently on the floor.

"I'll help you," he said.

His voice was quiet, reassuring, without rebuke, and she was immediately abashed. "I'm sorry . . . I thought . . ." She felt like the biggest fool in the world and her face burned with embarrassment.

In weighty silence, Durango carried in the rest of the boxes, disregarding her and the apology falling from her lips. When he finished, he returned to the main room without another word.

She stood a minute, waiting for the flush of humiliation to dissipate, staring at the spot where he'd disappeared from view. "*That* went well," she muttered lamely.

But she lapsed into silence as she looked around in dismay at her office-to-be. It was a mess. She wiped her finger on a tabletop and scowled at the dust and grit on her fingertip. It would take a week just to clean away the dirt and grime, and move the old furniture aside to make room, but she was determined to carve out a workspace for herself.

She spotted an old desk in the corner. She could use that. There was a wobbly chair with a broken leg and the back was loose. Maybe she could fix it. These weren't the best working conditions, but she'd manage. Pushing the exchange with Durango from her mind, she set about making a workspace.

Within a couple of hours, she'd managed to shove aside enough of the clutter to haul out the desk and clear it off, and find a chair strong enough to actually sit on, thereby making at least the semblance of an office. But she needed office supplies—pens and pencils, paper clips, cataloguing supplies, a phone, a computer to build a database. She had assumed those things would be provided for her. She breathed an impatient sigh. Well, she wasn't going to ask Durango for them. She'd buy them herself first, she decided, then wondered how far she'd have to drive to find a town with an office-supply store.

Afternoon heat pushed a stillness over the desert that rolled in through the open doors and windows of the fledgling Cultural Center. She cleaned and swept and dusted in determined silence so as not to disturb Durango or call attention to her presence. She was unaware he had a visitor until she heard voices raised in anger coming from the next room.

"What are you doing here?" There was no mistaking the enmity in Durango's tone.

"Just need your signature on this agreement and I'll be on my way." The reply carried a false note of conviviality.

A long silence was broken by the sound of papers rustling, then what sounded like papers being ripped to shreds.

"Here's your agreement," Durango said angrily. "Now get the hell out!"

Amanda couldn't ignore what was being said, the voices were at shouting level and the door was open. She knew she should probably not be hearing this conversation, but couldn't leave without being seen by the two angry men. Quietly, she stepped down from the ladder where she'd been clearing off the top of a bookcase. Her instinct to hide and not be caught listening battled with her desire to know what they were talking about. Curiosity overcame both gut feeling and good manners, and she stood in the middle of the room, ear cocked to the doorway, openly catching every word.

The visitor laughed, sounding unperturbed by Durango's

anger. "Hey, now. Is that any way to talk to your old buddy?" If the taunt was meant to be good-natured, it fell short. Amanda could hear the meanness in it.

"You're no buddy of mine, Buck Powell," Durango spat. "And I'm giving you exactly thirty seconds to get the hell out before I throw you out."

"Why don't you make it easy on yourself, Yazzie? Sign the damned papers," he said, no longer making any pretense at pleasantness.

"I'm not signing anything. Wild Horse Mesa is Yazzie land and you know it. What makes you think you have any kind of claim on it? It's been in our family for three generations. We own it."

"Prove it," the other man challenged.

Amanda heard a chair scrape back, slam against the wall, and topple to the floor. Then the man Durango had called Buck Powell fell, literally, into her line of sight, sprawling on the floor, holding his jaw where Durango had apparently punched him. She recognized him as the man she'd seen hanging around the trading post. He stared at her every time she went in or out of her room, making her skin crawl.

"Oh, I'll prove it all right," Durango said. He was standing over Buck, fists clenched, ready to make good on his threat. "Meanwhile, if I catch any of your men intimidating my mother and my grandmother, or stepping one foot on that land, you'll all answer to me."

As Buck scrambled to his feet, he caught sight of Amanda openly eavesdropping in the next room. Glowering under bushy eyebrows, he seared her with a look before stomping out.

Then Durango, his face a mask of scalding fury, stormed out, his boots clattering down the wooden steps. Moments later, a blue pickup truck with Durango at the wheel roared out of the parking lot. Once again, silence descended.

What was that all about?

She tiptoed into Durango's office and righted the chair he'd knocked over. The papers he'd torn up were scattered in scraps on the floor where he'd thrown them and she left them where they lay.

Wondering at the bitterness of the exchange between the two men, she went back to her own business of clearing a work-space. The sooner she got set up and finished archiving, the sooner she could leave here.

She gripped a tall bookcase and dragged it heavily across the room to position it against the wall near her desk, but howled in pain when it slipped out of her hands and pressed heavily on her big toe. She jerked her foot back, then crumpled to the floor, rising tears of pain burning her eyes. Quickly she untied her sneaker and winced as she slid it off. The injured toe, already swelling and turning purple, throbbed painfully.

She held her foot in her hand and rocked back and forth, gritting her teeth until the pain lessened enough for her to think clearly. She remembered seeing a medical clinic, but where? Through raging pain, it came to her—the Presbyterian Church mission about a mile down the road.

It was longer than a mile and by the time she got there, the pain had increased significantly. She hobbled into the squat adobe building under a hand-painted sign that said Monument Valley Health Clinic. A big-boned, plain-faced, red-haired woman in her thirties was standing at the counter in the tiny lobby talking to the receptionist. When Amanda hopped in on one foot, face contorted in pain, she immediately rushed to Amanda's side. The name engraved on the tag pinned to the front of her white coat identified her as Chamomile Drew, MD.

Amanda leaned on the freckle-faced woman who looked much too young to be a doctor and let herself be helped into the examining room. The woman didn't dress like a doctor, either, Amanda noticed. Under her white coat, she wore a long, granny-style dress, and her bare feet were fitted into comfortable-looking Birkenstocks.

With help, Amanda hitched up on the exam table, gasping as a dagger of pain raced up her leg.

"Thank you, Dr. Drew," she breathed as the spasm passed.

"Call me Cammie," the doctor replied with a smile that did wonders for her face. "Everyone else does."

She leaned over Amanda's foot, closely examining her toe through oval wire-rimmed spectacles, then touched it lightly. Amanda sucked in a breath and winced with pain. "Sorry." The doctor looked up, her eyes probing Amanda's face. "You're new here."

"Yes," Amanda replied. "I'm working on a project at the Navajo Cultural Center. I was trying to move a bookcase and it slipped and landed on my toe."

Cammie, gently cradling Amanda's foot, turned her attention back to the toe, which was now turning a stomach-churning greenish-purple.

"Hmmm. It's not broken. Just badly bruised." Cammie's panther-green eyes flicked up at Amanda. "You working with Durango?"

"No." She clenched her teeth as Cammie gently wrapped the injured toe, forming a fat, protective bubble around it.

"This should be enough padding if you bump it, but you probably won't be able to get your shoe on." Cammie helped her down from the examining table. "Where are you living?" Cammie asked.

"At the trading post. It's just temporary until I find something else."

Cammie wrinkled her nose distastefully. "Oh," she said. "Buck Powell's place."

"Buck Powell owns the trading post?" Amanda instantly

envisioned him as she'd seen him that morning—sprawled on the floor, rubbing his jaw.

"You might want to look for something else," Cammie went on. "Meanwhile, don't drink the water. He's been cited several times for leaky gasoline pumps contaminating the well."

Amanda suspected as much. The fumes while taking a shower almost gagged her. "Where else is there?" she asked.

Cammie nodded. "It's hard to find a place to live around here. But I have a friend who's renovating an old restaurant into apartments. I can call her and find out when something will be ready."

"That would be great," Amanda said, hope rising.

"I have a house provided by the Clinic," Cammie went on. "Otherwise, I wouldn't have been able to stay. I've been here nine years."

"Nine years! How have you lasted that long? People don't seem very friendly."

"Oh, that's just because you're new. Don't take it personally. The Natives are naturally withdrawn with newcomers." Cammie paused, then not so subtly changed the subject back to Durango.

"How are you and Durango getting along?"

The question was meant to be casual, but came out with meaning simmering just below the surface. Amanda caught the tone right away and wondered if Cammie had a history with Durango. She was tempted to ask the doctor about the strange dark eyed man. "He's tolerating me," she said.

Cammie nodded wordlessly then handed Amanda a clipboard. "Here. Fill out this medical record before you go. I'll give you some pain pills to take with you."

Amanda wrote her name, filled in the requested information, and handed the clipboard back.

Cammie scanned it and her eyes widened. She looked up at Amanda.

"Bell? Was that your father in that accident out on Comb Ridge a couple of months ago?"

"Yes. I'm here completing an archiving project for him."

Cammie's face got serious. "I'm so sorry," she said, meaning it. "I was on the search and rescue team that found the van and looked for him."

A hundred questions about her father and what happened to him jumped to Amanda's lips, but before she could ask them, a nurse rushed into the room, breathless and agitated, interrupting.

"Cammie? We have a little boy in emergency. Fell out of the back of a pickup. Come quickly!"

"Okay," Cammie replied and turned to Amanda. "Look, I've got to go, but here's my card. Call me if your toe gets worse or if you have any questions about anything. Can you make it back out to your car by yourself?" She grabbed a pair of crutches that were leaning against the wall in the corner and pushed them toward Amanda. "Here. Use these. Bring them back when you don't need them anymore."

"Thanks," Amanda said, but Cammie had already hurried away.

With her weight on her good foot, Amanda crutched out to her Jeep. She was sorry she didn't have a chance to ask about her father's accident, but Cammie had invited her to call if she had questions, so that's what she would do.

When she got back to the Cultural Center, Durango was at his desk deep in conversation on the phone. He barely glanced at her as she maneuvered awkwardly, clattering noisily up the steps and into the trailer on crutches. The pain pounding in her foot and his show of indifference to her obvious injury, combined to feed her pique. She threw him a screw-you look and proceeded stone-faced into the storage room.

Her ill will ground to a halt when her gaze landed on her desk. Its surface was piled high with office supplies—pens, pads of paper, tape, paper clips, and scissors—everything crisp and new in store-bought packaging. Again, her face burned with embarrassment as she mentally inventoried the supplies, feeling ever more ungrateful as she realized the completeness of the purchases. Everything she needed was there.

Durango's voice close behind made her jump.

"Your phone will be connected in a couple of weeks. It takes a while to get a phone on the reservation. I've borrowed a computer for you to use. It's not new, but should be good enough. It'll be here tomorrow."

She dragged in a long breath, let it out slowly, and turned to face him, ashamed of her churlish entrance. There was still no hostility in his look, but no benevolence, either.

"Thank you," she said, leaning on the crutches. "I know you weren't expecting me, and my being here has disrupted your work, but I want you to know I appreciate your forbearance." With a dip of her head, she indicated the items on her desk. "*And* the supplies."

He didn't reply, but stared in her eyes, his piercing gaze reaching into her, taking her measure as if trying to decide if he could trust her.

"I'm sorry about the way I acted before," she said, trying to fill the silence. She wished she could think of something more to say.

"No," he replied. "I'm the one who is sorry. For the incident here this morning." He tossed his thumb over his shoulder, and she knew he was referring to the clash with Buck Powell.

"That wasn't meant for you to hear," he went on. "And my actions were inappropriate. Violence solves nothing. Please accept *my* apology."

His skin was the color of pale cinnamon, taut over high cheekbones, and his shoulder length hair gleamed like polished onyx. *What manner of man are you, Durango Yazzie?*

"There's no need, really," she said, "but apology accepted."

His gaze slid down to settle at her bandaged toe. "How did you hurt yourself?"

She waved a hand in disregard. "Oh, it's nothing. I was just trying to move the bookcase and it slipped."

"Where do you want it?"

After she told him, he effortlessly positioned it where she indicated.

"If you want anything else moved, ask me," he said. He gave a brief nod, a pleasured smile, then went back to his work.

The arrogance was still there, the proud lift of the head, but it was tempered with a vaguely sensuous light in his eyes that she found most provocative. He didn't know it, but he'd already moved something inside her without her having to ask.

During the rest of the week, she found herself throwing expectant glances toward the door leading into his office, more and more turning her attention to his presence in the next room. He spared her only occasional brief notice through the doorway as he went in and out about his business.

And that was just fine with her, she decided. She wasn't there for the long term, wasn't looking for a romantic involvement, or any involvement at all. As soon as she catalogued the collection, she was done. She was leaving, going—where?

Back to rigid, insufferable, stick-up-the-butt Elliott? *Never!* She'd barely given him a thought since she left, and it surprised her a little to realize that a man she had nearly married had almost entirely disappeared from her mind. The longer she was away from him, the more she wondered why she had agreed to marry him in the first place. But it really hadn't been a case of agreeing or not agreeing. She'd just found herself borne along on the tide of his enthusiasm, and the staunch approval of her mother and stepfather.

She didn't know where she'd go or what she'd do, and frowned, considering. Clearly, she'd have to make some plans for her future.

By the end of the following week, her makeshift workspace in the storage room resembled an office. She'd set up files, got the computer up and running, and designed and readied a database to receive input. Her injured toe had faded to a sickly yellow-brown, the pain had all but disappeared, and she could get a shoe on her foot. She drove to the clinic to return the crutches.

Cammie came out of an examining room and greeted her at the front desk.

"You still looking for another place to live?" she asked. "My friend said the apartment's available now. If you want to, go look at it right away. It won't last long. They go fast around here."

Amanda loved the apartment on sight. Tucked into a grove of cottonwoods and looking out on twin red rock towers, the historic log-walled building had been updated with a tiny galley kitchen and a modern bathroom. It was called the Blue Daisy Café after a former owner's failed attempt at operating a restaurant on the premises, and though the business was long gone, the name had stuck.

She wrote out a check for the rent and the security deposit and went back to the trading post to pack her things.

When she drove up, Buck Powell was sitting on a bench outside the grocery store. She felt his eyes following her as she got out of the car, and unlocked her door. Two steps inside her door, she halted abruptly.

Once or twice since moving into the trading post, she'd had a vague suspicion that someone had been in her room while she was away during the day. Now she froze in place and regarded the room warily. A prickly sensation of displacement plagued her awareness as her eyes swept the room, taking in each detail.

Was that a wrinkle on the pillowcase she was in the habit of smoothing when she made her bed each morning? Did she leave her hairbrush in the bathroom or on the table where it was now? The book she was reading last night was on the nightstand. She distinctly remembered putting it on the floor next to the bed. Suitcases lay open on the floor against the wall where she left them, but she could tell the neatly folded items inside had been disturbed.

The room had not been rummaged exactly, just disarranged, and clearly an attempt had been made to put things back. She did not doubt that someone had been in there, but since nothing was missing, concluded they must have been looking for something. But what?

She turned at a drift of sound. Buck Powell filled the space in the doorway. He was hefty and blunt with a beefy face, and though his stomach lapped over his belt, his arms were muscled and thick as tree limbs. His leering appraisal chilled her.

"Rent's due today," he said. His red-rimmed eyes stroked up and down her body. "That Indian paying you enough to cover your bills? Huh? 'Cause if not, we can prob'ly work somethin' else out."

He smiled when he said it, showing yellowish teeth, his voice low and croaky. She shivered, an involuntary tremor.

"I'm moving out," she said. "I've found another place to live. I just came back to pack." She rudely closed the door in his face, cutting off his smirk. In a moment, she heard his boots tread slowly along the boardwalk and stop at the bench by the creaky screen door outside the grocery store.

Within fifteen minutes, Amanda was speeding down the highway to her new home.

CHAPTER THREE

A week went by and then another, each passing day bringing a sense of order to Amanda's work. She'd begun the tedious process of archiving, sorting the materials into categories—diaries, logs, registers, letters, memoirs and fictionalized accounts of life in the Southwest written by early settlers and residents, government employees, military officers, and Native Americans.

Next, she would peruse each document and write a summary of its contents. Then she would assign it a catalogue number, record the number, and type the summary into the database. After that, the work would be placed on a bookshelf, or in the case of clippings and letters and other loose papers, in a protective folder and put in a fireproof metal filing cabinet.

It was an exacting process, but the very minutiae of the work kept her mind occupied, and allowed her to pretend that the note left on her door her first night at the trading post was of no consequence. In truth, a tiny disquiet had nudged the edge of her consciousness ever since. That disquiet mushroomed into anxiety when a second note appeared.

It was there when she got home, a white rectangle stuck into the crack between the door and the doorframe. With shaking fingers, she plucked it from the tiny crevasse and unfolded it. The shock of the words hit her like a smack in the face, and she could do nothing but stare wordlessly at the message.

Come to Twin Rocks Canyon tonight at dusk. It's about your father. Come alone.

Instinctively she looked around as if the writer might be standing in plain sight ready to explain the meaning of the note, but there was no one. She looked up at the two red spires guarding the mouth of Twin Rocks Canyon. It was close, close enough to walk to, but a sixth sense told her to drive. She would go, of course, despite the warning bells going off in her head.

Still standing on the porch, she looked over her shoulder once more, then unlocked her door and went inside, half expecting to find her rooms had been searched again. Satisfied that nothing had been disturbed, she pulled out a chair and sat at the table, her eyes pinned to the note, reading it over and over, fearing she was missing some vital clue in the neutral, boxy, all uppercase letters, but the unfamiliar handwriting gave up nothing.

The enormity of it astonished her. Someone had information about her father. And it suddenly, jarringly occurred to her that her father might be alive.

It was well before dusk when Amanda set out in the Jeep. She turned west off the highway onto a thinly graveled two-track that dead ended at the mouth of Twin Rocks Canyon, a deep crease slicing through the surrounding red sandstone. Heat still fell in waves even this late in the day, and she parked in the shadow of an ocher-hued escarpment.

She got out and stood in the middle of the clearing, making sure she could be seen by whoever was coming to meet her. The sky had a violet cast, and stillness unfolded in all directions as if the world were holding its breath. Her eyes probed her surroundings, piercing the deepening shadows, trying to penetrate the darkness of a thick stand of cottonwood and conifer at the base of a steep rock rise. Suddenly there was movement in the trees and she strained to see, her eyes cleaving a gash in the quickly falling twilight.

Slowly a shadowy figure merged into view, an old woman, a Navajo grandmother with a deeply wizened face, gaunt and haggard, hollows showing under jutting cheekbones. She shuffled to the edge of the trees, not venturing into the clearing. Her birdlike eyes went to Amanda for a piercing instant, then shifted to the surrounding terrain. She wore the native dress of the reservation—brightly colored gauzy skirt topped by a drapey blouse. Her gray hair, pulled back into a fierce bun behind her small head, retained touches of its original blue-black luster.

Both women, the gaunt old one and the tall young one, stood motionless. Amanda stared anxiously at this woman who had information about her father. She wanted to rush to the bent figure, wanted to embrace her or restrain her, but dared not scare her off. The elder, seemingly reluctant to make herself vulnerable by coming out into the open, stood absolutely still.

A long silence stretched between them as the grandmother's eyes settled on Amanda, who remained transfixed, not knowing what to do, not daring to move. Suddenly the old woman's glittering black eyes darted away from Amanda's face and refocused at some distant spot over her shoulder. A wave of fear washed over the age-worn face before she turned and ran, disappearing into the trees and rocks.

"Wait!" Amanda called. "Don't go!"

She took a step to run after the old woman, but stopped when she heard a muffled scuffling behind her. Spinning around, she caught a glimpse of movement darting behind a boulder partway up the rocky incline.

Darkness was coming on quickly now and deep silence shrouded the canyon. She couldn't see into the gloom, but knew someone or something was moving up there as a fine spill of dirt and pebbles skittered off the high ledge and tumbled onto the path at her feet.

She fought against the instinct to flee. Curiosity and the hope of learning something about her father kept her rooted to the spot. A quarter moon topped the eastern horizon and the midnight-blue sky was filling with tiny stars. She smelled the real desert carried on a tiny breeze, but heard no sound and nothing else moved. The silence became a great stillness that little by little took on a sinister aspect, as of some unknown malice creeping into the canyon.

An eddy of wind stirred and faded, sounding like a sigh, followed by the shake and whisper of dry cottonwood leaves. Every shadow was an enemy, every rustle of the brush a warning.

Apprehension rising, Amanda broke and ran to her car, fumbled clumsily with the handle, then jumped in and yanked the door shut behind her. She flipped the lock, roared the motor to life, and sped out of the canyon, throwing a plume of dirt and stones in her wake.

Back in her apartment, the door bolted, the drapes drawn, all the lights on, she willed herself into a calmness she didn't truly feel. Her mind reeled with questions. Who was that Indian woman? What did she know about her father?

And what—or who—had frightened the Old One away?

CHAPTER FOUR

"You did what?"

Judy Moon peered at her younger brother Durango with the same expression she reserved for her three mischievous sons, and occasionally for her husband Jeremiah. To Durango, it brought to mind the look his mother often gave him when he was a child.

"I know. I shouldn't have hit Buck Powell," he replied, wilting but only slightly under his sister's disapproving gaze. His eyes were apologetic as he shoved a hand through his hair, pushing it off his face. Then his jaw tightened and he lowered his voice. "I wanted to kill him."

"Hush that talk," his sister admonished, eyes big, eyebrows popping. She glanced quickly into the next room where her little boys were playing.

Jeremiah Moon carried his lunch dishes to the sink, giving his wife a loving pat on the behind as he passed.

"Powell's been after that Wild Horse Mesa property for years," he said. "He wants it bad."

"Well, he's not going to get it, legally or otherwise. It's got cliff dwellings on it."

Durango pushed the food around on his plate while Judy waited patiently at the kitchen sink for him to finish his lunch so she could clear the table. Her homey kitchen was in the part of the house that overhung the San Juan River. The house itself was located forty miles off the reservation in the tiny town of

Bluff, a residential enclave of artists and writers.

"I hear you've got someone working out there with you now," Jeremiah remarked casually, changing the subject. "From California? Long blond hair?"

At that, Judy looked up interestedly but continued wiping the counter.

"Yeah," Durango replied.

"She's a tall cool glass of lemonade," Jeremiah observed. "Isn't she?" He exchanged a sly look with his wife.

"She's just here for the summer," Durango answered, purposely avoiding the invitation to discuss Amanda's looks.

Jeremiah acknowledged Durango's comment with a nod and a smile, picking up some paintbrushes drying on the edge of the sink. His ash-blond hair was in a long braid down his back, and half a dozen turquoise and lapis bead necklaces around his neck clicked softly as he walked out onto the screened-in porch that doubled as an artist's studio. He sat down in front of a large canvas and was immediately lost in concentration.

"Who is she?" Judy asked after a moment.

Her tone was breezy, as if it were an idle question, but Durango knew it wasn't, so ignored it and asked a question of his own.

"Do you remember any more of the story Grandmother told about how that land on Wild Horse Mesa came to be ours?"

"Just what I've already told you. It was given to Great-grandfather by the Indian Agent."

"How was it given? Was it signed over? Was there a deed recorded with his name on it?"

Judy thought. "I don't know about that. I was just a little girl when Grandmother talked about it. You'll have to ask her if she remembers anything else."

"I did. She doesn't remember. All she knows is what her grandmother told her when she was a little girl, and all her grandmother knew is what her father told her. Something about how Great-great-grandfather's medicine cured the Indian Agent's daughter from a terrible sickness. The little girl's father gave him that piece of land in gratitude and as payment."

Judy picked up Durango's dishes, ran them under the faucet and put them in the dishwasher. She sighed. "It didn't seem that important before. That land has always been in our family. Everyone knew there were Puebloan ruins out there, but they were so inaccessible, no one wanted to bother with them. And, you know, some people don't like walking around in ruins, afraid the spirits will make them go crazy. Then all of a sudden Buck Powell began claiming the land was his."

Durango's brow furrowed, and he absently fingered the pottery bowl in the middle of the table, tracing the painted designs.

"Did she ever mention the Indian Agent's name?"

"Not that I recall."

"Did she say when this happened? What year?"

Judy gave him a blank look. "Durango, I wish I remembered more. Why don't you go to Window Rock, talk to the Tribal Historian. Maybe she can help."

Durango nodded. Her idea was a good one. At least it was a place to start.

Judy, swiping a mop around the kitchen floor, spoke into his thoughtful silence. "So . . . who is working out there with you?"

Durango's thoughts of Window Rock instantly broke away. "She's not working with me. Her name is Amanda Bell. She's working on a project for her father. She's Dr. Bell's daughter."

The mop in Judy's hands came to a sudden stop. "The same Dr. Bell who was killed in the crash last May?"

Durango nodded, not really wanting to talk about Amanda. He had enough trouble keeping his mind off her as it was. For weeks he'd been trying to think of a way to ask her to stop calling him Mr. Yazzie. He didn't know why it bothered him so much, nor was he sure why he was reluctant to bring it up to her. It might be because he was afraid she'd read too much into it. He didn't want her to think it was some kind of invitation to get close.

"Oh," Judy said, then after a pause added, "How old is she? What does she look like?"

"Forget it, Judy. I know what you're getting at, and it won't work. I'm not interested in her."

"Why not?"

"You know why not."

A long silence lay in the room.

"Because of Sharron?" Judy asked finally.

"No."

The silence picked up again, but after a while Judy pressed on. "Then why not?"

"She's not Navajo," he replied.

Judy laid a stern eye on Durango. "Neither is Jeremiah," she said.

"That's different," Durango said, then blanched at the hurt in his sister's eyes. "Look, I'm sorry. I didn't mean anything by that. You know I love Jeremiah like a brother. It's just that . . . I can't get involved. I've got important work to do." Another long silence stretched between them. Finally, since it had come up, Durango asked the question that was hanging in the air.

"How is Sharron doing?"

"Not well."

"The kids?"

"They could be better."

Durango slammed his fist on the table, causing the painted pottery bowl to rattle. "What does she do with the money I send her?" he fumed.

"I don't know," Judy replied softly.

Durango stared out the windows at Comb Ridge, a jagged

rise in the distance. A dull ache of memories washed over him. "When I go to Window Rock tomorrow, I'll stop in Tuba City and check on them."

Judy and Durango turned at a knock on the back door. Jack Rice, smiling through his bushy beard, peered in the screen door at them.

"Come in," Judy called. "It's open. Would you like coffee?" she offered as he stepped across the threshold. "Or I've got fresh-made iced tea. Which will it be?"

"No, no thanks." Jack smiled and waved his hand, politely declining. "I just stopped by to see if I can get some information from Jeremiah about this year's Desert Dazzle Art Festival."

Jeremiah came out of his studio, wiping his hands on a paint-stained rag, smiling a welcome. He crossed the room to a desk, picked up a piece of paper and handed it to Jack.

"I wrote a press release. It's all there. Date, time, artist call, deadline for submissions, entry requirements. Let me know if you need anything else."

Jack glanced at it. "This'll do. Thanks. Ought to have another great turnout," he speculated. "This art festival has drawn bigger and bigger crowds to Bluff every year since you started it. Might even get some television coverage this year."

"That would be great," Jeremiah said.

Jack turned, acknowledging Durango. "I see Dr. Bell's daughter is working out on the reservation with you. She came into the newspaper office asking about a place to rent. Cute, isn't she?"

Judy and Jeremiah both hid smiles while Durango twisted his lips in exasperation.

"She's not working *with* me," he answered gruffly, doing a poor job of hiding his irritation at being asked to comment on Amanda's looks a second time. "She's doing something for her father, finishing some work he wasn't able to complete."

Jack waited for Durango to go on and when he didn't, the newspaper editor reached for the screen door and pushed it open. "Yeah, well, that's nice. Sounds like something a good daughter would do."

After Jack left and Jeremiah had gone back to his painting, Judy sat down at the table across from Durango, who had slipped back into pensive silence.

"Is anyone in your cultural preservation study group entering work in the art show?" Judy asked.

Durango nodded distractedly. "Sally Rainwater's boys are working on some oil paintings depicting historic events. Larry is painting The Long Walk and Albert is drawing reproductions of artifacts and petroglyphs. Maybe some of the others will, too." Durango drifted off in thought again.

"Go to Window Rock," Judy said after a while. She gave Durango's hand a sisterly squeeze. "Maybe you'll turn up something there."

Chamomile Drew, MD, skepticism plain on her face, narrowed her green eyes as she looked at Amanda. The two women were in a booth at the motel coffee shop across the road from the clinic, and the doctor's hands were folded loosely around a coffee mug on the table in front of her. Amanda had just told her about the aborted meeting with the mysterious elder at Twin Rocks Canyon the previous week.

"Amanda . . ." Cammie began. Her eyes softened as they skimmed Amanda's face, then she shook her head. A line creased her brow as she gazed at her new friend.

"Look, there's no easy way to say this, so I'll just say it straight out." She reached across the table and settled her hand lightly on Amanda's.

"Will you believe me when I tell you there is no way your father could be alive? From the looks of the van, he was probably injured pretty badly. And even if he was able to crawl out of the wreckage, well, without food or water . . ." She stopped again.

"Amanda, there are," she leaned forward and whispered the words as if doing so would lessen their impact, "*animals* out there."

Cammie wasn't telling her anything she hadn't already thought of. "I know, but look at this note. Somebody knows something. If I can find out who that is and what they know . . ." Her voice filled with determination. "If someone has information about my father, I've got to find whoever it is."

Cammie watched as Amanda silently reread the note she'd already read half a dozen times since they sat down.

"Here," she said holding out her hand. "Let me see it again. Maybe I can tell something by the handwriting."

Amanda handed over the note, and Cammie's eyes moved slowly over it. After a few minutes she shrugged and handed it back to Amanda. "Nope. I don't recognize it. Think, Amanda. Don't you have any idea who it might be?"

"None. And I haven't seen the old woman around. I've watched for her."

Everywhere Amanda went—the post office, the gas station, the clinic, the trading posts—her gaze flew expectantly to every face that came into view, hoping to find the mysterious elder she'd caught a glimpse of through the brush at the entrance to Twin Rocks Canyon.

People of all ages from the reservation came into the Cultural Center to talk to Durango every day—students from the high school or members of their family, Durango's student history group, teachers, visitors, researchers. No one escaped Amanda's scrutiny. She found it difficult to concentrate on her work.

Suddenly she had a thought. "Cammie, who would have the accident report? How can I see it?"

Cammie took a sip of coffee and put her mug down with a soft clunk. "Are you sure you want to?"

"Yes. Who do I see? Where would I go?"

Cammie gazed at her friend then caught sight of the time. "Oh! I've got to get back to the clinic." She pushed her coffee cup away and stood up to leave, then bent to give Amanda a friendly hug.

"Try Tribal Police Headquarters," she said. "In Window Rock."

The last person Durango expected to see at Tribal Headquarters in Window Rock was Amanda Bell. But there she was, with her fair skin and blond hair as noticeable as if she were illuminated by a stage spot, sitting at a corner table in the cafeteria, scowling.

He paid the cashier for his coffee then stood a moment watching her, wondering what she was doing there. When she looked up and caught his eye, something in her expression propelled him to her table.

"May I join you?" he asked as he approached. Haunted eyes shadowed with anxiety regarded him and he hesitated, wondering too late if he might be intruding.

"Hello. Yes, please sit down," she greeted him, but her smile was forced, and her fingers trembled slightly, fluttering the sheet of paper she was holding.

He took a seat next to her. "Is something wrong?"

"No," she replied averting her gaze. "Yes," she said, then laughed nervously and looked at him directly.

"Well, actually I'm not sure." She indicated the page in her hand. "It's the police report about my father's accident."

"Oh?" He waited for her to say more, but she didn't. "Is there something wrong with it?" he asked.

"Yes, I think there is. There's only one page here, and it's basically just the accident report. There's no follow-up report, nothing to indicate they investigated my father's disappearance."

"There must be," Durango said. "Let me see." She gave him the report and he skimmed it quickly.

"And look there." She moved closer and leaned toward him, her fair hair swinging free in front of her shoulder. He caught the scent of something herbal, like soap or shampoo and felt the warmth of her arm where it lightly touched his sleeve.

She pointed to the middle of the page. "It looks like they've closed the case and written it off as a case of suspected drunk driving. There must be some mistake. That can't be right."

Her voice caught, breaking on a swallowed sob and when he looked up, he saw that her blue almond-shaped eyes were glittering with tears. "Why not?" he asked.

"Because my father didn't drink," she replied.

"How do you know that?"

The heat on his arm dissipated as she bridled and pulled away, straightening in her chair.

"Because he never drank," she said icily. She pressed her lips and her mouth tightened as she took the accident report from Durango's hand and slipped it back in its manila envelope.

"I just meant so much time has gone by, maybe he—"

"No," Amanda cut him off. "He didn't." Her sharp look dared him to go on.

Durango let it go, but wondered at her innocence of human frailties. It was refreshing and, despite her worldly appearance, she was vulnerable somehow, in need of protection.

What she said next confirmed it.

"I think my father might be alive." Her voice was hopeful and she gazed at him expectantly, waiting for him to say something. Her shoulders rose and fell almost imperceptibly with the breaths she took.

"What makes you think that?" he asked carefully, not wanting to dishearten her yet knowing what she'd suggested was impossible. Even if her father had survived the accident, he couldn't have lived very long in the desert.

Amanda told him about the note in her door, about going to Twin Rocks Canyon, about seeing someone run away. "Someone knows something about my father," she said, "where he is or what happened. I just feel it."

Her blue eyes shone with conviction as she spoke, and she was a little breathless when she finished. He could see she was thoroughly convinced of what she was saying. She fixed him with a long searching look as if she hoped to wring some answers out of him.

For a moment their gazes held. The clink and clatter of dishes and glassware punctuated the buzz of collegial lunchtime conversation around them, visitors and employees making the most of the last few minutes of their afternoon break. The sounds drifted out of Durango's consciousness, and he was momentarily unaware of anything but her stricken look, the serious light in her beseeching eyes. Something inside him gave way, and he felt a warmth spread in his chest. He found himself holding in a breath and let it slide out before he spoke.

"I know someone," he began. "An acquaintance, an investigator in the department. I don't know if he worked on the case, but maybe he knows who did. I'll see if he can get a copy of the investigative report."

Amanda smiled at him, relief flooding her eyes.

"But I have to go now," he said. "I have an appointment with the Tribal Historian, then I have to stop in Tuba City on the way home. I won't be back in Monument Valley until after dark. I'll let you know tomorrow what I find out."

She put a grateful hand on his arm and squeezed lightly, holding on. "Thank you, Durango," she said.

The warmth in his chest deepened as it struck him that she'd called him Durango instead of Mr. Yazzie. Though it was what he'd wanted, suddenly a line had been crossed and he wasn't sure he was ready for it.

CHAPTER FIVE

The morning broke hot and bright, the sun reddening the roughened rock that sloped high to meet the sky. Gravel crunched under the Jeep's tires as Amanda pulled up in front of the tiny Monument Valley Post Office, an added-on trailer tucked into the base of a russet-colored monument a half mile down the road from the clinic. Inside, numbered postal boxes covered two walls, and a bulletin board with pictures of missing children and fugitives hung beside the door. Sitting behind the counter was the postmistress, Sallie Rainwater. She was reading a show-business gossip magazine, but looked up excitedly when Amanda came in.

"Did yah hear they're gonna make a movie?" Sallie was plump and pretty, and the smile in her round face brought added sparkle to her dark expressive eyes.

"No, I didn't hear," said Amanda.

"Yeah. I'm gonna be an extra. I've been an extra before, yah know. Three times. They make lots of western movies here."

Amanda nodded. That explained the encampment of motor homes and vans and eighteen-wheelers parked down the road from the trading post. Location managers and preproduction people setting up for filming.

"Next year I'm going to Hollywood," Sallie went on. "I'll have enough money saved up by then."

"Oh?" said Amanda. "Won't you miss your family here?"

Sallie nodded. "Yeah. But I want to be in the movies. And my boys. They're artists and musicians, yah know. They need exposure. There's more opportunities there."

Amanda unlocked her post office box, and retrieved her mail. She glanced through it, finding mostly solicitations and advertisements. There was an envelope with her mother's handwriting that she knew would contain another letter filled with entreaties to return to Los Angeles. She stuck it all in her leather shoulder bag and went to the counter.

"I might as well pick up Durango's mail for the Cultural Center while I'm here." She knew Durango wouldn't mind. She'd done it before and he hadn't objected.

"Sure." Sallie put the magazine down, got up and went in back where the mail was sorted. She returned with a stack of envelopes. "Maybe there's something in here to cheer him up, eh?"

Amanda tucked it into her shoulder bag with the rest of the mail. "What do you mean?"

"Oh, you know. The problems with his land and Buck Powell trying to claim it. I saw some pickups and a bulldozer lined up at the property line when I came in this morning. Wasn't fully light yet, but I saw them in the distance. Durango won't be happy about that."

Amanda didn't as a rule indulge in gossip, but she was more than a little curious about the dark, aloof man with the serious face. She hadn't worked up the nerve to ask anybody about him, not even Cammie. Trying not to be obvious, she approached the subject with Sallie in a roundabout way.

"What makes Buck Powell think the land is his?" she prodded, hoping her casual tone disguised what was really prying.

"Don't know." Sallie shrugged. "The trouble started last year after the oil and gas company surveyors left. We think they found oil. That's when Durango's mother and sister asked him to come home from California and deal with Buck. They were afraid of him. He made movies, yah know."

Amanda's eyebrows shot up in incredulity. "Who did? Buck?"

Sallie laughed indulgently. "No-o-o. Durango! He won an award for a documentary about Native Americans. He said he'd help me when I go to Hollywood, give me some names of people to see. But he's back here now, so I don't know. Maybe he forgot."

Amanda hoped he hadn't forgotten, and that he could help this charismatic down-to-earth woman who had lofty ambitions for herself and her children.

She patted her shoulder bag, indicating the mail inside and turned to leave. "Thanks, Sallie. See you tomorrow."

She was already out the door when Sallie called her name. Amanda stepped back inside.

"I almost forgot," Sallie said. "Someone was here looking for you yesterday."

"Here at the post office?" That was strange.

Sallie nodded. "Right after you left for Window Rock, he came in. He asked me where you lived."

"Who was it?" Amanda was curious but not alarmed.

"Don't know. Didn't say. There was a line-up at the counter so I was busy."

"What did he look like?"

A telephone rang on the wall behind Sallie, and she reached for it. "He was white," she said over her shoulder, then picked up the receiver.

"No, Albert," she said into the phone. "You can't stay home from school today and paint. You need to know about more than art. You need to know about math so you can count all the money you're going to make selling your paintings, okay?" She smiled at Amanda, then turned her back to speak privately to her son.

Amanda drove away, wondering vaguely who could be looking for her but quickly shrugged it off. Someone selling library or archiving supplies, no doubt. She'd probably gotten on somebody's mailing list through the Internet.

When she arrived at the Cultural Center, Durango was already there. For weeks, she'd watched him experiment with different ways to set up and display the artifacts and historical items in the Center's collection, including those sent by her father. Unfortunately, he didn't seem to have a knack for it, but so far, she'd resisted the temptation to offer any suggestions, afraid he'd see it as meddling.

When she walked in, he was standing with his back to the door, feet firmly planted, hands on his hips, staring at a loom he'd placed on top of a high cabinet.

His hair was gathered at the nape of his neck and held in place by a ponytail slide, a wide ring-sized band of hammered silver with an oval turquoise stone at its center. The contrast of the silver hair cuff encircling the inky-black ponytail that lay on his back was spectacular. He turned when she entered.

"Good morning," he said.

She lifted an eyebrow and suppressed a grin. This was something new—a morning greeting. She considered it a breakthrough. Of sorts.

"Good morning," she answered. "Here's the mail."

As she reached into her bag to retrieve it, her glance went to the loom. It looked out of place and characterless. Only the frame was assembled with side supports made of sections of small pine trees stuck into a base holding the crosspiece at the top. No wool was threaded on the spindles, and if Amanda hadn't already known what it was, she might not have guessed. *Such a beautiful thing,* she thought. Why would he put it there?

"What," he said.

The word, spoken so abruptly, was more a summons to comment than a question, and it jarred her from her thoughts. She looked away from the loom and shook her head.

"Is something wrong with it?" he demanded.

"Oh, no," she replied, placing the mail on his desk.

"You don't like it?" he asked gruffly, his black-clad body stiffening.

"No, I love it." She turned back and lifted her eyes to look at it again, then met his gaze. The sun streaking through the window lit the room with brilliance and gleamed on his sleeked-back hair.

"Then what's wrong? I can tell you're thinking something." His dark eyebrows slanted in a frown.

"Well?" he challenged when she didn't answer.

She hesitated a moment longer, then said, "The loom. Why don't you put it here on the floor so people can get close to it?"

He gave her a startled what-do-you-know-about-it look. "But then they could touch it," he said, explaining the obvious.

She laughed. "Well, isn't that the point? How else will anyone get to know it? They need to touch it, feel it. Use it! String some wool yarn; let them see how it works."

Dark eyes under lowered brows flicked to hers and held. She wasn't sure if he resented her comment or was inviting her to go on, but she went on anyway.

"Have Navajo elders come in to teach your cultural heritage group how to design and weave a rug."

During the long moment that followed, she feared she'd made him angry, but then his brow smoothed and his mouth tilted into a half-cocked smile, which she figured was better than no smile at all. She was encouraged by it.

"And here." She put her hand on a flat rectangular rock and stroked the wide, smooth indentation on its surface. "This *metate*," she went on. "If you put it on the floor and put some dried corn or beans in it, the kids can use the grinding stone and learn what it feels like to grind corn and beans."

Durango inclined his head and gave her a frank measuring look, his eyes quizzical.

She guessed he was wondering about the validity of her suggestions, whether or not he could trust her judgment.

"I worked for a historical museum before I came here," she said, offering up a mini-resume. "I have degrees in Archival Studies and Museum Design."

He considered that, eyes narrowed in contemplation, then nodded sharply, apparently finding her credentials acceptable. "Okay," he said. "What else?"

Her eyes scanned the room, picking out objects lying haphazardly about, or spilling from the opened, but as yet unpacked, boxes of donated Southwest historiana.

"Hang some of those Navajo rugs on the wall where they can be seen instead of folded up in that glass case," she went on. "Put some on the floor. And arrange something along this wall. Sallie Rainwater's boys are artistic. Have them paint a mural. Or better yet, have them make a life-size diorama of an Indian village. Let your students see up close how their ancestors lived. How better to help them understand their heritage?"

"Yes," he said, almost to himself. "That's what they must do."

His eyes were studying her so attentively she wondered what they saw. Since the day she met this enigmatic man, everything about him had said *I don't need you,* but the words he spoke now had a beseeching quality.

"Can you spare some time to work with me today?"

Her heart tripped over itself. "Sure," she said. "I'll make time."

They worked together all morning, Amanda giving thoughtful suggestions, Durango arranging and rearranging displays according to her bidding. In the near distance, the school bell rang for lunch, and they walked across the parking lot to the high school cafeteria to eat lunch and talk.

That they were still talking when the bell rang, signaling the end of lunch hour didn't go unnoticed by some of the senior students. Amanda saw the girls throwing sidelong glances, and heard them giggling and whispering behind their hands, and caught the boys' knowing smiles as the students left the lunchroom for their afternoon classes.

"I think we may have started a rumor," she said with a low laugh. "I hope the kids don't get the wrong idea."

Durango rolled his eyes and nodded. "These kids get all kinds of ideas. I never know what they're going to come up with next."

A lull followed, and she sat back, thinking hard for a way to keep the conversation going.

"Sallie tells me you're a movie producer," she said, breaking the silence.

Faint clouds settled lightly on his features when he replied. "I used to be."

"Why'd you stop?" she asked. "I know Los Angeles is a company town, but if you're in the company, it's not such a bad place," she teased.

He gave her a slightly sardonic grin of agreement, but didn't answer.

"Didn't you like the movie business?"

"Oh, I liked it," he said. "It didn't like me."

She had a feeling there was more, something more than not being liked by movie people, and that he was coping with a hurt that wasn't healing very well.

"I didn't fit in," he said flatly.

Amanda studied his face, and her heart ached as she recognized the same pain in his eyes that she saw in her mirror every morning. Being an outcast was nothing new to her. She knew what it was like to not fit in, and felt a kind of alliance with him because of it. It was the first time she'd felt connected to anyone in that way, and she wanted to acknowledge or comment on it, but didn't know how he'd react. She decided to keep her words light.

"Sallie said you won an award. What was it?"

Something flickered in his gaze, something sharp and tense, but then his expression eased.

"I produced a documentary about the importance of preserving Native American culture. It was voted 'Most Important Documentary of the Decade' at a film festival in Salt Lake City. The critics loved it."

"That's quite an accomplishment," she said, genuinely impressed.

"Yeah," he said, "it was. But after the film festival, I couldn't get anyone to finance distribution to theaters. No one was interested in it except Native Americans, and they weren't able to raise the kind of money it would take to get the film out where it would do the most good."

His tone roughened a little, not exactly bitter, but disappointed, hurt. If she'd realized talking about it would be painful, she wouldn't have brought it up, but he went on before she could redirect the conversation.

"Before that, I'd played the studio game, writing and directing the kind of movies Hollywood loves and clones at every opportunity. You know, car chase shoot-'em-ups, date flicks, buddy-type films. And a western. After I won the award for the documentary, I realized that's what I wanted to concentrate on, but suddenly nobody wanted to know me. I couldn't get any backers."

His voice was deep and resonant, and Amanda realized this was the longest she'd ever heard him speak.

"After ten years of making successful commercial films, my best work was being rejected by the establishment. But then it occurred to me that it wasn't my work they didn't like. It was my message, my very origins, and by extension . . ." He looked up. "Me."

He frowned, his black eyes darkening as he drifted back in time.

"Is that why you came back to the reservation?" she asked.

Durango slid his lips into a sad, grim smile and nodded. "I'd made a good amount of money over the years, so I decided that if I wanted to show Native Americans the importance of recording their history, I could do it better by coming back here and building a Navajo Cultural Center at the high school. And as an adjunct of that, form an interactive history club where students could be proactive in learning about their heritage."

Amanda nodded in understanding.

"At about that same time, my sister asked me to come back to help with a problem involving some land the family owns. So the timing was right."

Amanda's mind drew a picture of Buck Powell sprawled on the floor, rubbing his jaw. She remembered what Sallie had told her about seeing a bulldozer at the property line this morning and wondered if Durango knew.

"By the way," he said abruptly, changing the subject. "I found the letter from your father telling me you were coming to Monument Valley. It fell behind my desk before I had a chance to open it. To be honest, I don't even remember receiving it."

Amanda figured that was as close as she was going to get to an apology for his rudeness when she arrived, so smiled her acceptance.

At Durango's mention of her father, she was reminded to ask if he'd been able to talk to his friend about the accident investigation report.

Durango shook his head. "Not yet. He's visiting his sister in San Diego. I left a message for him to call me when he gets back."

Amanda looked away quickly to hide her disappointment, not wanting him to think her ungrateful of his efforts to help. She noticed the lunchroom was completely empty now, even the cooks and cafeteria servers had left.

"I've got to get back," Amanda said, not really wanting to. She liked being with him, talking to him. "I have to begin sorting and cataloguing some early-century diaries today. I don't want to get behind schedule."

As they stood to leave, Durango's eyes washed over her with an expression she couldn't read. *What are you thinking?* she wondered, trying to interpret his scrutiny. Then she blushed and hoped he couldn't read *her* thoughts, which were distinctly inappropriate and involved bare skin.

In darting glances, Durango watched her as they walked back to the Center after lunch. She was natural, unpretentious, honest. All the things that had been missing in his life for a long time. Or maybe they'd never had been in his life, but still he felt a longing as if they had.

Of course, she's in a hurry, he thought. She has a schedule. A deadline to meet. She's anxious to finish cataloguing the diaries and all the rest of it. Because the sooner she's through, the sooner she can leave. Then she'd go back to a life as different from his as the night was from the day. Nothing about their lives was the same, and never could be.

He held the door open, and Amanda gave him a smile as she walked through it. She was nice and tall and walked proudly on long, strong legs that swung easily from her slender hips. He wondered what it would be like to kiss and hold someone as tall as he was, eye to eye, mouth to mouth, one long body pressed against another long body.

His thoughts dissolved as she went directly into her office, and immediately busied herself pulling books and journals out of dusty boxes.

He sat at his desk. With effort, he turned his thoughts away from Amanda, but then found himself thinking about Sharron, the reason he'd left the reservation in the first place.

His mind burned with the memory, and suddenly he was seventeen again and so hotly in love with Sharron, it took his breath away. They hadn't meant to fall in love, but they did and wanted to marry. Their parents were outraged. Navajo tradition prohibited marriage between a man and a woman of the same clan.

"But father," Durango had argued, "we're not related by blood." His hands were clenched into fists, and the pain of a thousand red-hot knives tore at his chest.

"It doesn't matter, my son. You cannot marry Sharron."

"But I will be a *good* husband. I will love her and take care of her and keep her safe. You'll see. I swear to you I will."

His father shook his head, his mouth a tight, hard line. "It is forbidden. We must follow the tradition of our people."

When Sharron's family moved and took her away, Durango was sure he'd die. He lay in the desert under the midnight sky and pounded his fists in anger, protesting a tradition that would keep lovers apart. Over time, he renounced those traditions and drew away from the beliefs of his people until he felt he no longer belonged. He stayed just long enough to graduate from high school, then left the reservation, vowing never to return.

Sounds from the next room came to him now—boxes being ripped opened, books being placed on a table, pages riffling. Amanda was singing quietly to herself as she worked. Her voice was serene, warm as sunlight. He pushed noisily away from his desk and stomped out.

For the next couple of hours, Amanda worked without stopping. She was aware that Durango had left shortly after lunch, his boots punishing the wooden steps as he went, and she found herself wondering where he was. As she pored over aged and faded journals, his face superimposed over the yellowed pages. She tried to be realistic and not consider him in a romantic way, but every time she thought of him at all, her heart thumped alarmingly.

She stood up from the worktable where she'd been sitting, shoulders slumped, reading diaries for hours. She put her hands behind her hips, and stretched and arched her back, feeling the tension release. Through the windows, she could see the last of the daylight slipping away. Time to go home, before it got too dark.

She went to her desk to write out a to-do list for the next day. As she took a pen from the drawer and pulled a note pad toward her, something at the edge of her desk caught her eye. She picked it up and held it to the light.

It was a small stone pendant hanging from a thin leather cord. The flat stone was triangular in shape, but polished to a shine, angles smoothed and rounded. It looked old and the colors were odd. Reddish on top, black on the bottom. A tiny hole drilled in the stone accommodated the leather cord, making a primitive sort of necklace.

She wondered how long it had been on her desk and who had put it there, then realized one of the students must have dropped it accidentally. Students often came in on their lunch hour to talk to Durango about a history project, or browse through the books in her office, or sometimes just to peek curiously at her.

Or was there another possibility? Did someone bring it to her as a gift? It didn't look casually dropped; it had the appearance of having been deliberately placed.

Carefully, Amanda laid it back on the desk. If someone lost

it, they'd come looking for it. She decided to leave the pendant exactly as she found it.

CHAPTER SIX

What Jack Rice liked best about owning a newspaper was that he got to know everybody's business. And that business could be pretty interesting, considering the town was full of strays and misfits. They all had pasts that were dubious at best, and they all had stories. Jack was no exception. He shook his head, banishing the fragmented memory of that little episode back in the sixties with the police officer in Chicago. That was a long time ago, before he came West. But, what the hell. Everyone here had secrets. Why couldn't he?

Jack gazed at his image in the back-bar mirror and reflected that not only did people readily, eagerly even, tell him things, but he could ask anybody anything and get away with it. Nobody questioned his right to ask—he was a newspaper editor, after all—and he usually got answers, too. It's amazing, Jack marveled, what people would tell him, not only when they wanted to get their names *in* the newspaper, but also, and especially, when they wanted to keep their names *out*.

Jack puckered his lips around the business end of a longneck beer bottle and swigged deeply. His gaze idly swept the nearly empty café. He put the bottle on the bar, motioned for another, and went back to pondering the advantages of his chosen career.

Sometimes Jack didn't even have to ask questions to find things out. People just naturally sought him out. Like the day that tall blond girl walked into the newspaper office looking for a place to live. She was a puzzler at first, but then he heard she was the daughter of that professor who crashed in the desert.

It didn't take much inquiring for Jack to find out she was working with that snotty Navajo out at the high school. The Indian said he was building a cultural center for his people, which Jack thought was a pretty strange thing for someone who had turned his back on his people, and only came home when someone laid claim to his property.

The girl—what was her name again? Oh, yes, Amanda. Jack figured she came to Monument Valley to find out what happened to her father. He wondered if he should tell her what he saw in the desert that day.

Jack put the bottle to his mouth, tilted his head, and drank thirstily, recalling the events in detail.

He'd been hiking on Comb Ridge when he saw smoke lifting above the rim of the canyon. Hurriedly, he clambered up a pile of tumbled rocks to gain a vantage point. The canyon gaped below, a wide crevasse like an earthquake's yawn zig-zagging across the dun-colored desert. On the canyon floor far below, flames licked and smoke billowed from a van that had dropped nose first into a shallow erosion gully. A man was hauling cargo out of the van through the hatchback.

Jack had immediately pulled his cell phone from his pocket to summon help, but stopped when he saw the man drag the cargo he'd pulled from the blazing van to a cave partially hidden in the rock wall. He watched in astonishment as the man put the boxes inside the cave, covered the entrance with boulders, then ran into the desert away from the fire, which by now was on its way to engulfing the van.

Scrambling from the rock pile, he made his way down the steep trail, occasionally losing his footing on the glacial drift that made up the surface of the slope in his hurry to get to the bottom. It was a good ten minutes before he got to a spot where he could again look down into the canyon. He saw another sight he almost couldn't believe.

Now there were people down there, Indians. Two of them pulled a man from the driver's side of the flaming van. Five or six others rolled the boulders away from the cave's entrance and dragged the boxes out.

Chest heaving, heart pounding, Jack pulled his binoculars from his backpack and sighted on the hurried activity below. Two things confounded him right away.

First, all of the Indians were wearing red bandanas folded and tied around their foreheads. Second, the boxes they were taking out of the cave held antiquities. Jack got a good look when one of the boxes broke open and the contents tumbled out.

The Indians laid the van driver's body in the back of a pickup, piled the cartons of rugs, pots and other artifacts around him, and drove off into the desert, disappearing in a cloud of red dust.

Not much stunned Jack Rice after sixty-five years, but this had put him butt down on the rocky trail. He sat there, his mind awhirl, trying to make sense of what he'd seen. He wasn't close enough to recognize the Indians, and he had no idea where they went, but he meant to find out. It wasn't the driver of the van he was interested in—he looked dead anyway. It was the boxes.

Jack had done some quick calculations in his head and concluded that his contacts in Phoenix and Albuquerque would pay a good price for the contents of those boxes. If only he knew where they were.

His mind drifted back to the present when his attention was pulled to a family in a corner booth of the dimly lit cafe. Two children squabbled noisily over the menu while the mother gently tried to resolve the dispute. Jack sent a smile in their direction and nodded cordially. Always pays to be neighborly.

Yep, he'd be a fool to tell Amanda—or anyone—what he knew. Instead, he figured to wait and see if she'd lead him to the artifacts. Who was it that said all good things come to those who wait? Well, that's what he was doing. Waiting. Following that girl around . . . and waiting. Along with the nose for news all good newspapermen possessed, Jack had the patience of a saint. Well, maybe not exactly a saint, he amended, smiling to himself.

He put some bills on the bar, gave a two-fingered salute to the barkeep, and slid off the stool. Only time will tell, he reminded himself. As Daddy used to say, give *anything* enough time, and it will come around again.

CHAPTER SEVEN

August came in a rush, surprising Amanda with its arrival, and bringing with it a bittersweet uncertainty. Though she loved where she was and the work she was doing for her father, six weeks into her new life, she had to admit to fleeting moments of homesickness. Those moments did not include Elliott Sheffield. She hardly thought of him at all, and the idea of having almost been his wife was a barely perceptible memory.

As well, each passing day brought more anxiety about what had happened to her father.

No more mysterious notes appeared on her door. She received no more invitations to attend secret meetings in remote canyons, nor admonitions to go home though she was sure the latter sentiment remained. She was disappointed that the long-awaited investigation report from Durango's friend provided no new information, and drew the same conclusions as the initial accident report she'd already read. *Cause of accident: suspected drunk driving. Dr. Maynard Bell: missing and presumed dead.*

She knew any reasonable person would drop the matter. But she'd stopped listening to reason the day she walked out of her stepfather's mansion. Now she was listening to her gut, and her gut was telling her there was more to it. Since being on her own, she was learning how to pay attention to her instincts. She had to. There was no one else to depend on.

Included in her uncertainty was the matter of Durango.

Why did she feel stabbed in the heart when she thought of

him? She had memorized things about him that no sensible woman would have noticed. Like the way his Levi's snugged his behind, and his habit of standing hipshot with his thumbs stuck in his belt loops. The little concentration crease on his forehead when he was deep in thought. Sometimes in the middle of the day, she'd find that her attention had strayed from the pages she was reading to a picture of Durango Yazzie's face in her mind.

Lately she'd been seized with the irrational notion that it would be nice to lay her cheek against his. She even imagined for a moment what it would feel like to kiss him, then mentally kicked herself for being so stupid.

Because that was never going to happen.

For one thing, it would be pointless; she was leaving in a few months, just as soon as she finished archiving her father's collection. For another, and it pained her to think it, Durango obviously didn't have any similar feelings about her. Since the day she'd helped him with the museum displays, he'd indulged her with the sparest of smiles, the barest of glances, reinforcing what she already knew about how she looked. She was plain, as her mother had often reminded her.

She gave a regretful sigh, eased her Jeep to a stop, and set the parking brake in front of Cammie Drew's low-slung, board-and-batten house. The house, within sight and walking distance of the Medical Center, overlooked a broad sweep of tableland.

The sun, making its descent, limned the western rimrock with gold while washing the desert with an amber afterglow. Quiet settled in. Except for some nightbirds circling overhead, nothing much moved. Amanda strode the powdery red dust path to the front porch overhang.

Cammie, barefoot and wearing one of her many flower-print granny dresses, flung open the front door at Amanda's knock. The enticing aroma of coffee beans wafted across the threshold, drifting into the night air. Amanda sniffed appreciatively.

"Guatemalan," Cammie announced, tilting her head over her shoulder toward the kitchen. She stepped back to let Amanda enter. "From the central highlands," she went on. "Antigua, to be exact. My mother sent them. They arrived today." She looked over the tops of her wire-rimmed spectacles and smiled at Amanda. "Glad you could come and share them with me."

The two young women could not have been any more divergent in looks and background, but had become close friends since meeting at the health clinic in June. Amanda admired the strength and independent spirit of Cammie who, as a wide-eyed Native American advocate, had come fresh out of medical school to this largely inhospitable part of the country with a single-minded goal of providing some much needed health care to the Navajos in Monument Valley.

Amanda sat at the scarred kitchen table while Cammie attended to the coffee, effortlessly performing the precise and unchanging ceremony. Rich dark-roasted beans rattled into a coffee mill then were reduced to savory granules that filled the kitchen with delicious aromas.

When Cammie was satisfied with the texture and consistency of the grains, she scooped them into a gold-plated filter that she fitted into a sleek Euro-design drip-style coffee brewer, her one indulgence in an otherwise austere lifestyle. She filled the water receptacle, flicked the switch, and within seconds coffee began dribbling gently into a sparkling glass carafe.

Leaning her hip against the edge of the counter, she folded her arms loosely at her waist while she waited.

"That's pretty," she said, her eyes at Amanda's throat. "What is it?"

Amanda fingered the black and red pendant hanging around her neck. "I found it on my desk. I think it belongs to one of the students, but no one's come back for it. I'm wearing it hoping the owner will notice and claim it."

Cammie's cool green eyes appraised her kindly. "I like the way you're doing your hair, too. Indian-style."

Amanda smoothed her palm down the thick blond braid laying over the front of her shoulder, a slight flush warming her cheeks as Cammie's unexpected comment defined her new look. It was only when she heard the words *Indian-style* that Amanda realized she was unconsciously emulating the hairstyle of the young Indian girls at the high school by plaiting her hair.

"Thanks," she replied.

When the coffee finished dripping, Cammie filled two mugs and set them on the table along with a bowl of sugar and a cracked crock of real cream. She sat opposite Amanda and let out a long satisfied sigh. For a moment, the two friends sipped their coffee in companionable silence.

Amanda hadn't had any close girlfriends growing up so she enjoyed the camaraderie of these moments with Cammie. Since arriving in Monument Valley, she'd often sought Cammie's counsel and advice, and Cammie didn't seem to mind taking on the role of confidante.

Now, in the comfortable warmth of Cammie's kitchen, Amanda was working up the nerve to bring up the one subject they hadn't ever discussed at length. With a sudden burst of courage, she set her mug on the table in front of her, and cupped her hands around it as if to ground herself to something solid.

"Cammie, can I ask you something?"

"Of course. What is it?"

"What do you know about Durango?"

Cammie cocked an eyebrow and studied Amanda over the top of her skinny eyeglasses, her mouth in a one-sided smile. "I know he's devilishly handsome, but that's stating the obvious. What exactly did you want to know?"

Suddenly embarrassed that she'd asked, Amanda inclined her head and frowned slightly into her coffee mug trying to hide her discomfort. Cammie, her usual perceptive instincts in high gear, sensed her uneasiness and nodded knowingly.

"Well," she began, "he's not married. He's not gay. He's not attached—unless you count his attachment to the Cultural Center. Is that what you wanted to know?"

Amanda nodded. "He just seems so . . ."

"Distant?"

Amanda nodded again.

"Unfriendly?"

"Uh-huh."

"Lost?"

Amanda looked up, eyes wide. "Especially that."

"Are you falling for him?" Cammie asked after a moment.

"No." The word rose and fell uncertainly from Amanda's lips and didn't fool Cammie for a minute.

"Don't, Amanda. There's no chance. I don't mean just no chance for you. I mean there's no chance for any woman who isn't Navajo. Since he's come back to the reservation, he's recommitted to his culture. He won't get involved with a white woman." She paused. "At least not in any long-term permanent way, not the way you'd want."

Disappointed, Amanda slid her glance outside the window and watched for a moment as long shadows slipped away with the last of the daylight.

"Trust me on this," Cammie added thoughtfully. "I know. There was a time I thought differently."

Amanda took that to mean that Cammie was speaking from experience, and it confirmed what she'd first suspected, that Cammie and Durango had had a personal relationship at one time. How far it had gone, she didn't know and wasn't going to ask. It was Cammie's business, and she'd share it when she was ready.

"But didn't his sister marry out of their culture?" she asked instead.

"Yes. Many Navajo do nowadays. But Durango . . ." Cammie trailed off. "I think it's guilt."

"Guilt?"

Cammie's gaze rested softly on her friend.

"Well, I guess I'm not telling any secrets. It goes back a lot of years, but it's pretty common knowledge that Durango's family wouldn't allow him to marry his high school sweetheart because she belonged to the same clan. That's when he left the reservation and basically . . ." she turned her hands palms up and hiked her shoulders, "left his culture behind. He was angry. But then he had some disappointments out in Hollywood, too."

"Yes, he told me about that." But not about the other.

"Well, now that he's embraced his culture again, he's done it completely. Sort of an atonement for turning his back on it when he was young. Now he feels he has to make a choice. The white way or the Navajo way, but not both."

That must be what he meant about not fitting in, Amanda thought, recalling their conversation at lunch that day. Her heart gave a painful squeeze as she recognized that particular pain.

From outside, headlights flashed and dimmed through the windows as a car pulled into the driveway.

"Who's that?" Cammie craned her neck to look down the hall through the living room windows. The headlights blinked out and a car door thunked shut. "I never have visitors after dark. Unless maybe someone's sick or hurt."

Cammie padded barefoot down the hall into the living room and after a moment Amanda heard a delighted cry when the front door swooped open.

"Noah!" Cammie's surprised but welcoming voice floated into the kitchen.

"Hey! Cammie!" hailed a cheerful male voice. Then there were sounds of bear hugs and greetings, the reunion ritual of good friends.

"Come on in, have some coffee. It's fresh. My mother sent the beans from Central America."

"Mmmm," the man said. "One of the perks of being the love-child of sixties hippie parents."

"Yes, it is, actually." Cammie laughed good-naturedly. "They're down there with Habitat for Humanity, building houses in an earthquake-damaged village."

She came back into the kitchen, her wrist slung loosely through the arm of a slim but well-built man with a suntanned, boyish-looking face and a killer smile. He was wearing jeans, Gucci loafers, and a forest-green V-neck sweater. The red baseball cap turned backwards on his head didn't cover the escaping wisps of short, sun-streaked hair.

Cammie introduced him. "This is Noah Tucker. He's a friend of Durango's from Los Angeles."

"And a friend of yours, I hope," Noah interjected, his eyes seeking hers.

She laughed lightly and gave his arm a quick comradely squeeze. "Noah's a movie director," she told Amanda, then turned back to Noah. "Sit down. Have some coffee."

Noah had large glamorous blue eyes that sparkled when he smiled. He sat at the table and accepted the mug of coffee Cammie put in front of him.

"I'm looking for Durango now. Do you know where he is? I went to his house, but he wasn't home. He wasn't at his mother's, either."

Cammie shrugged and looked at Amanda as if expecting her to know Durango's whereabouts, as if Amanda kept track of his comings and goings. Which she secretly admitted she made an effort to do, but didn't want them to know it, so she rounded her eyes, lifted her shoulders and shook her head.

"No. I don't know where he is," she answered truthfully.

Noah sipped his coffee, gave an appreciative hum, sipped again and set his cup down.

"We don't start work on my movie until next week, but I came early for the art festival. I'm anxious to see Jeremiah's new work. It's all the buzz in L.A. You got anything to eat?" he asked abruptly.

Noah's gaze settled on Cammie with affection, and it became instantly clear to Amanda that he was madly in love with her. Apparently, Cammie's powers of perception didn't extend to matters involving herself, because she didn't seem to notice. Instead, she got up, went to the refrigerator and looked inside.

"I made chili, you want some?"

Noah nodded. "Sounds good."

"Where are you staying?" she asked, busying herself at the stove. "At Durango's?"

"Yeah. In the gourd house. But I don't have a key. That's why I'm looking for him."

At Amanda's blank look, Noah explained. "Durango has a guest house on his property that is decorated inside and out with ornamental gourds. It's very cool."

"You haven't been there?" Cammie glanced at Amanda over her shoulder. "You've got to see it. The patio in back and the veranda in front are draped with live, growing gourd vines. Hundreds of gourds, all colors, all sizes and shapes. It's a curiosity."

"Are you working with Durango on the Cultural Center?" Noah asked Amanda.

"No. We share office space." Amanda explained her project to Noah who was interested and asked a lot of questions.

"Have you known Durango long?" Amanda asked, curious to know how these two men with such opposing personalities and characteristics got along and came to be friends in the first place.

"We were at UCLA Film School together. We shared an apartment and after graduation worked on a couple of film projects together."

Cammie put a steaming bowl of chili in front of Noah, then sat down next to him, oblivious of his lingering gaze when he thanked her. He picked up his spoon, talking while he ate.

"Durango is a genius of a filmmaker. I was sorry to see him leave the business." His tone approached near reverence when he talked about his friend. "He has this uncanny ability to see the minutest details in a frame of film. It's amazing. He never missed anything; rarely had to reshoot a visual. I call it the film-maker's third eye. Every director in Hollywood envied him." Noah turned his attention to the chili, eating hungrily.

"How long are you staying in Monument Valley?" Cammie wanted to know.

"Well, we shoot here for four weeks with the extras, then the cast and crew go back to California for postproduction. But I'll be staying on. I'm scouting some Native American music for my next film, so I'll spend a few days in Window Rock, hit the local clubs there, then go on to Albuquerque. Maybe later to Phoenix. I'm looking for a dynamite homegrown band. You know, Native American Rock. Something more traditional than commercial. Something authentic. I'm looking for a . . ." he hesitated, his chili spoon suspended in the air while he sought words, ". . . a Reservation Sound. I'll know it when I hear it."

"Have you met the Rainwater boys?" Cammie asked.

Noah shook his head, his mouth full, obviously enjoying the meal, more so, Amanda guessed, because Cammie had made it.

"They play in a band that's scheduled to perform at Desert Dazzle," Cammie told him. "People around here think they're pretty good."

"I'll check them out tomorrow."

Amanda listened to Noah and Cammie's friendly relaxed bantering, and felt a fledgling sense of belonging that making friends in a strange place brings, but at the same time her heart was swept with a strange loneliness. Her mind wandered and she found herself thinking about Durango. Again.

She would have liked it if he were here in this room with her, would have liked to be connected to him if only in casual intimacy. No, that wasn't true. She wanted more than that. She wanted Durango to look at her the way Noah looked at Cammie, with eyes full of promise and desire. She wondered where Durango would be on a Friday night.

Tomorrow she would see him, actually be with him, at the art festival. He had asked her to help him out at the Cultural Center booth, and she had eagerly agreed. It crossed her mind to wonder if he had asked her because he wanted her there, or because he needed a couple of extra hands. It didn't really matter. She wanted to be with him.

The sound of Noah's laughter broke her reverie, and she let her mind be pulled back to the warmth of the kitchen. Cammie was laughing, too, and had placed her hand lightly on Noah's arm in casual affection as they shared a joke Amanda had not heard. There was something warm and enchanting in their gentle camaraderie, and she envied them a little. Tears gathered and burned behind her eyes. When they threatened to spill down her cheeks, she lowered her head and blinked them back, looking at her watch as if checking the time.

"It's getting late," she said. "I've got to go. I'm meeting Durango tomorrow morning at seven to help him set up his booth. Some of his cultural heritage students are exhibiting historical displays, and I promised to pitch in for the day."

Noah dragged his gaze away from Cammie and glanced at his watch, then yawned and stretched. "I should go, too," he said. "I left L.A. this morning and drove all day. I'm beat. Can I use your phone? My cell can't pick up a signal way out here. I want to see if I can track Durango down."

"Sure," Cammie replied and pointed down the hallway. "It's in the bedroom."

Amanda helped clear the table as Cammie rinsed cups and dishes and put them in the dishwasher. At the front door, Amanda hugged her friend good-bye.

"He's really cute," she said, her voice low so it wouldn't carry.

Cammie tilted her head and raised her brows, taken aback at the comment. "Noah?"

"He adores you," Amanda whispered.

"Noah?" Cammie said again and looked toward the bedroom where he was talking on the telephone. "Noah Tucker?"

Amanda laughed lightly and hugged her speechless friend again, their cheeks touching briefly.

"Yes," she said. "Noah Tucker. How many Noahs do you know? He's crazy about you."

"Ohmigod," Cammie said in disbelief, blushing mightily.

Amanda made her way out the door and across the porch. "See you tomorrow at the art festival," she called back as Cammie waved and closed the door.

A full moon hung high, lighting Amanda's way down the path to her Jeep parked next to a silver Mercedes that she assumed belonged to Noah. The blue-black sky was filled with stars and she paused a moment to take in the overwhelming vastness of it. No sound but the passing air broke the stillness, air so clean and clear she could feel the tangible, palpable presence of nothing.

She hugged her sweater closed against the night chill and made her way toward her car, then stopped as her heart kicked up into her throat, cutting off her breath.

She stood rooted to the spot, a scream stuck in her chest as her mind first denied then struggled to process what her eyes were seeing. Something red was smeared on her windshield, a message written in blood—*GO HOME.*

Her frantic gaze swung around to pierce the darkness at the edge of the driveway and into the shadows beyond. She saw no one and nothing moved. Her heart beat wildly as she turned and ran back to the house where she hammered furiously on the door.

"Cammie! Cammie! Open the door!"

Noah flung the door wide, his face perplexed, the telephone receiver still pressed at his ear, his conversation having been interrupted by her urgent pounding.

"Amanda! What happened?"

Cammie was coming up behind him from the kitchen, peering over his shoulder, her startling green eyes filling with alarm. She squeezed past him to reach out and pull Amanda inside.

"Someone slashed my tires!" Amanda's breath was being swallowed by fear and she gasped, forcing the words out. "And smeared blood on my windshield!"

"It's Amanda," Noah said into the phone, his boyish face hard and serious. "Someone slashed her tires," he said, repeating her words and nodding as he listened to instructions coming from the other end of the line.

"Okay," he said, and nodded again. "Okay." He hung up.

"That was Durango," he told Amanda. "He said to stay here. He's coming to get you."

Cammie put her arm around Amanda and led her to the sofa where they sat down. She slid a Navajo blanket from the sofa back and hugged it around Amanda's shaking shoulders.

"Noah, would you bring her a glass of water, please?"

He went into the kitchen and when he returned with the

84

water asked, "Do you have a flashlight? I'll go out and look around."

Cammie told him where she kept it, then held the glass to Amanda's trembling lips. "Here, drink this. I'm going to give you a sedative. Doctor's orders."

Amanda took a sip, and shook her head. "No, I don't need it. I'm fine."

But she wasn't. She gulped at the jagged rock of fear in her throat. Her stomach was rolling and she took some deep breaths trying to settle it.

Cammie got up and peeked through the blinds, watching Noah outside. After a few moments, he came in, shivering, ears red from the night chill.

"Well, it's not blood," he announced. "It's red spray paint."

Amanda went from shock to disbelief, not quite sure if she should let fear or anger take control.

"Paint? Who would . . . ?" Her fuzzy brain could barely formulate the questions, let alone come up with any answers. She was sure that whoever did this also left the note on her door at the trading post. But why? What had she done? Who hated her enough to want her gone?

"We'd better call the police," Cammie said. She took a jacket from the closet and handed it to Noah, who was still shivering. "Here, California guy. Put this on." She reached for the phone, but Noah stopped her.

"No. Let's wait for Durango."

As if on cue, Durango's big blue pickup roared up the driveway.

"Here he is now," Noah said.

Heavy footsteps pounded on the porch decking. When Noah opened the door, Durango rushed in, his eyes stormy, a worried line carved deep between his eyebrows. His eyes sought and caught on Amanda's before she leaned forward, braced her elbows against her knees, and took a deep breath. Her stomach was rolling again.

Hurried strides took him to the sofa, and he sat down beside her. His clean male scent filled her head as she breathed deeply, trying to get a grip on herself. He took the glass from her hand, sliding his fingers over hers. With extreme gentleness, he took her hand in his and held it. She caught a whiff of something sweet on his skin.

"Tell me what happened," he said. His eyes roamed her face, and strange feelings stirred inside her. She started to answer his question, but her voice caught on a sob as he opened his arms and she fell into them.

Suddenly Noah, Cammie, and Amanda were all talking at once, relating the events of the evening. Amanda, sniffing a little, described what she'd seen, her words muffled against Durango's leather jacket. She shuddered as the sight of her car, red-smeared and all four tires slashed, replayed itself over and over in her mind.

"I called the Tribal Police from the car," Durango said. "They should be here any minute."

"I'll watch for them." Noah went to the window and peered outside.

But it was more than a few minutes and by the time they arrived an hour later, Amanda wasn't so much frightened as angry. The attack on her car was almost as much an outrage as an attack on her person would have been.

A young, nice-looking Navajo police officer took a report, asking questions in a calm voice, while two other officers walked around outside. Through the window, Amanda could see their pale yellow flashlight beams drilling into the darkness and dragging convulsively along the uneven red earth as it rose and fell into the distance.

So many cars had been in and out of Cammie's driveway, it

was impossible for them to identify whose tires made which treads. One of the policemen came in gingerly carrying a plastic bag containing the used can of spray paint that had been tossed into the brush across the road. They promised to drive around the area looking for anything or anyone that appeared suspicious.

Durango went outside with them for a few minutes then came back in and went right to Amanda's side. He took her hand and laced his fingers through hers.

The four of them sat together a while longer, speculating and making futile attempts to come up with answers to who had damaged the Jeep. Who was trying to frighten her away? And why?

No one had to say aloud the thought that hung in the air, so heavy and oppressive she could feel the weight of its presence on her skin—the violence against her car was a not-so-veiled threat of violence against her.

She shuddered involuntarily and Durango gave her hand a light, quick squeeze. "It's all right."

But Amanda knew there wasn't anything all right about any of it, including the fact that she was being drawn to a man she shouldn't want and, according to Cammie, couldn't have.

"I don't think I can get a flatbed here to tow the Jeep away until tomorrow," Durango said to Cammie.

Another wave of desolation washed over Amanda as it hit her what not having a car really meant. In the far-flung emptiness of desert living, a car represented independence and a measure of security. Now she had neither.

"Can someone drive me home?" she asked in a small voice.

"Home!" The word flew from Durango's mouth, and his black eyebrows dashed down between his darkened eyes. "You're not going home," he told her. "You're coming with me."

Amanda, not wanting to weaken, not wanting to rely on someone to hold her up who might not be there tomorrow, started to protest, but Durango deliberately cut her off.

"Don't even consider it. You're staying at my house. You'll be safe there."

Durango's tone made it clear that he would brook no argument, and when Noah and Cammie quickly agreed it was a good idea, Amanda gave in, silently grateful that she would not have to spend the night alone in her apartment, which suddenly loomed cold and forbidding.

CHAPTER EIGHT

Cars, vans and trucks had begun streaming into Monument Valley the day before the Desert Dazzle Art Festival officially opened, causing a giant crush on the highway. The temporary campground that had been set up a half mile from the festival site was filled by noon. By ten o'clock opening day, the crowd had grown to thousands.

Amanda leaned out of the Cultural Center booth and peered up the two-lane blacktop leading to the Navajo Tribal Park. As far as she could see, both sides of the road were lined with display tables and makeshift booths. Artists had come from as far away as New York and California. Many had been up all night arranging their artwork on primitive canvas-and-plywood display backdrops.

The road itself had been closed off to vehicle traffic forming a giant outdoor pedestrian mall. Hundreds of people poured through the entrance gate. Musicians carrying their instruments. Native dancers in showy costumes. Strutting, gun-toting Old West reenactors. Navajo families in traditional dress. Everyone looked as if they'd stepped straight out of the pages of history.

Amanda quickly realized this was more than a local art show. Durango told her that Jeremiah had been approached many times about changing the name from Desert Dazzle Art Festival to something which more appropriately described what it really was, a celebration of Native American and Southwestern art and lifestyles.

She couldn't help being carried away by the exhilarating sights and sounds. The excitement was contagious and she allowed it to blunt the sharp edges of her fear and anger. But not her determination. She was convinced that what happened last night was somehow related to her father's accident. All she had to do was stick around long enough, and stay alive long enough to figure out the connection.

Except for the few hours she slept, Durango had kept a protective eye on her since they'd left Cammie's house the night before. He had taken her to her apartment to pack some clothes and toiletries, then driven directly to his sprawling adobe house adjacent to the reservation's northern boundary.

There he had hustled her inside, showed her to her room, then locked the doors and windows and turned on all the outside lights.

"The dogs outside will bark and wake me if anyone comes around," he'd told her. "No one will get past them."

This morning he had hustled her right back out as the sun was coming up, hurrying to the festival site to help his students put the finishing touches on the display booth. As it turned out, plenty of students showed up to help, so there wasn't much for her to do. She pitched in anyway, handing out to interested passersby brochures that outlined Durango's lecture schedule and explained the many Cultural Center activities.

In the end, she was glad she had stayed at Durango's house. Despite the sedative Cammie had given her, she'd slept fitfully, waking twice with a start before realizing where she was. She probably wouldn't have slept at all if she'd gone to her apartment, but letting him take her in had aroused plenty of uncertainties. Was she in danger of incorrectly interpreting a simple act of kindness as a deeper kind of caring? By allowing her into his personal space, had he opened the door to some sort of connection between them? Or would two troubled misfits eventually find a bit of temporary comfort in each other's arms? Maybe she should be content with that and not press for more.

Her gaze glided to where he was standing a few feet away from her with two of his students, talking to a Navajo family, speaking his native language to them as easily as he spoke English to her. Side lit by the morning sun, the angles of his face were striking, the features distinct, each pronounced and definite as if carved by an artisan obsessive over details. She was attracted to him strongly and against her will. What kind of sense did that make for a liberated woman? Absolutely none. Falling for him was just an unforeseen hitch she'd have to get over.

A man with a camera, who Amanda had noticed waiting at the edge of the crowd around the booth, found an opening and approached Durango, introducing himself.

"I'm from the *Salt Lake City Tribune*. We heard about your historic preservation activities with the students. Would you mind telling me more about it?"

"Not at all." Durango smiled, his face animated as it always was when he talked about his work. While he was speaking, a Native American drum ensemble began a subtle, percolating percussion somewhere in the distance, providing what Amanda felt was a fitting musical accompaniment to Durango's words.

"Its mission is historical rediscovery and preservation," explained Durango to the reporter. "My students are interested in actively protecting elements of their culture, especially those in danger of being obliterated.

"Whenever possible we combine old ways with new ways if it results in learning." Durango stepped over to where a group of students and elders were together giving a rug-weaving demonstration. He motioned with his hand, touching and stroking the thick wool rugs as he talked. Amanda's eyes were drawn as they always were to the chunky silver-and-turquoise watchband clamped around his wrist. It looked solid and substantial. A man's watch.

"For instance," Durango was saying, "some of these rugs were woven from a design the students developed on a computer program. It was a way for them to learn about one of the traditions of their culture while at the same time developing their math skills."

The reporter was holding up a palm-sized tape recorder to catch Durango's words. Amanda was sure Durango was giving him enough information for several newspaper articles.

"The Student Cultural Heritage Club is like a Navajo rug design. When we started, we weren't sure how it would end up. We only knew that we were starting something good. As time went by, just like a traditional Navajo rug, it became a beautiful combination of creative effort and hard work. And it's still evolving. For the most part, the students decide on and develop their own cultural preservation projects and I encourage that."

Out of the corner of her eye, Amanda caught a glimpse of a heavyset woman walking with the side-to-side gait of old, bowed legs, her ankle-length crush-pleated skirt swaying above sneakered feet. Out of habit, Amanda centered her focus on the old woman's face. She hadn't given up the hope of finding the Navajo grandmother from the failed meeting in Twin Rocks Canyon.

As the old woman melted into the flow of people, Amanda's line of sight filled in with Jack Rice, smiling and waving from across the way. He was standing next to a Navajo taco stand, eating the traditional native meal from a limp paper plate. Seeing him there, she found herself inexplicably irritated for a brief moment as it struck her that she seemed to run into him everywhere. But of course he'd be around. He owned a newspaper. The art festival was news.

"Pretty."

Amanda's thoughts were interrupted by the sound of a tiny voice. She looked down into the small round face of a child. Ebony eyes glittered against the toffee-colored skin of a little Indian girl licking a dripping ice cream cone. She pointed a sticky finger at Amanda. "Pretty," the little girl repeated.

"Thank you," Amanda said before realizing the child wasn't talking about her, but about the pendant she was wearing around her neck. "You mean this?" she asked, rubbing the smooth surface of the red-and-black pendant between her fingers.

The child nodded. "Picture," she said. "Like the picture."

"Picture? You mean you saw a picture of this?"

The little girl nodded again.

"Where, honey?" Amanda asked, doubtful, but curious.

"Over there." The little girl pointed again, but this time to her left, down the mall toward the exhibit gallery and the bandstand.

"Lorita!" An attractive teenaged girl Amanda recognized from the high school hurried over, took the child's hand and led her away. "Stay with Mommy, Lorita. Don't run off again. Sorry," she said over her shoulder to Amanda as she, tugging on the little girl's hand, joined her friends waiting for her in the middle of the thoroughfare. The child stumbled along reluctantly, looking back, sneaking one more peek at Amanda's pendant.

Intrigued by the prospect of learning something about the pendant, and the possibility of locating its rightful owner, Amanda laid the brochures on the counter and turned to speak to Durango.

"I'm going over to the gallery . . ." But he didn't hear her. He was still talking the ear off the newspaper reporter.

The kids seemed to have everything under control and she wasn't really needed at the booth, so wouldn't be missed if she slipped away for a few minutes to take a look at the painting of the pendant.

She fell in with the wave of people headed toward the giant white tent anchoring the center of the art festival, the main exhibit gallery. On the way, her attention wandered and she ambled along, stopping and starting as the mood struck, or as something piqued her interest—beadwork, pottery, or handmade jewelry.

Singers had joined the drum ensemble and she paused at their performance platform to listen, letting herself be caught up in the spellbinding rhythms and chants of Native American ceremonial music.

When the performers took a break, Amanda continued on toward the exhibit gallery, trying to ignore the aromas coming from the food booths that were already attracting long lines of hungry people. She was hungry, too, and was tempted to stop and eat something, but she and Durango had promised to have lunch with Cammie and Noah. She looked at her watch. She had an hour to herself. She'd be back in plenty of time if she hurried.

Suddenly, an icy chill slithered down her spine, the unmistakable sensation of someone's eyes boring into the back of her head. She spun around, her gaze slicing the crowd, searching for the interloper. Someone was watching her. She knew it, could feel it.

Native women showing off a splendor of turquoise jewelry walked beside men wearing big silver belt buckles and black wide-brimmed reservation hats. Drowsy-eyed young Navajo boys testing out their new machismo sauntered by in baggy jeans and T-shirts, ogling and flirting with pretty raven-haired girls.

As Amanda searched the crowd, she found herself blocking the way, the flow of people separating briefly then reuniting as they swarmed around her. She stepped off to the side out of the walkway, and ducked behind a display of Navajo Chief blankets hanging from pine pole racks.

She studied the moving sea of faces, seeking some sign of recognition. Seconds piled on top of each other before her gaze landed on an old man standing near a pottery display, and she stared. His hat was pulled low, covering his eyes. He was just far enough away that she couldn't make out his face, nor could she distinguish his features. His sun-burnished skin led her to believe he was Navajo, but she couldn't be sure.

When their eyes met through a break in the passing crowd, he turned away. Amanda blinked and he was instantly swallowed up by the river of people. She continued to peer at passing faces, but no one gave her a glance. No one was paying any attention to her except the woman selling the Navajo blankets.

"Can I help you?" the woman asked, her expression probing and curious. "Would you like a blanket?"

Amanda shook her head and moved on, making her way toward the art gallery, shaking off a vague sense of disquiet.

The bandstand was in its final stages of readiness for the concert that would begin at noon and go until midnight with ten bands scheduled to play. She knew Noah was anxious to hear some of them in his search for music for his next film.

Earlier she'd caught brief glimpses of the Rainwater boys as they hurried back and forth between the gallery where their artwork was being exhibited and the bandstand where their group was setting up to play. Amanda was thinking that Sallie must be very proud to have two such talented and good-looking sons.

When she reached the exhibit tent and stepped inside, it took a minute for her eyes to adjust from the glare outside to the dimness within, but when they did, she spotted it right away. There, along the far wall, in the center of a display of paintings illustrating nineteenth-century Native American craftsmanship was a painting of *her* pendant.

She stared, speechless, her gaze riveted on the four-by-three-foot canvas. It was part of a series of vivid visuals, individual canvasses each with a singular item—a colorful beaded pipe pouch, an earth-toned, hand-coiled basket, a distinctively decorated Southwestern clay pot, every item depicted in near documentary accuracy. Her breath caught at the stunning clarity and detail of the work.

She moved forward, gaping as if her eyes played tricks, but there was no mistaking it. It wasn't a similar pendant, it was the *exact same* black-and-red perforated stone portrayed in exquisite detail right down to the shallow chip on the top point of the stylized triangle, and the minute hand-pecking along the bottom edge.

"Excuse me. Sorry, pardon me," Amanda said as she elbowed her way, rather rudely she knew, to the front of a group of spectators so she could read the white card attached to the bottom of the canvas frame.

The title of the painting was "Charmstone."

The artist was Albert Rainwater.

A soft gasp escaped her.

It wasn't just a piece of jewelry, it was an amulet, she realized in slight amazement. And it belonged to Albert. But why hadn't he claimed it? He must have noticed her wearing it; she'd seen him several times since finding it on her desk.

She reached up to curl her fingers around the cool, smooth stone on the leather cord around her neck. An amulet. She wondered at its significance, wondered what spiritual meaning was attached to it.

As she was leaving the gallery, a commotion broke out at one of the antiques booths across from the bandstand. Albert Rainwater himself was arguing with a vendor, his irate voice lifting above the noise of the crowd.

Albert, short, stocky and tough-talking was as charismatic and outgoing as his mother. He was hugely popular in school; the girls particularly were drawn to his flashing black eyes, fascinated by his bad boy image. Amanda moved closer, wondering what the argument was about.

The vendor had come out from behind his plywood display table and was gesturing furiously at Albert, who jabbed an angry finger at the items being offered for sale.

"Thief! You're a thief," shouted Albert, holding a white flintstone arrowhead two inches in front of the man's face. "You steal from your own people!"

"No, no." The frightened vendor, a middle-aged Indian with no front teeth, protested. "Get away. Leave me alone."

People quickly gathered around as the argument raged on. Amanda saw Jack Rice pushing through, camera and notebook at the ready.

Suddenly Albert reached down, gripped the edge of the plywood table with both hands, and flipped it over, sending the display items flying into the dirt.

"You stole these! You dug them up in the desert!"

"No. I didn't."

"I saw you!"

Albert's arms were cocked, his hands tightly fisted, ready to throw some damaging punches. It was all he needed when the vendor reached out and gave him a shove. Albert sprang at the man, knocking him off his feet, and they both fell to the ground, Albert on top swinging wildly.

Larry Rainwater, the older, taller, sullen-faced brother, his jet-black hair parted severely in the middle and tied in back, bolted out of the crowd. He twisted his hand in the fabric of Albert's shirt and tried to pull him off the other man. Albert wouldn't let go, and he and the vendor scrabbled in the dust as Larry, his waist-long ponytail whipping back and forth, struggled to break up the fight.

"No," Larry shouted. "Stop! Don't do this!"

Suddenly Durango appeared.

"Larry! Albert! Knock it off!"

At the sound of Durango's voice, Larry backed away. Durango put his big hands on Albert's shoulders, and lifted him off the man who instantly drew his knees to his chest and put his hands over his face.

"What's going on?" Durango demanded as the man scooted away from Albert, then stood and wiped blood from his mouth with the back of his hand. Albert was unmarked, but there were patches of red dust on his clothes.

"He stole those things," Albert shouted, still standing his ground even with Durango's hands constraining him.

The man, on his knees now picking up his wares scattered in the dust, had stopped denying it, in a hurry to pack up and leave. Durango's eyes darted over the artifacts the man was hastily throwing into a cardboard box.

"Where did you get those?" he asked.

"My family," the man answered. "They belonged to my great-grandfather."

Angrily, Albert started to go after him again, but Durango held him back. "That's not true," the boy shouted. "I—"

"Albert, let's go," Larry interrupted, edging nearer to his brother.

"Take your things and get out of here," Durango told the man whose lip had started to bleed again. "You can get your booth fee refunded at the gate. Go on."

Durango loosened his grip on Albert's shoulders and stood in front of the boy, his face a mask of stern disapproval. He towered over Albert who had the good sense to hang his head and look contrite.

"Albert, you can't go around making those kinds of accusations when you don't know they're true." Durango's voice was mild, robbing his remark of any real sting.

"But Durango, I—"

Larry immediately stepped in, cutting Albert off again.

"Come on," he said. "The band plays in an hour. You have to clean up before we go on stage."

He flicked a quick look at Durango. "It won't happen again," he said, avoiding Durango's eyes. Larry closed his fingers around Albert's arm and pulled his brother away.

As the crowd dispersed, Durango noticed Amanda standing off to the side. His expression softened and he went quickly to her side.

"I came looking for you. Are you all right?" His voice and the look on his face expressed anxiety. He put his hand on her arm, letting it linger there a moment. Then he dropped it.

Before she could tell him she was fine, Cammie and Noah drifted over.

"What was that all about?" Noah asked, his eyes on the boys as they hurried away.

Durango heaved a breath and turned his head to join Noah's gaze. It looked like the boys were arguing.

"I don't know. Something's going on with them. They've been missing a lot of school this year. I'll talk to them on Monday."

Cammie arched her eyebrows, slanting her eyes to the booth the vendor had hastily vacated, the site of the scuffle. "Sallie would be disappointed if she'd seen that. She tries so hard to keep a rein on those two."

Durango nodded in agreement.

"Yeah," he said. "Unfortunately, there's no way she won't find out about it."

On the stage, musicians were setting up their instruments, dragging sound equipment into place, and Noah spoke up.

"There's just enough time to eat lunch and get back before the bands start if we go now."

"How about if Amanda and I grab seats while you and Durango bring some food?" suggested Cammie. "We can eat during the concert."

Everyone agreed, and the two men headed for the food court.

"You buying?" Noah asked affably as they walked away.

"No," Durango shot back, clapping Noah on the shoulder. "You are. You're the big Hollywood movie director."

Amanda gazed after them. Durango, in jeans and boots, his long legs half-striding, half-loping along, looked so infatuating, she couldn't drag her eyes away and watched until he was out of sight.

By the time the Rainwater boys took the stage, every chair was filled, and an overflow crowd packed the standing-room-only perimeter of the seating area. A slender Navajo girl named Jeleeda, beautiful as a Mongolian princess, and a good-looking longhaired drummer, a varsity football player from the high school, completed the band. They called themselves Harmony, and Amanda soon discovered the name referred to more than just their music. The band's name was both a message and a plea, their music an intriguing Native American folk-rock sound.

Jeleeda's high sweet voice, backed by guitars and drums and shaker gourds, floated out over the crowd, telling a story every Navajo present could identify with—the Long Walk of their ancestors and other old injustices.

After Jeleeda finished the opening number, Larry and Albert stepped to the mike to speak, but couldn't be heard above the clamor of the crowd. Teenage fans both Navajo and Anglo were cheering the music, many of them standing on their chairs, some of them symbolically raising their fists. On stage, the musicians motioned for the crowd to quiet down, and eventually it did.

Albert spoke first. He'd put on clean clothes and showed no sign of having recently been in a fight. Feathers and beads fell from the thong in his sleek, black hair.

"Our songs may sound angry, but they're really about hope. Don't forget your connection to the land. Don't forget your connection to the elders."

The audience erupted, roaring their approval, and then it was Larry's turn, but he had to wait for the noise to subside before he could talk. Even then, he had to shout to be heard.

"It doesn't matter where we are," he called out, "we can have our culture as long as we have our prayers!" Cheers exploded again, and Larry shouted into the uproar, thrusting his fist for emphasis. "Our songs! Our language!" Impossibly, the crowd noise swelled to deafening levels as he hammered home the point.

"Our history!"

At that last, the crowd went wild, cheering and stomping and whistling. The emotional outpouring continued for several minutes, and didn't wane until the band began strumming the opening chords of their next number.

Amanda was mesmerized by the music, impressed with the tone of the message. It was mildly activist, but far from militant, urging respect for all cultures and condemning discrimination or exclusion of any kind. It was conciliatory and angry at the same time, born of the musicians' Navajo heritage.

She looked around at the excited faces. These were good kids having fun, celebrating their youth, kids with a mission, proud of their heritage, but seeking direction. She'd heard them talking in the library; many of them were torn between life on the reservation, a land within a land where quaint and ancient customs still thrived, and life outside with all its perceived freedoms.

She looked at Durango. That was the same dilemma he

struggled with, and was still struggling with according to Cammie. He looked back at her with a smile that took her breath away. Gently, he wrapped his fingers around hers and held on, his smile lingering, a hint of sweet evil behind his eyes. A tug low in her belly became a throb of wanting.

When Harmony finished its set, the audience reluctantly let the musicians leave the stage. A few more bands played, then at intermission Cammie suggested dinner at her house, and the four of them rose to leave.

It was the hat that caught Amanda's eye. Black, wide-brimmed with a silver medallion circlet around the flat crown, the same hat worn by the man at the pottery stand whose gaze had connected with hers earlier. He was outside the concert area, standing on the other side of the fence. Amanda strained to see through the moving mass of people.

"What's the matter?" Durango asked, noticing her distraction.

"That man," Amanda said. "There's something familiar about him."

"What man?" Durango tried to see where she was looking. "Where?"

"Over there." She indicated with a tilt of her chin. "Talking to Larry and Albert."

The boys stood close to the old man, gesturing with their hands, coaxing and cajoling. They appeared agitated. Amanda thought it looked like they were trying to talk him either into or out of something, but the old man stood firm, shaking his head and backing away.

Durango narrowed his eyes, sighting in where Amanda had indicated, then hunched his shoulders in a shrug.

"I don't know who he is."

Suddenly Larry turned and looked in their direction. He spoke sharply to Albert who grabbed the old man's arm and with Larry on the other side, took off at a fast clip through the parking lot, hustling the old man along with them.

Amanda stared at the spot where they had disappeared into the late afternoon throng and stood very still, blinking with bafflement. Durango's fingers were warm and strong where they grasped hers. He regarded her soberly, and quirked his eyebrows in question.

"Is something wrong?"

"For a minute, I thought . . ."

She shook her head as if to clear it and took a deep steadying breath.

"I thought it was my father," she murmured.

CHAPTER NINE

Amanda didn't believe in happenstance. Long ago, she'd adopted a personal philosophy similar to the Navajo way of looking at the world, a holistic approach that implied that life flowed in a circular motion with all things beginning and ending at the same point, and everything in between connected according to natural law.

True coincidences were rare, she felt, so when a whole series of unexpected, seemingly related incidents occurred in a short period of time, she didn't believe they were serendipitous. They were caused and connected at the core, just as all the strange events since she'd come to Monument Valley were somehow linked. She just didn't know the source of that connection. *Yet.*

It took four days to get her car back—washed, clean, new tires all around—and she'd used that time to think, to plan, and to make a decision. That decision was to take matters into her own hands.

Now, driving across the Utah state line into Colorado, she was taking the first step in that direction, which she hoped would lead to finding the core connection.

She paid scant attention to the topography as it changed from red to gray, from sandstone to granite, or to Sleeping Ute Mountain, a stunning profile in the distance. Her mind was filled with questions.

She was already convinced that whoever vandalized her car was the same person who left the note on the door of her trading post room. In spare moments, she'd pored over the note, trying to come up with anything that would help identify the writer, but the way the words were written looked forced and unnatural, an obvious attempt to disguise the handwriting.

And she'd never stopped wondering about the Navajo grandmother who was frightened away in Twin Rocks Canyon, and the message she'd carried about Amanda's father.

But most of the questions had to do with the Rainwater boys.

Amanda had the distinct impression that Larry had deliberately tried to silence Albert after Durango stopped the fight with the festival vendor. Those boys were hiding something. What was it?

And the fight itself was puzzling. Albert had called the vendor a thief, accused him of stealing, and claimed to have seen the vendor in the desert. Seen him doing what? If, as she surmised Albert's meaning, the vendor had been doing something illegal in the desert, how was it that Albert had witnessed it? What had Albert been doing in the desert?

And what about the old man at the art festival, the man who stared at her through the crowd, the man Larry and Albert had been talking to? There'd been a fleeting moment when she'd thought it was her father. Durango and Cammie told her that was impossible, insisting again that her father couldn't have survived the accident. Maybe so, but a notion dredged from a place beyond reason or logic told Amanda that everything that had happened since arriving in Monument Valley was somehow related to her father and his accident.

Then there was the amulet. Someone had deliberately placed it on her desk so she couldn't miss finding it. But who put it there? And why?

She'd hoped to talk to Albert about it, but he'd been making himself scarce since the art festival. He hadn't been to the Cultural Center, and she wasn't at all sure he'd been attending classes. Even if the amulet didn't belong to him, he was connected to it somehow.

When she'd asked Durango about the stone, he'd peered at it for several seconds then said he thought it had ceremonial significance, but without knowing its context couldn't tell her more. "I'd need to see the provenance to know for sure," he'd told her.

That's what had given her the idea to go to the Museum of Southwest History in Cortez, Colorado. She had an appointment with the curator in an hour.

She nosed her Jeep into a parking spot on Market Street behind the museum, and was instantly taken by the *trompe l'oeil* mural of a cliffside pueblo painted on the back wall of the three-story building. So skillfully had the artist used light and shadow to give the illusion of texture and space, that for a split second her eye tricked her mind into believing the scene was real. The life-sized Puebloan inhabitants were painted so faithful to form she almost wouldn't have been surprised if one of them had moved.

Next to the entrance, a flint-knapping tool display filled the front window and an overhead marquee announced the lecture schedule for the month. Wooden plank steps led to a carved wooden door.

Inside, a receptionist announced her and, in a minute, hurried footsteps clattered unseen on the marble floors somewhere in back. Then, as if blown in on a breeze, Dr. Sarah Hardy appeared. Wispy gray hair framed her lined, tired-looking face, and her rushed movements sent a clear message that her very busy day had been interrupted. Nevertheless, she beckoned Amanda into her office.

"Thank you for seeing me on such short notice," Amanda said. "I'm sorry I'm late, I didn't realize how long a drive it was. I appreciate your time."

"Yes, well, when I made the appointment, I'd forgotten that a major collection was due to arrive this morning. It's out at the loading dock now. I'm afraid I can only give you a few minutes." The curator attempted a friendly smile, but it fell short. She sat down behind a disorderly desk.

"What can I help you with?"

Amanda took the only other chair in the cluttered office, then slipped the leather cord holding the pendant over her head and handed it to the curator.

"I wanted to ask you about this."

"Oh." The curator drew out the word, delight momentarily animating her face. "A charmstone."

She held it to the light with both hands, moving it this way and that, admiring the workmanship, a thin smile on her lips.

"I was hoping you could tell me something about it," Amanda went on. "How old it is, what it was used for."

Sarah Hardy studied it a moment. "Well, it's hard to tell its exact age, but I'd say . . ." She contemplated the stone, her eyes taking a lingering assessment of its attributes. "Perhaps late eighteenth or early nineteenth century, but I could be wrong."

She continued looking at the pendant, turning it over in her hands. "The Indians ascribed supernatural powers to these amulets. This would have been worn as a talisman. Sometimes several of them were carried in a little leather pouch. You know, for protection. This one in particular was carried for protection against enemies."

The phone on the desk sounded a discordant summons, bringing an impatient wince to the curator's face. "Excuse me." She reached for the phone with one hand and handed the amulet back to Amanda with the other, her movements rushed and jerky.

As the stone slid into Amanda's palm, she closed her fingers tightly over it, a satisfied ripple of warmth and relief moving through her. It was for protection.

Then her fingers flew open and she stared at it, urgent new questions forming in her mind. Even more than wanting to know who was trying to protect her, she wanted to know who were the enemies she was being protected against.

Sarah Hardy finished her phone conversation and hung up. "I have to go now," she told Amanda. "The deliverymen won't unload the truck without my authorization."

She rose and hurried out of her office. Amanda followed, falling in step. "Where can I get more information on this piece?" she pressed.

Dr. Hardy replied, speaking over her shoulder, talking as she walked. "We only have a few of them in our collection, but the foremost authority on Southwest charmstones is a professor from the University of Colorado. He had a rather large personal collection."

Amanda hurried to keep up. "Could you tell me his name?"

The curator's brow puckered as she answered. "His name escapes me, but I recall that about ten or fifteen years ago when he and some of his students were digging an Anasazi site in Bluff, there was some sort of scandal. I don't know the details."

Her flat-heeled shoes thudded on the wooden ramp leading to the warehouse entrance. "Of course the university covered it up. The man is dead now, died in an automobile accident in Utah. Oh, yes," she said then, remembering. "His name was . . . Maynard Bell."

Her voice broke and languished to a near whisper when she said the name, belatedly making the connection between the dead professor from the past and her current visitor, realizing too late that the names were the same.

She halted her hurried step and turned to Amanda. Neither spoke. The silence lengthened until a young woman carrying a clipboard hurried toward them through the cavernous warehouse. Distress had arranged itself into a frown on her face.

"Dr. Hardy! Come quickly! We need you right away. The driver dropped the crate containing the Worrell sculptures."

Dr. Hardy's agitated expression deepened. "I'm sorry," she said to Amanda. "I must go." She turned, clearly anxious to be away, and disappeared through wide metal double doors that clanked shut, leaving Amanda staring dumbly into space.

Scandal? What scandal?

A huge pressure was building inside her head. If she didn't know the answers, she at least thought she knew the questions, but everywhere she turned, a new level of mystery revealed itself.

She'd never heard about any scandal involving her father. Dr. Hardy said it had happened while on a dig in Utah. Did her father have a misadventure with one of his female students, that kind of scandal? It certainly wasn't out of the realm of possibility. It was no secret that emotions and tensions ran high on an archaeological dig just as they did on a movie set, and romances however short-lived often blossomed. But so what? Her parents were divorced by then.

Or was it something else, something directly related to the excavation itself—like illegally digging artifacts. Or worse, stealing them.

Something clicked in her mind. That's what Albert Rainwater had accused the art festival vendor of doing. *Stealing from your own people,* he'd said.

Amanda had plenty of time to ponder on the long drive back to Monument Valley. This new information seemed to be a piece of the puzzle, but where it fit, she had no idea. Something told her the answer was right under her nose.

Her thoughts faltered and returned to the fight—Albert Rainwater with fists clenched, filled with rage, standing over the frightened vendor sprawled in the dust; Larry, tense, nervous, interrupting and speaking for Albert, anxious to take him away.

By the time she crossed the San Juan River onto reservation land an hour and a half later, she hadn't come up with any answers. She was still so deep in thought, it didn't immediately register what she was seeing up ahead.

A car partly on but mostly off the two-lane blacktop angled into the drainage ditch on the right. A man standing alongside was waving his arms over his head, the unmistakable stranded motorist distress signal. Long-remembered admonitions against picking up hitchhikers leaped to mind, but she ignored them and slowed cautiously as she approached.

It was an ancient Navajo man whose equally ancient pickup tilted crazily on a flat tire. She hadn't decided whether or not to actually pick him up or merely summon help for him when he made the decision for her by stepping into the middle of the road, forcing her to stop.

She powered down the window to speak to him, but the man put his hand on the door handle, opened the door and looked in, measuring her with his gaze. Seemingly satisfied that she was harmless, he lifted a bony finger, pointed down a road that ran through the sandy nowhere and spoke to her in Navajo. The only word she understood was Texaco, so guessed he was asking to be taken to a gas station somewhere up ahead.

When she nodded, he climbed in, settled himself into the seat then stared straight ahead presenting her a strong profile with a sharp hawk-beaked nose.

Hardship and age had etched lines over the old man's face, creasing the parchment-like skin of his cheeks, curving beside his mouth, and making hatch marks along his lips. Skin and flesh caved in under high wide cheekbones, forming deep hollows. His mouth was set as if it had never known how to smile. But his eyes were engaging, deep-set, very black, but not cold. A wide black headband held long gray streaked hair in place. A few strands lifted and settled, moved by the air coming in the vents.

He didn't speak again nor did Amanda. On either side of the road squat red mesas rose from the earth, flat-topped islands in a rolling sea of sand. The smell of the dry sage came in through the air vents.

Out of the corner of her eye, she saw him turn to look at her, his teardrop-shaped turquoise earrings swinging with the movement. Dark eyes touched her face with a long expressionless look, then glided off to stare at the distant monuments when she attempted to meet his gaze.

In a few minutes, she reached the gas station. It was one of those all-purpose highway havens where customers could rent a video, pick up a gallon of milk, buy a bucket of chicken, and, oh yes, get gas. She steered off the pavement and braked next to the door, getting as close as she could so the old man wouldn't have to walk too far. He opened the car door, but sat there stone-faced and unsmiling. When he captured her eyes with his, he spoke to her in Navajo.

"Ni zhee'eh ya ah teeh."

She didn't understand what he said, but something stirred inside her and she sensed the words held significance, expressing something more than mere gratitude for the ride. He gazed at her so intently, she felt he was trying to infuse the meaning of the words into her brain with his eyes. Her hands gripped the steering wheel and she shifted in her seat.

The silence between them grew beyond comfort and not knowing what else to do, she nodded and smiled, but he made no move to get out. Their eyes held a long moment and when she spoke, it was to break the awkward silence.

"I'm sorry. I don't understand."

The old man nodded, then lifted his hand, extended his forefinger and put it to his lips in a gesture of secrecy.

"*Ni zhee'eh ya ah teeh,* Amanda."

"Damned if I know, Amanda."

She sat at Durango's kitchen table leaning on her elbows, her hands framing her face, watching him toss a salad. "But you speak Navajo."

"Yes, but it hasn't all come back to me. What did you say it sounded like again?"

She had pronounced it phonetically as best she could, but tried again. "Well, it sounded like he said, 'shut up today'."

Durango halted his dinner preparations, cocked his head and let his expression become thoughtful, but couldn't stop his mouth from twitching into a partial grin.

"Were you talking at the time?" he asked with exaggerated seriousness.

"No." The word rose and fell, then catching the glint of humor in his eye, Amanda laughed, responding to his subtle tease.

Her laughter ended in a radiant smile, warming him and brightening his kitchen. He was glad she was there with him. When she wasn't around, he felt an extraordinary void.

When she returned from Cortez and came to the house to pick up her belongings so she could move back into her apartment, he wished he'd bribed the mechanic to take more time repairing her car. He'd seen her Jeep pull into his driveway and went out to greet her, trying to hide how glad he was to see her with an elaborate show of watching the sunset. He'd hoped to delay her departure with a dinner invitation and was a little stunned when she accepted.

He checked the steaks sizzling under the broiler and finding them to his liking, speared them onto warmed dinner plates, which he placed next to a heaping salad bowl on the table. He pulled up a chair and sat across from Amanda.

"Here. Eat. I'll bet you haven't had a decent meal all day."

He liked watching her eat. She did it with an appetite, enjoying every bite, not like the women he'd known in Hollywood who ordered dry salads and meals with no dairy or fat, then forked tiny bites from their dinner companion's plate as if those calories wouldn't count. Amanda ate heartily, chewing deliberately, taking earthy pleasure in the nourishment.

After her car was vandalized, he'd realized with fearful clarity that the vaguely threatening notes she'd found on her door could be more ominous than he'd originally thought. He examined the dreadful possibility that her suspicions about her father's accident might not be unfounded. He'd worried about her all day wondering where she was, hoping she was safe.

He ate thoughtfully, trying to come up with a way to keep her from going back to her apartment. He wanted her to stay at his house where he knew she'd be safe and where he could keep an eye on her, but knew he had no right to insist on that.

Instead, he asked a question that was none of his business.

"When you finish your work here . . ." He suddenly had second thoughts about asking it after all, but was committed to going ahead. Either that or look like a tongue-tied fool.

"Is there someone waiting for you back home? A husband? Boyfriend?" The words came out jerkily with nervous pauses in between. Was there any really comfortable way to ask a nosy question?

But Amanda didn't seem to notice his awkwardness and shook her head in reply. "I was engaged to someone, but . . ." She shrugged and let the sentence trail off.

When she fell silent, he studied her face, trying to discover her secrets. He couldn't tell if the memories she was reliving were painful or not. He waited for her to go on, trying to hide his anxiety about her answer.

"I broke it off when I came here," she said finally.

A bubble of something that felt like pleasure rose in his chest, but he didn't take time to examine why that should be. He concentrated instead on her voice. Earthy. Sexy. He asked another question to keep her talking.

"Why'd you do that? Break it off, I mean."

This time she answered without having to think about it.

"Because my father asked me to come here and finish his work, and I wanted to do it. It was important to me. Elliott didn't understand that. He didn't want me to come. We argued, and I gave him his ring back."

"Elliott . . . ?" He coaxed her to go on, for some reason needing to put all the pieces together. The vague note of jealousy in his voice when he said the other man's name surprised him. He hoped she didn't detect it.

"Elliott Sheffield. He digs. He's an archaeologist. Of course, his students do most of the actual digging, but he's very well known in his field. He specializes in Native American antiquities. Several years ago, he made some significant finds at Mesa Verde in Colorado. His colleagues were quite impressed."

Durango wondered if she was impressed as well. She sounded like she was. They ate in silence for a few seconds, but he was reluctant to let the conversation drop.

"You didn't have to break the engagement. Why didn't you just postpone the wedding until you were finished here?"

"I could have done that if I'd really wanted to marry him."

"If you didn't want to marry this . . . Elliott, why'd you get engaged to him?" The question slipped out before he could stop it. He watched her push food around her plate with her fork and hoped he hadn't crossed the line by hammering her with personal questions. Curiosity about her was getting the best of him.

He watched her face change as she went deep inside for the answer to his question. It looked like she was trying to figure it out for herself.

"I just sort of fell into the engagement." She laughed lightly. "Because it was easier, I guess. He was a family friend, well, actually his father and my stepfather were friends, played golf at the country club, did some business together. And I'd known Elliott a long time. He was older, and very intelligent. We had some things in common. He was a decent guy, really. Just . . . boring." She let a silence string out. "But my family approved, and it just seemed . . ." She shrugged. "Easier."

He stared at the twinkling lights in her eyes. He'd been right about her, at least about some things. She'd led a sheltered and protected life, no match for what she was apparently up against here. Someone, some unknown person wished her harm, and despite the strength of her words, she had to know she was vulnerable.

"What about you?" she asked, breaking into his thoughts.

"What?"

"Is there someone . . . special . . . in your life?"

A heartbeat went by. "No. Not anymore," he grunted.

Now she was looking at him with an expectant look, demanding he say more. *Payback time.* That's what I get for prying, he thought, awash in a strange, sweet aggravation at being expected to rip open his heart and actually talk about Sharron.

"A long time ago there was a girl." The words broke off abruptly as a familiar pain, though not nearly as sharp as in the past, came to the surface. "We were very young and wanted to get married. Our parents forbid it. We were from the same clan. In Navajo tradition, that isn't allowed."

He hoped that would end that particular line of conversation, but Amanda's eyes shimmered with interest.

"What's her name?"

"Sharron Begay. When we were kids, they called her Running Girl."

"Where is she now?"

"She moved away. Got married . . . to a not very nice guy. And she's had a hard life."

His mind called up the rundown trailer where she lived on a sparsely populated two-track in the desert near Tuba City. "I've sort of looked after her over the years."

Amanda nodded her head as if in understanding. "You still love her."

Her remark caught him up. *Did* he still love Sharron?

"No," he said with finality. "It's not love, not anymore." He paused. "I guess I feel responsible."

"Why?"

"Because if she'd married me, she'd have had a good life. She wouldn't be drinking. She wouldn't be taking drugs." He knew it wasn't as simple as that, but he chose to believe it was true. "I send her money for the kids."

Amanda's blue eyes widened with astonishment. She was clearly surprised at that.

"They're not mine," he put in quickly. "They're her husband's, at least two of them are. But he took off three years ago, so . . ." He hesitated again. "I don't know who the father of the third child is, and I don't think she knows, either."

Amanda didn't respond to that and, not being as unpardonably rude and nosy as he was, didn't press him further. She searched his eyes in a noncommittal way, and he wondered if she was judging him and how he fared.

"I guess I can't see letting kids suffer for the sins of their parents," he said in explanation even though she didn't ask. "It doesn't seem fair, does it?"

He didn't add the part about the guilt, that there was a part of him that felt he should have tried harder to keep Sharron safe instead of running off to Los Angeles.

"No, it doesn't," she agreed.

Amanda sat back. Her lashes were lowered, sweeping her cheeks and he wondered if she was avoiding looking at him because he'd said too much, if the circumstances of his personal life were too complicated. Maybe she thought they were sordid. Even so, a strange sense of relief lifted from his heart. He hadn't really talked about Sharron with anyone, not even his sister, though she would have been happy to let him unburden himself on her.

"Durango?"

Amanda's voice derailed his thoughts abruptly.

"Yes."

"I want to go to the crash site."

His fork made a soft clink on his plate when he set it down. He knew what she meant, but was caught off guard by her request and feigned bewilderment.

"What?" He needed a few moments to shift gears and think of a way to talk her out of *that*.

"The site of the accident. Where my father . . . where he crashed. You said you'd help me. In Window Rock. You said then that you'd help me in any way you could. I'd like you to show me where the accident happened."

She sounded like her mind was made up, but he hoped to stall her anyway. He didn't see that going there would do anything but deepen the hurt she already felt about the death of her father. Mentally he shook away the traditional Navajo dread of the *chindi*, of contamination by the dead that despite his years away from the reservation couldn't be suppressed.

"Why? What do you hope to find there?"

Pushing away her empty plate, Amanda heaved a sigh. She drew her eyebrows together as she thought about it, fingering the fringe on the edge of her placemat. "I don't know."

She looked up. Her bright blue eyes, steady and direct, shined like cobalt. "But I want to go. Will you show me?"

117

He wanted to say no. He wanted to scoff and tell her it was a crazy idea, but there was enough determination in her expression to stop argument. It was important to her and he knew she'd go alone if he didn't take her.

There was a soft knock at the kitchen door and a voice called from outside. "Hey! It's me. Noah."

Durango, grateful for the unexpected interruption that would give him time to consider what she was asking, greeted Noah and offered to fix him a plate.

"Are you hungry?"

"No. I just ate at Cammie's. But I'll have a quick cup of coffee if you're making some."

Durango made the coffee, filled three thick mugs and set them on the kitchen table along with cream and sugar, as Noah talked about his first day of location filming in the desert.

"It went great," he went on, excitement animating his voice. "The light was perfect and the blue sky was right out of Central Casting. We're right on schedule." He stirred sugar into his coffee then lightened it with cream.

"By the way," he said to Durango, "I upgraded Sallie Rainwater's part into a speaking role. Just a few lines, but it'll make her eligible for a SAG card before she moves to L.A. I can help her get some film and TV work once she gets there, but it's easier if she already has her SAG card."

Durango reached out and clasped his friend's arm in a comradely gesture. "That's great. Thanks, Noah. I owe you one." Durango remembered his promise to help Sallie. He knew how much she had her heart set on getting into the movies.

Noah nodded. "Not a problem. Sallie's really good, actually. She's got an unusual look and is comfortable in front of the camera. She should be able to get enough work to support herself and the boys until they start selling some artwork."

Durango's gaze slid to Amanda as she listened to Noah talk

about the film. He concentrated on her mouth when she interrupted to ask interested questions. Her lips were full and sexy. They looked soft and slightly dewy as if she'd just stepped out of the shower. A sudden rush of wanting those lips rose in his chest.

Noah drained his cup. "Well, I'm off. Got an early call tomorrow. We start shooting at dawn."

Durango had difficulty tearing his eyes from Amanda long enough to say goodnight to Noah, but he did and when Noah was gone, saw that she had gathered her things and was holding her car keys. Despite his disappointment, he managed a good-natured grin.

"Do you have to go?"

The big leather bag she always carried hung from her shoulder, and she stood between the deep-cushioned sofa and the blazing fireplace, her thumb hooked on the strap.

"You could stay here, you know." Quickly he examined the possibilities that offered and just as quickly banished them, considering the real intent of his offer. "You might feel safer."

She shook her head. "No. I'll be fine. I'm not afraid and besides, I need to go back to my place and . . ." She hiked the leather strap, repositioning it on her shoulder.

"And?"

"I have things I need to do," she said with finality.

Her lips had settled naturally into a full glossy pout that he found sensuous. He was standing close to her and she tried to step around him, but he reached out and brushed his hand down her braid, his fingers lingering at the soft leather thong on the end. His touch neither asked nor demanded a thing from her except her presence.

He moved his hand to her face, traced a finger along her jaw and tilted her chin up. For a moment, her posture was as tense as an animal trying to choose between fleeing and standing off an intruder. His gaze caressed her face then stopped at her eyes. She looked back at him wordlessly, her lips parted slightly.

"I love looking at you," he said. "Sometimes I see your pretty face at night when I'm falling asleep."

Her mouth dropped open. "You think I'm pretty?"

"No," he said. "I think you're beautiful."

His arms encircled her waist and pulled her up against him. He could feel her warmth and vulnerability. They were the same height, chest to chest, hip to hip and for some reason that turned him on. He savored the wildflower scent of her hair.

When he kissed her, she didn't pull back, but rather gave in to it, and pressed her body the tiniest bit closer to his. Still holding her car keys, she wound her arms around his neck. He could feel her heat, inhale her scent, and against his mouth was the sweetest, most tender, most arousing touch he'd ever experienced.

A long time ago, he'd deadened his emotions on purpose and thought he wanted them to stay that way. But this was something new, a heat he'd never felt before. No, not just a heat, it was something more than that. It was an intense connection.

Her hands moved to his shoulders, and she pushed gently away. A soft gasp escaped her.

"I'm sorry I did that," he said.

"Oh, I'm not," she said, so he boldly kissed her again, letting the touch and smell of her take away the last of what breath he had left.

When at last he lifted his lips from hers, she inhaled deeply then let it out in a slow stream that he could feel on his cheek. She regarded him with a speculative gaze before she spoke again.

"Will you take me to the crash site tomorrow?"

Her eyes were compelling, magnetic, and he hiked a grudging shoulder, giving in. "I guess I could do that."

"Thank you." She hugged him then pulled from his embrace, and he let his hands slide along her waist not wanting to break his touch.

"How about if we leave at ten from the Cultural Center? Bring hiking boots and a windbreaker. We'll make a day of it."

She nodded and smiled, lifted a hand in farewell, and then she was gone, taking those blazing, joyful stirrings she'd roused in him along with her.

He stood at the window, staring into the inky blackness of the desert long after she'd gone. The last of the embers flamed in the fireplace, snapping and cracking into the silence as their glow diminished. Her touch stayed maddeningly on his mouth as he relived their kisses, and he beat back a growing fire in his belly. *She isn't Navajo.*

The phone rang jarringly, irritating him. *Who the hell is calling so late?*

He snatched up the receiver and barked into it. "Who is it?"

"It's Judy."

His sister's voice did nothing to dispel his agitation, but only added to it as visions of car wrecks and feverish children rushed to mind.

"Judy. What's wrong?"

"The police in Window Rock just called me looking for you. Sharron's in the hospital. She gave your name as the emergency contact. Her kids are at the police station. They'd been alone for three days. A neighbor called the cops when the youngest one knocked on their door asking for food. You have to go to Window Rock right away."

Chapter Ten

Durango's kiss had lingering power, no doubt about it. The touch of his lips on hers was the last waking thought Amanda had before she'd drifted into sleep the previous night. When she caught her reflection in the bathroom mirror this morning, she was still smiling like she had a most delicious secret.

She showered and dressed, eagerly anticipating the day, not only because she'd be spending it with Durango, but because he was taking her to the site of her father's accident, and her curiosity would be satisfied. She still didn't know what she expected to find there, but felt it was a step toward unlocking the secret of what happened to her father, and maybe explaining some of the other mysterious happenings.

In her office, she had a hard time wrapping her mind around her work. Her eyes traveled restlessly over the books and papers on her desk. Some of the books, their pages marked by yellow sticky notes, lay open while others waited to be read, summarized and documented, preserved for posterity in her father's name. She fingered them idly, involuntarily calculating how soon she'd be finished with her work. *Soon.*

Students from the high school woodworking class had built floor-to-ceiling shelves on two walls of her office that she'd filled with numbered and catalogued books, biographies and handwritten journals. Three storage cabinets held files of clippings, letters and odd snippets of historiana numbered and cross-referenced to a master log in her computer. She was almost finished with her work. A little stab of regret pierced her heart and stayed there.

Vaguely, she wondered what she'd do and where she'd go. She remembered her resolve to make a plan for her future. And she would. But not today.

It was almost ten o'clock, and she glanced expectantly out the window to the parking lot. Durango would be arriving soon. Her hand went to the freshly plaited braid that lay over her shoulder, and she remembered how he had stroked it.

He thinks I'm beautiful.

She closed her eyes and Durango's face immediately filled the void. His voice flowed into her consciousness and she concentrated on it. Deep and close inside her head, his words blended together and drifted around her like music.

He was a man of this century, but with a soul from the past, a mixture of masculinity and sensitivity. There was a sexiness there, too, and a sense of mystery. She wondered if she would ever have the chance to find out what was behind the man. Intense desire overcame her with a warmth that spread through her middle. She wanted him, and that scared her more than the undercurrent of danger she'd been aware of even before her car was vandalized.

She opened her eyes, took a quick, sharp breath and stared wordlessly, startled.

Buck Powell was standing in front of her. His pudgy hands were resting on his thick hips, pink lips were warped into a sneering smile. His eyes drifted over her, taking their time.

"Where's the Indian?"

The question was either a challenge or a threat, she wasn't sure which. "He's . . . he's on his way," she stammered more from surprise than fear.

She knew he'd like to think she was frightened of him, and she was a little, but wouldn't give him the satisfaction of showing it. "He'll be here any minute."

Buck whipped a folded sheet of paper out of his shirt pocket and flung it on her desk. It glanced off a stack of books and landed on the floor.

"See that he gets that. It's from the court. And tell him he can kiss his land good-bye. He's got thirty days." With that, he turned and walked away. She watched his fleshy backside disappear out the door and down the steps.

She bent to retrieve the sheet of paper, unfolded it and read it with an odd twinge of disappointment. It was a court order that confirmed Buck's statement. Durango had thirty days to present legal title or some other proof of ownership of a parcel of land, or a deed would be conveyed to Buck.

Amanda wondered if Durango had been successful in his title search. He told her he'd contacted the Bureau of Indian Affairs when Tribal records hadn't turned up anything. The plot of land in question wasn't actually on the reservation, but rather adjacent to it on the northern border, butting up against the eastern edge of Buck's spread. Sallie Rainwater suspected oil had been found there. Amanda wondered if it was true.

She dropped the notice on Durango's desk and glanced at the clock. Almost eleven. Her hiking boots and nylon windbreaker were in the car. She'd packed sandwiches and ice water in insulated containers. Durango said he wanted to make a day of it. So, where was he?

Slightly agitated, she wandered around the one-room museum, looking at the new displays, noticing that Durango had incorporated more of her suggestions into their design. From outside came the sound of hammering and sawing; workaday voices called and cajoled. Construction had begun on a new larger museum building behind the temporary structure. The crew, helped by boys from Durango's cultural heritage group, had already put the finishing touches on a hogan and a replica ceremonial kiva that would be used for Native dance exhibitions and rock concerts.

At eleven thirty, she snatched up the phone on Durango's desk and dialed his number at home. She caught his lingering scent on the receiver and a heaviness settled in her chest.

Hope flared briefly when there was no answer. He must be on his way, she thought.

Unless he didn't plan to take her.

She considered that briefly, but dismissed it. She didn't think he'd disappoint her.

Unless she had read more into those kisses than was meant.

She replaced the receiver like she was mad at the phone and checked the time again. He lived twenty minutes away.

At noon, all remaining pleasure left her, and a sourness burned in the pit of her stomach. She'd been ditched, stood up, brushed off. Adding to her disappointment was humiliation at the thought of his kisses and the way she'd responded to them. She swallowed dryly, stopping the lump in her throat.

Well, what did she expect? She was no beauty. She was just boring Amanda. Boring, boring, boring. And she couldn't say she hadn't been warned to keep her distance or risk being hurt by him.

Determination worked its way through the emotion. She didn't need him. Not to take her into the desert and not for anything else. She'd go to the crash site by herself. If only she knew where to go.

She folded her arms at her breast in a belligerent attitude and brooded out the window.

Across the parking lot, Sallie Rainwater, worry in the hunch of her shoulders, pushed open the double doors of the high school and headed toward the Cultural Center. She strode with purpose, her expression fretful and anxious. When she saw Amanda in the window, she gave a half-hearted wave.

She came in, her face pinched, her black eyes flashing. "I'm looking for Durango."

That makes three of us, Amanda thought sourly, including Buck in the tally. "He's not here. I expected him two hours ago, but he hasn't arrived."

Sallie stood uncertainly near Durango's desk, eyes averted, misery written clearly on her features.

"I don't know if I should wait or . . ." Her voice trailed off and she stood there, nervously twisting her fingers. Held-back tears glistened in her eyes. One of them spilled over.

"What's wrong, Sallie?" Amanda came to the woman ready to comfort her. "Did something happen? Are the boys all right?"

"I'm not sure." Sallie sniffed. "I just came from a meeting with the principal." She took a deep steadying breath. "Mrs. Seltzer told me Larry and Albert have missed a lot of school this year. She asked me why."

Amanda plucked a handful of tissues from a box on Durango's desk and handed them to Sallie. "Do you know why?"

Sallie gently wiped her eyes and shook her head. "No. I didn't know they weren't in school. They leave every day at the same time. Sometimes they leave early. I don't know where they go." Her expression was tight with strain, but she had checked the flow of tears. "I wanted to ask Durango. Maybe he knows."

A little warning bell went off in the back of Amanda's mind, faint and far away, the kind of message she was paying attention to these days.

"I worry about them," Sallie went on. Her head was down and she was looking at the crumpled-up tissues in her hand. "There are gangs on the reservation now. My boys are artists, musicians. I'm afraid for them if they get involved with the gangs. When they graduate from high school next summer, we're moving to Hollywood."

She glanced up shyly, catching Amanda's eye through thick

dark lashes. "Noah gave me a part in his next movie, yah know." She tried for a smile, but it collapsed before it reached its full potential. "I hope they're not in any trouble."

Amanda gazed at her with sympathy, certain the boys were involved in something that at the very least they didn't want others to know about. She put her arm around Sallie's ample shoulders and gave her a quick hug.

"I wouldn't worry. Larry and Albert are intelligent boys. I'm sure they're not in any trouble," Amanda told her, wishing she believed it.

Sallie nodded, gave her eyes a last dab and heaved a shaky sigh. "When Durango comes in, would you ask him to call me?"

"Maybe you'd better leave him a note," Amanda suggested. "I'm not sure when I'll see him. He was going to take me to where they found my father's van, but he hasn't shown up. I'm going alone, but I don't know how to get there."

Sallie blotted her nose with the tissues and cleared her throat. "You mean in the canyon? Behind Comb Ridge?"

"Yeah, I guess so. Do you know where it happened?"

"Not exactly. I have a general idea."

"Can you draw me a map or tell me how to get there?"

Sallie's round face puckered in thought. "No," she said. "But maybe I can find it if I went with you."

Relief and gratitude flooded through Amanda. "You could do that?"

Sallie straightened her shoulders and started in on a fresh handful of tissues. "I'm too upset to go back to work anyway. I'll finish sorting the mail later. Let's go."

Amanda closed and locked her door then hurried down the steps to her Jeep. Sallie followed to get in on the passenger side, but stopped and looked back.

"Your phone is ringing," she said. "Do you want to get it?"

"No," Amanda replied, anxious to be off. "Whoever it is will call back."

As Amanda turned the Jeep onto the highway, Sallie studied the horizon. "I hope we get there before the storm hits."

Amanda looked where Sallie's steady gaze probed the distance. She saw no sign of an impending storm, only miles of red desert being sunburned to death.

Durango let the phone go on ringing, ten times, twenty times, even though he knew Amanda wasn't there when she didn't answer by the third ring. His watch read ten minutes after noon. Maybe she'd gone to lunch.

He terminated the connection, then tried her cell phone, but heard only blank silence. He glanced quickly at the phone, saw *searching for signal* scrawled across the display screen, so clicked off, waited a minute, then tried again. Nothing. Frustrated, he folded his cell phone and tossed it on the passenger seat. He'd try again when he got closer.

Now, with both hands gripping the steering wheel, it was all he could do to restrain himself and keep his speed legal. The last thing he wanted was to get stopped by a Tribal cop and be held up through the interminable process of having his license checked and getting a ticket.

He knew he'd let her down, but it couldn't be helped. He only hoped she'd let him explain. But even then, would she understand? He wasn't sure he understood it himself.

If he didn't run into traffic or construction on the highway, he'd reach Monument Valley in ninety minutes. If the storm held off, there'd still be time to go to Comb Ridge.

He pressed his foot a micrometer on the accelerator and flicked a glance at his rearview mirror.

It struck Amanda right away as an unlikely spot for an automobile accident. Desolate and far-flung, an alfresco kiln miles from the highway, reached by nothing that even resembled a road, she and Sallie hit on it more by luck than by design.

The mesa thrust itself abruptly out of the desert floor, and boulders balanced on seemingly inadequate pinnacles on the rise of land. To the east, the slope was a low, relatively gentle ridge connecting the mesa with a dry basin at the mouth of a canyon.

To the west, rocks as large as pickups were strewn like pebbles across the receding landscape, piled into occasional bluffs and tall unbalanced outcrops. Farther beyond, hazy ghostlike sandstone monoliths shimmered like hallucinations through the heat rising from the desert floor.

Steep striated walls of sandstone rose on two sides of the crash site, a flat-bottomed wash tucked into a dry swale at the bottom of the canyon. The twisted, burned-out hulk of her father's van was still there, a cremated remain in the center of an unevenly charred circle. Amanda stared, speechless, her mouth agape in astonishment. Durango and Cammie were right; no one could have survived that inferno.

But doubt still nagged at the back of her mind.

When she opened the door of the Jeep to get out, it felt to her eyes like getting too close to a bonfire. The air was drugged with heat and her stomach lurched sickeningly, reminding her that she hadn't eaten since dinner last night. *With Durango.*

She got out and let the enormity of what occurred here wash over her. If not a death, something else equally malevolent had left its mark and her stomach rolled again. She had to eat. It was either that or get sick.

She stared at what was left of the van, nose down in a shallow gully. Attached to the rear window frame was a jagged shard of glass showing a scorched University of Colorado parking sticker. A few yards beyond, the lowland rose to meet a stretch of talus at the base of the mesa. Sparse vegetation marked the site, a little sagebrush, some Mormon tea.

"Come on, Sallie. Let's find some shade."

The two women hauled a cooler from the Jeep's cargo hold and dragged it to a flat-topped rock out of sight of the soot and ashes. Amanda took out sandwiches, handed Sallie a bottle of ice water, then leaned back against the rocky wall and considered the route they had used to get to this place.

Somewhere between Mexican Hat and Bluff, Sallie had directed her to turn off onto a barely visible dirt road that opened at right angles to the highway. Within minutes, the road had disappeared completely, and they'd driven in an as-the-crow-flies direction, using as their beacon a V-shaped notch cut into one of the rounded peaks of Comb Ridge.

"That's where most of the smoke was coming from," Sallie had recalled.

When the notched peak blended into the landscape, and after what seemed like an hour of circling and backtracking, they'd come upon the clearing. Now Amanda wasn't sure that if left to her own devices, she'd be able to find her way back to the highway. She was glad she hadn't tried it alone after all, and trusted Sallie's native instincts to get them home.

"Thanks for bringing me here," Amanda said. She remembered the traditional Navajo fear of *chindi* and wondered if Sallie was uncomfortable in this place.

Sallie shrugged. She took a bite of her sandwich and chewed and swallowed before replying.

"Anglos are fascinated by death. It was important to you to come here. Maybe it will bring you closure."

Far from closure, being there had opened up a vast black morass of turmoil and more questions. Amanda didn't know what exactly had happened here, but it was no accident, she was sure of it. She'd heard the rumors about a passenger in the van, and with that came another more terrifying thought. It was murder.

"It's more than closure," she said thoughtfully. "I want to find out the truth about what happened to my father. Maybe I should have told you. I think my father might still be alive."

Sallie stopped her sandwich midway to her mouth and raised her eyebrows, signaling Amanda to go on.

Amanda related the series of events, beginning with the notes on the door of her trading post room her first night in Monument Valley and ending with the strange words said to her by the Navajo elder she'd picked up on the highway on the way back from Cortez.

"I need to find out what the words mean. And he knew my name."

Sallie didn't seem to find perplexity in that last part. "Everyone in Monument Valley knows your name."

"They do?" Amanda was genuinely surprised.

Sallie nodded. "Tall, blond white girl in Monument Valley?" She smiled. "When you came, before the day was over, everybody knew your name. Some of us here, especially the elders, always seem to know things."

She looked meaningfully at Amanda who interpreted the remark as a reference to the well-known telepathic abilities of many Navajos in Monument Valley.

"What were the words the old man said to you?" Sallie asked after a stretch of silence.

Amanda gave her the same phonetic version she'd given Durango. This time she tried for the throaty, glottal sound characteristic of Native speech.

"Say it again," said Sallie. "The first part."

Amanda did.

"That first part—*ni zhee 'eh*—I think that means *your father*," Sallie said.

Elation spiked through Amanda, but not total surprise. She'd already sensed the message had to do with her father.

"Say the rest again," Sallie prompted.

For the next several minutes, Amanda recited over and over, trying to recall the exact pronunciation she'd heard come from the old man's lips.

Sallie, gazing into space, finally shook her head. "I don't know. Let me think about it."

Distant thunder rumbled, echoing against the walls and promontories of the clearing. A cloud momentarily blocked the sun. Other clouds rushed from the faraway jagged horizon. Amanda and Sallie collected the picnic things and stowed them in the Jeep.

"I want to look around a little before we go," Amanda said.

She eyed the spit of rock that lay on the desert floor like a pointing finger. Walls sheered almost straight up toward the top, and in the middle, a stratum of sandstone met a stratum of slate, forming a layer cake effect. Gingerly, she approached the base, making her way around refrigerator-sized boulders, then halted abruptly.

"Hey, look. A cave," she called.

Sallie waved, but made no move to take a closer look. Taking a cue from Sallie, Amanda backed away, changing her mind about checking it out.

She squinted up the incline, but could see no hand or footholds in the steep rock face that she could use to begin an ascent. She was thankful she'd followed Durango's suggestion about hiking boots.

Where *was* he?

She hiked toward the far edge of the bluff, hoping to find a way to the top. For one thing, she'd lost all sense of direction hours ago and wanted to get up high where she could look around and get her bearings. For another, she wanted to see . . .

Well, she just wanted to see.

Sallie, shod only in sneakers, opted not to follow. Instead, she walked around the clearing, giving the burned-out van a wide berth, casting nervous glances at the advancing clouds. "Don't be long," she warned as thunder rumbled far away.

"I won't," Amanda promised.

She soon lost sight of Sallie, so paid careful attention to her immediate surroundings, memorizing nearby landmarks and rock shapes so she wouldn't get lost. On the south side of the finger-like outcropping, she found what she'd hoped for, a slightly less angled incline. Boulders, smaller than those on the north face, would allow her to reach the crest.

At first, it was more a walk than a climb, but as she neared the top, it got steeper, and bits of stone and dirt clumps under her boot soles broke apart and rolled away in mini landslides. She slowed her pace so as not to lose her footing. She had to use her hands and arms to pull herself along the last several yards until her shoulders, which by this time were burning with effort, topped the rim. Then, levering with elbows and knees, she hauled herself up over the edge.

The plateau was about half the size of a football field. Its eastern end melded seamlessly into a mountain range that climbed in ever higher peaks into the distance. Below the juncture of mesa and mountain, she caught sight of a wide sandy creek bottom, dry at this time of year, forming a fragment of trail that led away toward the farthest end of the canyon. Hop brush and chaparral sage flourished on either side of the rough trail, becoming taller against the cliff. Brush growing across the trail indicated it was seldom used.

To the southwest, silhouetted against a thickening purple gray mist, were the soaring red rock formations known as The Mittens, so named because of their unmistakable similitude. Located on the grounds of the Navajo Tribal Park in Monument Valley, park authorities claimed they were the most recognizable tourist attraction in the world. From Amanda's vantage point, they looked like game pieces on a Monopoly board.

She walked to the edge of the mesa and peered over the rim when Sallie's voice drifted up from the clearing below.

"What are you doing?"

"Nothing," Amanda called back. "I just wanted to see what was up here." She saw the Jeep where she'd parked it in the clearing, but couldn't catch Sallie in her line of sight without getting dangerously close to the drop off, so tossed her words into the void. "I don't know exactly where we are, but I can see all the way to Monument Valley from here."

"Who are you?"

This time Sallie's voice was oddly pitched and had a quaver Amanda didn't like. She froze and in that instant, realized Sallie's questions had not been directed to her, but to someone else.

Who was she talking to?

"Sallie?"

Amanda's call bounced back, repeating and retreating, diminishing to a distant echo. Somewhere below out of sight, a hail of pebbles skidded down the incline. Then rocks clattered, and she looked over the edge in time to see a boulder as big as a laundry basket roll past her Jeep to the periphery of the clearing.

"Sallie!"

Fearful images began forming in her mind as she loped to the spot where a moment ago she'd crawled up onto the mesa, and searched for a more precipitous way down. Finding none, her stomach pitched with the knowledge that trying for speed on the unstable talus would be dangerous and foolhardy. But she had to risk it. She had to find out who Sallie was talking to, had to find the cause of the fear in her voice.

Somewhere below a car engine rumbled faintly to life. She cocked her head to fix the sound in her ear, then jerked her eyes toward the slickrock where mesa flowed into mountain. The sun, before it disappeared for good behind an opal cloud, threw a final ray of light onto the fragment of rocky trail she'd seen earlier and glinted off the chrome rear bumper of a sport utility vehicle retreating out of the canyon.

Unbelievably, the sound of another car motor droned in the distance, and she spun toward the flat expanse of desert behind her. There, a fast moving cloud of sand, the telltale sign of a vehicle speeding through the desert, raced toward the horizon.

As Amanda stood stupefied, wondering at the absurdity not to mention the odds of two strange vehicles in this godforsaken place, the first bullet-sized pewter-colored raindrop fell like a bomb, forming a crater in the dust at her feet.

CHAPTER ELEVEN

Raindrops suddenly plummeted to earth accompanied by crashing thunderclaps that bounced across the desert, echoing and reverberating against the buttes and mesas in a deafening discordant symphony. A male rain, according to Navajo legend, not the gentle, soothing female rain that restores and nurtures, preparing the earth to bring forth new life. Some of the elders believed that if you have no respect for the rain, the sacred forces will punish you. Amanda instantly regretted misjudging the speed of the swiftly approaching thunderheads, and narrowed her mind to the task of getting down off the mesa.

Fearing a lightning strike, she immediately dropped to the ground and swung her feet over the verge. Then, using the heels of her hands and the soles of her feet slowly pushed herself off the edge, sliding on her butt and back, dropping six feet to a rock ledge. Two more sit, push, slide and drops and she had put the steepest part of the descent behind her. The rain had picked up speed, barreling down with an intensity that threatened her footing. Carefully placing each booted foot and steadying herself with her hands, she made her way, moving crab-like, to the less angled part of the incline.

By then, she found herself battling a deluge. It felt like she was fighting her way through silver-lined sheets flapping and twisting on a backyard clothesline. Lightning seamed the leaden sky, which had forsaken all signs of the sun.

Her windbreaker didn't keep the biting wetness from soaking

through to her skin and she shivered with the cold. Slipping and tripping, her feet squishing inside her boots, she moved blindly toward the wide clearing where she'd left Sallie.

Ignoring the scrapes and cuts on her hands and legs, she paid attention instead to how long she'd been gone. Frantically she tried to calculate the number of minutes it had taken her to reach the top. Ten? Twenty? How long to get back down? Each passing second was a fearful reminder that Sallie had not answered when she called.

At last Amanda entered the clearing and peered through the saturated air, searching for some sign of Sallie. It was now raining sideways and thick gusts of wind and water obstructed her view and stung her eyes. She called Sallie's name, but the words blew back into her mouth.

Lightning, like ancient atalatl, speared into the clearing, momentarily lighting it up and illuminating her Jeep. A deafening bolt cracked to the ground, the flash momentarily blinding her. For a second she thought it had struck the grille guard on the front of her truck and blown the vehicle up.

When she saw the Jeep still intact, she headed for it hoping Sallie had taken refuge inside. She reached the driver's side and fought against the wind to open the door, but the Jeep was empty. A moment of panic brought the notion that Sallie was in one of the 4×4s speeding away from the clearing. She didn't know whether to pray it was so . . . or not.

The interior of the Jeep was warm and dry and tempting, but she closed the door and called out again.

"Sallie!"

She thought she heard an answer under the noise of the torrential downpour, and hitching her shoulders against nature's onslaught, slowly picked her way over the uneven ground toward the sound. After a few minutes, she hunkered down on the lee side of a stone block, and strained to hear the sound again. At her feet, water ran in rusty rivulets through the ocher dirt, forming ever deepening erosion gullies and reminding her that at any moment a flash flood could rip through the canyon without warning. She slowed her breathing and opened her senses.

Suddenly she caught a faint moan, and tracking the sound, crawled on her hands and knees toward it. Sharp stones scraped and punctured tender skin, but she kept going until she found Sallie on an elevated piece of ground near the entrance to the cave. She was curled in a fetal position, her hands and arms wrapped around her head as if to protect it. It looked to Amanda like she had crawled there, scrabbling on her belly, seeking shelter from the fearsome storm. Or something else.

A river of rocks that began partway up the red-and-beige-banded sandstone had avalanched down, small ones at first, then gradually, larger ones. The deadly barrage of brutal rocks had been too much for her, and cuts and bruises marked Sallie's hands and forearms. Blood flowed from a wide gash in her head, mixing with the rain and forming a pink pool on the ground. Her hair had come undone from the bun on the back of her head and trailed in the mud.

Gently, Amanda cradled Sallie's head in her arm and spoke her name. Sallie's eyes fluttered, but didn't open. Squatting on her heels, Amanda lifted the injured woman from behind, then wrapped her arms around Sallie's chest, grasping her wrists to lock them in place, and dragged Sallie through the wet sand to the cave. It would provide a measure of shelter until they could make it to the car.

Suddenly, the yawning darkness from inside the cave overwhelmed Amanda and she hesitated, an old horror of small enclosed places momentarily crushing the breath from her lungs. With a shiver, she braced herself, letting the dread wash over her. When it finally ebbed away, she tightened her grip on her wrists and pulled Sallie inside the cave out of the rain.

It was dry inside with room enough to stand. Dim light bathed the floor and walls near the opening, but further back it was pitch black. The sound of the storm now that they weren't being pounded by it was somewhat muffled. She heard skittering coming from the darker reaches of the cave.

Gently, she laid Sallie on her back, cooing and whispering to her as she wiped long snaky strands of wet hair from Sallie's face.

"Okay. It's okay, now," she soothed as if to a frightened child. "You're going to be all right. I'll get us out of here."

A tremble ran through Sallie's body and she coughed. She wasn't dressed for the cold and wet and was shivering uncontrollably. Amanda considered the difficulty of getting Sallie to the Jeep where she'd be relatively comfortable. She was strong, but Sallie was heavy. She dared not try to carry her through the howling storm lest she fall, injuring herself and further injuring her friend. Dragging Sallie that far presented the same risk. Best stay in the cave where they were out of harm's way. At least for now.

Her mind flew to the blanket and sleeping bag in the back of the Jeep, and she looked at Sallie shaking pathetically on the cold stone floor. Sallie needed the warmth they would provide, so during a temporary surcease in the downpour, Amanda dashed back into the storm to retrieve them.

Struggling against powerful wind gusts, she wrestled the Jeep door open, grabbed the blankets and sleeping bag from the back seat, and snatched her cell phone from the center console cup holder, unsure how helpful it would be in the confines of this wild canyon.

On the way back to the cave, her foot slipped in the muddy talus, and she went down, breaking her fall with the flat of her palms, the cell phone flying from her hand into the mud. As she struggled to regain her footing, she felt something small and hard roll under her fingertips. She could see tiny glass beads under a sheer layer of sand being uncovered by the rain. She scooped them up, letting the rain wash the dirt away between her fingers, then stuffed them in her pocket.

Blinding rain made her attempts to find the phone futile, and she was forced to return to the cave without it. Once there, she unfolded a blanket, and wrapped it around Sallie, then, averting her eyes from the gaping wound in Sallie's head, she sat down next to her, opened the sleeping bag and covered them both with it. Circling her arms around Sallie's bulky middle, she pulled her friend partway onto her lap, holding her as tenderly as a baby.

By then, any thought of driving them out of there in the Jeep was out of the question. She couldn't see through the murky fog, and didn't know where she was anyway.

"When the rain stops, I'll get you out," she whispered in Sallie's ear. "It looks like it's about over now," she lied.

Sallie moved her lips, struggling to speak. At first Amanda tried to quiet her, but stopped when she realized what Sallie was saying.

"There was a man," Sallie whispered hoarsely.

Chindi? Or a real man? Fear knotted inside Amanda as she waited for Sallie to go on.

"Not *chindi*," Sallie said, and Amanda knew her mind had just been read. "A real man."

"What did he look like? Where did you see him?"

Blankness settled over Sallie's face, and her eyes closed again. Amanda didn't know if she was asleep or unconscious. She wiped Sallie's face with a corner of the blanket and tried to blot some of the water out of her sopping hair. Sallie's breathing was shallow, but even.

From where they sat, Amanda could see the steep wall of the

mesa as it curved toward the flat expanse of sand. Rain fell over the cliff from pour-overs smoothed into troughs edging the rim. Thin ribbons of silver cascaded outside the entrance to the cave forming an opaque watery curtain.

She remembered the beads she'd found in the mud and shifted position so she could take them out of her jacket pocket. Squinting through the dim light, she could just make out quarter-inch black and white glass beads, and recognized them as pony beads, trinkets used two centuries ago by European merchants to trade with the Indians in the Southwest. She rolled the tiny spherules in the palm of her hand trying to remember where she'd seen them before. Not these exactly, but similar. The thought floated up. Durango had some beads like this in the boxes he received from her father.

Sallie groaned softly and Amanda pulled her thoughts in. She choked back a sob when she saw a tear sliding down Sallie's cheek.

"Afraid," whispered Sallie.

Amanda tightened her arms in a gesture of comfort and gently stroked her forehead. "Don't be afraid. I'm here with you. We'll go home as soon as the rain stops."

Feebly, Sallie moved her head from side to side. "My boys . . ." she croaked, a sob breaking from her throat, her eyelids drifting closed again. "What will happen to Larry and Albert now?"

A chill that had nothing to do with the weather settled in Amanda's bones. Her breath solidified in her throat. *Don't die, Sallie. Please don't die.*

"Nothing," Amanda replied. She tried to sound upbeat, but spoke through a throat constricted with sorrow. Taking a deep breath, she swallowed past the pain. "Nothing is going to happen to them except what you've planned."

Her heart was breaking, but she forced her voice to fill with hope and good cheer. "Next summer you're moving to Hollywood just like you said. You're going to be a movie star, and the boys will be famous artists, you'll see."

Amanda crooned and rocked until Sallie's body relaxed. She pulled her fingers through Sallie's hair, brushing it back off her forehead, finger-combing out as best she could the dirt and twigs that had streaked and tangled in the long, wet tresses. Meanwhile, the storm raged.

"The words . . ." Sallie's voice was hoarse and so weak Amanda wasn't sure she heard.

"Yes?"

Sally coughed and a gurgling sound in her chest made Amanda cringe. "The other words . . ."

Amanda leaned over and laid the side of her face cheek to cheek against Sallie's. Sallie drew a breath to speak and moved her lips against Amanda's ear.

"They mean 'all is well'. *Ni zhee 'eh ya ah teeh.*" Sallie's body tensed as a new wave of coughing took hold, but she struggled to continue.

"It means your father . . ." She choked and a thin dark red line of blood spilled over and ran down from the corner of her mouth. "It means your father is safe." She tried to say more but instead pulled in a long breath, then slowly let it out along with the essence of what had been Sallie.

Amanda began to cry, great whopping sobs that hurt her throat. The storm kicked up a notch, and she pulled Sallie closer and dragged the sleeping bag up over their heads, hoping this was some sort of a terrible nightmare and not the real thing. Later, when the sound of the storm began to subside, she lowered the sleeping bag to peek outside. Through the rising and falling virga, she saw a high-riding four wheel drive rumble into the clearing and park next to her Jeep. The door opened and Durango stepped out. The real thing.

It had nearly killed Durango to see her that way, sopping wet, smeared with mud, bloody cuts and scrapes all over, holding Sallie's body and rocking back and forth. And it was all his fault. He'd broken one promise to keep another.

Cammie Drew had led the rescue effort, summoned by Durango over a fractured cell phone signal, and Noah Tucker had come along. When Amanda refused to ride in the ambulance, Durango insisted on driving her to the clinic in his car, Noah following behind in her Jeep.

The Tribal Police were waiting in Dr. Drew's office at the clinic, and after Amanda gave them her statement, Cammie tried to keep her in the hospital overnight, but she refused to stay. Overruling both Cammie's and Durango's protests, and pushing their hands away when they tried to stop her, she drove herself to her apartment. Durango followed, right on her bumper all the way, then insisted on coming in with her.

She unlocked the door and stormed inside, turning on a light with an angry movement, almost knocking the lamp over.

"They didn't believe me," she seethed with mounting rage, eyes blazing blue fire. "They think we got lost in the storm. They didn't believe Sallie saw a man on the mesa, or that I saw two other cars there. They think I'm making it up."

Furious, she strode into the bedroom and threw her leather bag on the bed.

Durango stood in the combination kitchen-living-dining room watching her through the bedroom door. She ducked into the adjacent bathroom, and in a moment he heard the sound of water gushing into the tub. When she came out, she stood in front of the mirror over the dresser and lifted her arms.

Her braid had come loose and she unwound it, stopping every few seconds, using her fingers to pull out the tangles. He wanted to go in and help her. He wanted to bury his hands in that beautiful buttery hair, and bury his face in it, too. He made an involuntary movement and she turned on him, searing him with a look. He recoiled as if struck.

He let out a breath, a long, drawn-out exhalation, and drew a shaky hand down his face.

"Amanda."

She didn't look at him, just kept working with her hair, her mouth set, her movements jerky.

"I believe you," he said.

Her hands trembled at the sound of his words, but she didn't turn to him and didn't speak. Her face was tight with sadness and anger.

The only sound was the water running, and he wondered if she'd forgotten about it, wondered if it would flow over and flood the bathroom. He wanted to say something. He wanted *her* to say something.

She picked up a brush from the dresser and began pulling it through her hair, starting at the ends and working up, one handful at a time. The water kept running in the tub. The air was electric with words unsaid.

He'd started to explain in the car why he hadn't shown up that morning, tried to tell her about Sharron and how she'd gotten drunk and blacked out and left the kids alone. But he wasn't sure she'd been listening. Her head was turned away, and she'd stared silently out the window, wringing her hands.

"Amanda, about this morning."

She put the hairbrush down, walked into the bathroom, and turned off the water. When she came out, she glanced at him in the doorway as if she'd just realized he was there. She held his gaze in wordless challenge.

"You'd better go," she said, and closed the bedroom door.

He wasn't going anywhere. He let out a breath in a frustrated burst, plopped on her sofa, and pushed his fingers through his hair, sweeping it off his face. For a moment he held his head in his hand, then leaned forward with his elbows on his knees and his hands clasped between them as if in prayer.

His gaze swept the apartment. From where he sat, he could see every inch of it except what was behind the closed bedroom door, but he could hear her moving around.

Across the room, cupboards hung on the wall above a small kitchen counter and a pint-sized sink. Against another wall were a refrigerator, quite old, and an electric stove, equally old. A thick oak pedestal-table and four wobbly-looking chairs were in the corner next to the sofa where he sat. Behind him was part of the original building, a chinked log wall that had been built at least a hundred years ago.

He was quite sure this was a comedown for her, nothing like what she was used to in Beverly Hills. He knew what the homes there were like. In his moviemaking days, he'd spent a lot of time in mansions just like those, homes with lofty living rooms and great rooms and screening rooms, owned by people safe and protected from the harsher realities of life.

Here, she was living, if not in squalor, certainly miles from the lifestyle she'd lived before. And besides that, she was in danger. There was no question of that anymore. The frustrating part was the total lack of any clue as to who was trying to harm her. Now a friend had died in her arms and she was torn apart over it, maybe blaming herself for it.

No. He was quite sure she was blaming him, and rightfully so. If he'd been there, none of it would have happened and Sallie would be alive.

His hands began to shake and with effort, he pulled himself together. He'd been pushed back to the reservation after many years away from it by bitterness, but a different bitterness than what had sent him away in the first place. Was he letting bitterness rule his life? Was he making decisions based on resentment? He shuddered to think that was the kind of person he'd become.

It was something he would have to think about, not now, but later. For now it was important to save his family's land from Buck Powell, take care of Sharron, make sure the children were safe, and fix things with Amanda. Not necessarily in that order, that's just the way it came out. He had no idea how he'd make it all work. Maybe he couldn't.

Anger brought him to his feet and he stood, his thumbs hooked in his belt, looking down at the floor as if the answers to his troubles were written there.

The bedroom door opened, and Amanda stood in the threshold in a pink terrycloth robe tied at the waist, a towel wrapped around her head. Now that she'd washed off the mud, the scratches and scrapes on her face and neck looked raw and sore. A cut on her shin was bleeding a little. His heart wrenched.

She fixed him with a gaze, freezing him where he stood.

"You're still here." It was a statement, not a question.

The silence between them grew heavy and thick, its substance threatening to displace the air.

"Look," he began. He put his hand to his head, the heel of his palm on his forehead, his fingers buried deep in his hair. He stood that way a moment, his hand pressing his brow as if that would somehow bring forth the right words, then he plowed on as best he could.

"I made a vow. A long time ago."

Her eyes fixed on his face. At least she was listening now.

He brought his hand back to his belt, looped his thumb, and stood with his shoulders slumped. He'd made that vow so long ago, he'd almost forgotten when and why. But it came back to him now, and he found it vaguely disturbing. He'd spoken that vow to his father. Is that what this was all about? Proving something to his *father?*

"When I was gone, it meant sending them money. But I'm here now, so . . ." He lifted a shoulder and let it drop. "Sharron depends on me. The children depend on me. They always have. They have no one else."

Blank silence was all she offered, and he let his eyes fall from the accusation in hers.

"I tried to get back in time to meet you, but there were some legal complications. And then there was construction on the road. I called your office to tell you, but there was no answer, and when I tried your cell, the call wouldn't go through and . . ."

Helplessly he let the words trail off into infinity. Her face was impassive except for those pained eyes. Would anything he said make a difference to her?

"Sharron is in the hospital now. She's going into rehab when they release her. After that, she'll be arrested for child abuse. The children are in foster care, split up, all three of them." He shifted his weight from one leg to the other, feeling as repentant as if he were standing in front of his father, making excuses, defending himself for mischievousness or disrespect.

"But I care about you. A lot. And I want to help you find your father. And I want to keep you safe."

At that, a response formed on her lips, but she didn't let it out. He was afraid she was going to say she didn't need his help, didn't want his help. He was thankful when she didn't. She stood in the archway where she'd been since she'd opened the bedroom door.

After a long silent minute, he began again.

"Tomorrow I'm going back to Window Rock. I'll be gone a couple of days. I'm . . . bringing the children back. To live with me."

The words lingered in the air, and he could do nothing but wait for her reaction. There was none. "I'm not their father," he said, but she already knew that. "They call me Uncle Durango." He paused. "The littlest one calls me Uncle Dee."

Her rigid composure gave way and she heaved a sigh, but otherwise didn't move. She stared at him, and he thought he could read some of the emotions sweeping behind her stony face. Not so much anger anymore, but disappointment. Resignation.

He wanted to go to her, wanted to hold her, close those haunting eyes with his lips and let her use his shoulder as a pillow. He wanted to do that more than anything, but read no such invitation in her expression.

"I have to do this," he said.

"You'd better go then," she said quietly, and closed the door again. He heard the click of the lock from the other side, and the sliver of light under the door went out.

He turned away in anger and frustration. What was he going to do now? How had he gotten into this? Was it because he was trying to prove something to his father?

Well, it was too late now. The children had nowhere to go. Their fathers had disappeared into the mean streets never having shown a moment's interest in them from the beginning. There was no family left on Sharron's side, and her friends were just as unfit as she was to care for children. Social Services had told him she couldn't have them back, but agreed to let him take them into foster care because he was willing to keep them together.

Durango planted himself on the sofa where he remained for the night. In the morning when he heard her stirring behind the closed bedroom door, he let himself out and headed for Window Rock.

CHAPTER TWELVE

Amanda parked her Jeep in front of the *Desert Times Weekly*, opened the door, and gingerly slid out, favoring the ankle she had twisted in her climb down the mesa three days before. Jeans and a long-sleeve shirt covered the cuts and bruises on her arms and legs, but soreness swept through every muscle of her body even though her movements were slow and deliberate.

Morning sun lavishly illuminated everything it touched, and she squinted against the glare. It was dry and bright, and it might have been easy to forget there had ever been a rainstorm except that Sallie was dead. News of her death shared the front page of the *Desert Times Weekly* with news of looting.

Amanda snatched the top copy from one of the stacks on the ground next to the open door of Jack's hippie van. Her picture was on the front page next to Sallie's, along with information from the police report about what happened at Comb Ridge. They got it wrong, of course. They called it a rockslide caused by rain-saturated earth breaking loose from a sandstone ledge. It was a rockslide, but Amanda was quite sure the storm hadn't caused it. The rocks fell before the rain hit.

Halfway down the front page was a story with the headline, "Pothunters Arrested for Looting." An anonymous tip to the FBI in Monticello had resulted in the arrest of two New Mexico men who had been caught illegally digging artifacts in the desert. A search of the house trailer in Bluff turned up a sizeable collection of ancient pots, primitive hand tools and weapons, and other freshly dug artifacts. Neither man could produce a permit allowing them to excavate. Jack had split the front page with news of both events. Protection of Indian artifacts was taken seriously, and an arrest for illegal excavation was just as big a news item as the death of a beloved local resident.

She was still reading when Jack hurried out carrying more bundles of the freshly printed edition.

"Morning," he greeted then tossed the wire-baled bundles into the van. The movement wafted the smell of printer's ink into the air. "Help yourself if you came to pick up a paper."

"Thanks." She folded the newspaper she'd been reading and put it in her leather bag. "Actually, I came by to ask a favor. I'd like to do some research in your old issues." She followed Jack inside the office where he picked up two more bundles from the service counter.

"I was just getting ready to close for a while. Gotta get these papers to their pickup points."

"Oh." Her voice fell in disappointment, and Jack hesitated, looking from her to the bundles of papers yet to be delivered. "Well, I guess it wouldn't hurt to let you go through the morgue while I'm gone."

"Thanks, Jack. I appreciate it. Are your old issues on microfilm or computer?"

"Only the last couple of years are on computer," he said, hurrying out the door again. "Everything else is hard copies and clippings. But the files are clearly marked by date. You shouldn't have trouble finding what you're looking for. Some of the really old issues are out back in the shed."

From the doorway, she watched him finish loading the van then slide the side door shut, yanking on it two or three times before it caught. He wiped his ink-blackened hands on his pants, climbed into the driver's seat, and rolled down the window to talk to her.

"What are you looking for?"

"News reports about my father's crash." She refused to call it an accident. Whatever happened at Comb Ridge, it was not accidental. But she couldn't call it murder anymore, either, not after what Sallie had told her in the cave. *Your father is safe.* Amanda could probably call it attempted murder. But at least now she knew her father was alive. And she intended to find him.

Jack nodded, turned the key in the ignition and the van choked to life. "They're in there. Lock up when you leave, 'cause I'll be stopping for breakfast when I'm done. Won't be back for a while."

The van bumped over the lip of the pavement then braked abruptly as a pickup hauling a huge polyethylene water storage tank lumbered by. Then Jack floored the accelerator, and the van disappeared down the highway. Quiet descended along with a cloud of dust as Amanda closed the door, shutting herself inside the tiny office.

Jack's desk was as disorderly as it had been the first time she'd seen it. She shook her head regretfully at all that had happened since that innocent day, and walked around the counter to a door on the left. It wasn't marked, but she guessed it was the archives, and when she opened it, discovered she was right.

A computer, a scanner, and a printer were on a table against the wall. Next to it, a small, three-step wooden ladder stood open, its stout legs and cross brace forming the letter A. Metal floor-to-ceiling racks lined the other three walls and held dated banker's boxes filled with old newspapers. Some of the boxes had been hauled off the racks, and sat open in the middle of the floor, their lids askew or removed entirely. It looked to Amanda like someone had done a hurried search and neglected to put things back where they belonged. Despite that, the room was surprisingly orderly considering the disorder in the rest of the office.

She dragged Jack's desk chair into the room and sat down, trying to ignore the pain in her body as well as the pain in her mind. She knew exactly what she was looking for, so turned on the computer and waited while it booted.

She rubbed her temples with her fingertips, then touched the charmstone on the leather cord around her neck. It had worked. It had protected her in the storm, and from the enemy on the mesa. She shuddered to think where she'd be now if she hadn't been wearing it. What happened to her father out there was somehow connected to what happened to Sallie, despite the fact that police were calling her death an accident, too.

It was no accident.

She'd told them Sallie had seen someone, a man, and that Amanda herself had seen two cars driving away before the storm began. But she hadn't seen the man, and wasn't able to describe the vehicles, so no one believed her.

Except Durango.

A pain squeezed her heart as she thought about him. If only he had come at ten o'clock like he'd said he would. If only he'd been the one to take her to Comb Ridge. *If only.*

An incredible wave of guilt washed over her for blaming him. It wasn't his fault Sallie was dead. It was hers.

He'd been attending to a family matter. Not family, she corrected herself. Sharron wasn't family. Yet, he felt responsible for her, and had made a promise to look after her, a promise he was keeping even though Sharron messed up her entire life. He was an extraordinarily honorable man to care for another man's children, but the pain of it hurt Amanda more than she'd ever thought possible.

She had closed the door in his face while he was trying to make her understand, then hated herself for doing it, hated herself for wishing he'd chosen her instead of Sharron. She'd lain in bed and berated herself for being so selfish. She thought of the children and how much they'd already suffered from the selfishness of adults.

That's where Durango was now. Paying Sharron's hospital bill, putting her in rehab, picking up the children from foster care and bringing them to Monument Valley. And she loved him all the more for doing it even though she knew there was no room in his life for her. He said he cared about her. He said he'd help her find her father. He didn't say she meant any more to him than that.

She swallowed a lump in her throat and blinked back tears. No. She wasn't going to cry anymore, not another tear, not for him, not for anyone. She had things to do. She had to find her father. She had to find out who caused Sallie's death. It was the least she could do for Sallie's boys. Then she was leaving.

Her body heaved in regret and she held back a sob in her aching throat. *Oh, Durango! I'm going to hate leaving you.*

She pressed her hands convulsively to her face as a raw and primitive grief overwhelmed her. She hadn't known a woman could want a man so much. But if there was this much pain connected with loving a complicated man like Durango, she wasn't sure she wanted any part of it. Her life before had been so easy. Elliott had been easy, getting engaged to him was easy. Being married to him would have been easy. Easier than this, anyway.

The computer beeped and she slowly lifted her head. With effort, she collected herself.

A search page flashed on the monitor, and she studied it for a few seconds figuring out how the program worked. She knew the date her father disappeared, but didn't know when Jack would have written about it in the paper.

She keyed in a range of dates and a subdirectory of newspaper issues appeared. Scanning it, she discovered irregularities in the dates with gaps of weeks or as much as a month between issues. Jack hadn't been kidding when he'd said weekly didn't necessarily mean every week.

She typed in key words and pressed enter. Bold headlines appeared on a white background, and she slowly scrolled through them looking for her father's name or something that referred to an accident in the desert.

She stopped. There it was. "University of Colorado Professor Dies in Flaming Crash." Using the mouse, she pointed the arrow, highlighted and clicked, bringing up the story.

Dr. Maynard Bell, professor and well-known collector of Southwestern art and artifacts, has been missing since last week when his van was found in flames in the desert near Comb Ridge.

Search and Rescue teams were delayed in their attempts to reach the site because the accident went unreported for several hours, but also because of the isolated, rugged location. Authorities at first speculated that Dr. Bell was knocked unconscious from the impact then consumed in the flames, but a thorough search of the wreckage revealed no human remains. They later concluded that he crawled from the wrecked van, attempting to reach safety, but never made it. Professor Bell is missing and presumed dead.

The next couple of paragraphs summarized her father's career and contributions to anthropology, but it was the last paragraph that made her heart ram her ribs.

Police are calling the incident a case of drunk driving based on an unnamed witness's report that Dr. Bell was seen in a bar in Cortez just hours before the accident.

Neither the authorities in Cortez nor the owner of the bar, were available for comment. Information for this article was provided in part by the Cortez Sentinel.

Her mouth fell open as if she'd been punched in the chest. She blinked twice, read the article again, and quickly turned on the printer. This was impossible. Her father didn't drink, and he wasn't the sort to sit in a bar by himself.

She pressed the start button on the printer. The roller mechanism snicked a sheet of paper from the bottom tray, and the ink cartridge began its noisy tracking back and forth across it, producing hard copy of the article on the monitor. Impatiently, she watched the printed page roll slowly into the bottom tray. When the printer stopped, she snatched the page, her eyes glued to the last paragraph.

"A bar in Cortez," she murmured.

Cortez was a town of 8000 people. She had no idea how many bars a town that size would have, but it didn't matter. She would visit every last one of them if she had to.

And the *Cortez Sentinel,* too.

Her thoughts whirled. There was something else she had to remember. Something about Cortez . . .

Then it came to her.

Sarah Hardy, the curator of the museum in Cortez, had mentioned a scandal, something to do with her father at an excavation site in Bluff. That was ten or fifteen years ago. But what was the date?

She looked dispiritedly around the storage room, immediately daunted by the thought of a blind search of hundreds if not thousands of newspapers. She got up from the chair, every joint and muscle in her body protesting. Stepping lightly on her throbbing ankle, she examined the dates on the stack of boxes. It didn't look like there was anything as old as fifteen years in there, and she cringed at the thought of going into Jack's shed.

She went out the back door of the office and hobbled her way across the dusty yard toward a green metal storage shed at the back. It was the kind sold in home improvement stores and used to store garden tools, but this one was old, its color dulled and sun-faded.

And it was locked.

The hatch-type lock hung from the door clasp, the U-shaped hasp arm fitted into a thick base. She cupped the lock in her palm and examined the bottom. It required a key. Disappointed, she gave the lock an exasperated yank and turned away.

And it came open in her hand.

Quickly she turned back. The lock arm had been inserted into the base, but the locking mechanism was broken, so it didn't latch. Apparently, Jack left it on the door to discourage the curious and the mischievous.

The door was dented, badly bent, and didn't open easily, but with effort, she managed to pull it wide enough to squeeze through.

But she hesitated at the sight of the mouse droppings on the floor, and shuddered. There had been reports of Hanta Virus in the area, and several people had died from inhaling the highly contagious airborne dust from infected mouse droppings. Cautiously she reached inside and felt for a light switch, but her fingers found nothing. On the ceiling was a bare-bulb fixture with a string tied to the end of a chain. She gave it a yank, and the interior filled with a dim, yellowish light.

Inside were more boxes, mostly labeled, but many of them lopsided and broken from age, from dirt, from who knew what. At one time, water had leaked in through a hole in the roof, weakening the corrugated boxes and staining the old newspapers. The dust was thick, and she scanned the surfaces looking for signs of mouse visitation. Finding none, she went inside.

Her eyes traced the dates scrawled on the boxes, confirming that this was where Jack kept the really old issues, like he said. In those years, the newspaper had been called the *Red Desert Times* and was formatted into a four-page broadsheet unlike the *Desert Times Weekly*, a tabloid.

As she started on the boxes nearest to her, she noticed smudges in the dusty lids, impressions of hands and fingers, evidence that someone had recently preceded her. Apparently, whoever searched in the archives had looked out here, too. She wondered vaguely who it might have been.

The first box yielded nothing, nor did the two that came after. An uneasy feeling raised the hairs on her forearms, and she found herself looking over her shoulder. She didn't like being in enclosed spaces. She was reminded of the cave at Comb Ridge, but she quickly dampened that memory, and continued searching, determined to look through five more years of newspapers.

At last, she found some references to a major excavation at an Anasazi site partway up Cemetery Road in Bluff. The University of Colorado Archaeology Department had sponsored the dig, but Jack's reportage was sketchy, the details vague. It looked like Jack had a journalistic history of using secondary sources of information for his stories, mainly, bits and pieces of articles from other newspapers. She hadn't noticed many firsthand interviews, or much personal observation in Jack's reporting. Lots of opinion, though.

Stories of the dig went on intermittently for several issues, then suddenly stopped. She picked up an issue with a gaping hole in the front page where someone had cut out an article, and after that nothing more was reported about the university dig.

She skimmed subsequent issues then went back to the tattered front page of the issue dated May 22, 1990. No doubt about it, someone had deliberately clipped out nearly half the front page.

Warning bells were going off in her head again, and she acknowledged them, but tried not to jump to conclusions. She had no proof that whatever was clipped from the paper had anything to do with her father. Following false leads now would be time-wasting and could be dangerous.

She didn't know where her father was or what condition he was in. Was he sick? Was he injured? The old Indian said her father was safe, but that was three weeks ago. A lot could happen in three weeks.

"A lot did happen," she said out loud. "Sallie died."

She replaced the lid on the box and lifted it back in place. Her arms and back were sore, and she would have loved to go back home to bed. But, she couldn't. She had work to do.

Looking at her watch, she re-sorted priorities in her mind. It was too late to go to Cortez today to try to track down the witness who claimed to have seen her father. Instead, she'd head back to Monument Valley, and spend the afternoon working on her father's collection.

She pulled the light chain, bringing semi-darkness to the shed, then went out, closing the door and resetting the lock the way Jack had rigged it. She picked up her leather bag from the office, then turned the lock on the front door and closed it firmly, checking to make sure it was secure.

As she was getting in her car, a wave of low-energy hunger pangs hit her in the gut. She had to eat something, had to keep up her strength. She had a feeling she was going to need plenty of it.

CHAPTER THIRTEEN

Jack Rice sat at a corner table in the Turquoise Café, feeling immensely pleased with himself for getting the latest issue of the *Desert Times Weekly* out so quickly. The last thirty-six hours had been hectic, a challenge to his aging newspaperman's body, but he'd proven himself up to the task.

After he'd heard about the rescue at Comb Ridge on his scanner, which was tuned to the local frequencies at all times, he'd had to wait for a copy of the police report before he could write the story. Just as he was wondering what he was going to use to fill up the rest of the issue besides school sports, church news and recipes, his contact at the FBI office called to tell him about the looting arrests.

Jack had grabbed his camera and raced twenty miles to Blanding in time to snap a photo of the men in handcuffs as they were led to court the next morning. Then, back to Bluff to write up the story.

After that, he'd prepared the page layouts in a design program on his computer and pasted the printed copy onto storyboards, then driven the camera-ready copy to the *Cortez Sentinel* to be printed on their giant presses. He'd returned to his office to re-sort the bundles for distribution only minutes before Amanda arrived to go through the morgue.

He pondered her for a moment. He was right about her. She hadn't come to Monument Valley to complete a project for her father. At least, that wasn't the only reason. She was looking for the artifacts that were in the van when it crashed. That's why she went out to Comb Ridge. And now, she thought she'd find a lead in the article he wrote about it at the time. Well, she wouldn't. He didn't include in the story what he'd seen from the overlook at Comb Ridge that day.

Hell, no!

He wasn't stupid.

At mid-morning, the cafe was nearly empty. Jack was just finishing his breakfast of pancakes, orange juice and coffee, enjoying the enormous sense of satisfaction that comes with a job well done, when a man came in and took a seat at a table against the wall, away from the windows.

He paid no attention whatsoever to Jack, but all of Jack's senses leaped to attention. Jack had seen him around off and on since the middle of June. He seemed to show up everywhere Jack went, which was an especially curious circumstance considering how much time Jack was spending following Amanda Bell.

Who, the newspaperman couldn't help wondering, was watching who? Or was it whom, he wondered idly.

The first time Jack had seen the man, something nudged his recollection. He wasn't a stranger. There was something familiar about him, something about the self-important way he carried himself that stood out. The memory had stirred around the edges of Jack's mind, but didn't come to the surface right away.

But last week, he had remembered and spent a complete morning searching back issues of the newspaper until he found what he was looking for. In a fifteen-year-old issue, right there on the front page.

A waitress went over, smiled, gave the man a menu, and set down a glass of water, then began noisily clearing dirty dishes from nearby tables.

Jack put his napkin to his lips, pushed his plate away, and

pretended to be absorbed in the newspaper. But he was really studying the man's face.

Appearing engrossed, Jack turned the front page, then casually slipped his hand into his pocket, and took out a yellowed newspaper clipping. He unfolded it, adjusted his eyeglasses, glanced at the headline—*California Student Charged With Digging Indian Burials*—and surreptitiously compared the face in the photo to the face across the room.

By damn, it was the same person! Older now, with a beard, and Jack wondered on the reason for *that,* but the curly hair was the same. So were the piercing eyes and the high-bridged nose. And the superior attitude. The man hadn't acknowledged the waitress's greeting with so much as a nod.

Elation raced through the newspaper editor, and it was all he could do not to squirm in his seat with excitement. Was this a lucky coincidence or what?

Quickly, he went over his plan in his head, then folded his newspaper, and tucked the clipping back in his pocket. He stood up, dropped some money next to his coffee cup, then walked over to the man's table and slipped into the empty chair.

"Hello, Elliott," Jack said.

Eyes, the color of blue steel and just as hard, lifted from the menu.

"Do I know you?"

"I'm your new best friend," Jack replied, holding Elliott's gaze and smiling big for the benefit of the other people in the place. He didn't want curious onlookers thinking this was anything but a friendly chat between acquaintances. "And I have a secret to share."

Mild curiosity flickered and died in Elliott's face. "I'm not interested in your secrets, old man." He turned back to the menu, dismissing Jack.

"Oh, I think you'll be interested in this one."

Jack took out the newspaper clipping, laid it on the table, and with a great show turned it so Elliott could read it.

Elliott slid a disinterested glance toward it, and Jack enjoyed watching as tension gripped the muscles of Elliott's face and pressed his lips into a mean line when he caught sight of the headline and photo.

"Where did you get that?" he asked Jack, the words pushed through his teeth, his mouth hardly moving at all.

"I wrote it," Jack said simply.

Recognition crossed Elliot's face causing him to take a quick, sharp breath, but he collected himself immediately and Jack couldn't help admiring the man's powers of self-control.

"I remember you now. You're that newspaper guy." Elliott darted a nervous glance around the room. "What do you want?"

Jack, pleased to have caught Elliott off guard, pressed his advantage. "I'll get right to the point. I share your, uh, interest . . ." Jack stressed the word, deliberately pronouncing all three syllables and ending on a high note, as if presenting the word for consideration. "In Indian antiquities," he finished.

Elliott didn't reply, but his body pulled up tight and he stared at Jack, his face a stony challenge. The raw defiance emanating from Elliott shook Jack's bravado, and he wondered for a brief moment if he'd overestimated the man's interest in the proposition he was about to make. But he continued.

"Isn't it nice," Jack said with a laugh, a sound utterly devoid of humor, "how rich people all over the world will pay lots of money for these old things just lying around here in our desert?"

Elliott started out of his seat. Jack's hand shot out and gripped Elliott's arm. He held on, hoping to quell the rising surge of anger about to explode. Their gazes locked in a steely glare until Elliott, apparently considering the inadvisability of making a scene in a public place, composed himself and settled back. Then, glancing around the room again, he lifted his head disdainfully, and picked up the glass of water, his manner lofty and deprecating.

"I don't know what you're talking about."

Jack, cutting his smile short, refused to be dismissed again. "I think you do. And I have a proposal to make that will benefit both of us, and no one will get hurt."

A long silence went by during which Jack calculated his chances of being punched in the nose in reply.

Elliott's gaze hardened, and he raked Jack with an appraising once-over before saying benignly, "I'm listening."

Relieved, Jack hitched his chair closer, rested his elbows on the table and leaned forward in a confidential posture.

"Last May," he began, "an old man, a college professor, was killed in an accident in the desert. He was bringing a shipment of Indian artifacts to the Navajo Cultural Center. The Center's run by an Indian. Durango Yazzie." He fed the information a little at a time, like playing out a fishing line, waiting for the strike.

"I'm listening," Elliott repeated, his face blank.

"The artifacts never made it to the Center. Somebody in the van with the professor hid them in a cave and ran off. But some Indians came along and took them out of the cave, and drove away."

Elliott's eyes flared, but he said nothing.

"Don't ask me how I know this," Jack said in response to Elliott's questioning look. "I just do."

He paused a moment to let that sink in, then went on eagerly. "Here's the deal. You help me find the artifacts, we split the proceeds fifty-fifty."

"And why would I want to do that?" Elliott replied with a burst of sardonic laughter.

The laugh was too loud, and Jack glanced around nervously to see if it had attracted any notice, but none of the other customers looked their way. Jack tapped his finger on the incriminating newspaper clipping and leaned forward so his voice couldn't be heard at the other tables.

"Your family bought you out of this one fifteen years ago. Hushed it up all nice and tidy with their money. Suppose an article appears in my newspaper now stirring it all up again. Suppose it got out on the wire services, and hit the big city papers. Your colleagues would be more than a little interested in knowing about your grave-robbing sideline, don't you think?"

From the stricken look on Elliott's face, Jack had a pretty good idea what the man thought of that. He'd be ruined.

Jack sat back and let Elliott stew a while. In academic and scientific circles, reputation and credibility were everything. If even a hint of involvement in grave desecration got out, Elliott would be scorned, shunned. He'd probably be kicked out of the university, tenure be damned. At the very least, Jack was quite sure Elliott would never be awarded another research grant.

Elliott cleared his throat. "Look. You've made a mistake. I'm not into that anymore. You've got the wrong man."

Jack caught every false note in the denial, but said nothing.

"I've made important archaeological discoveries since then," Elliott continued his protest. "My work is highly respected, and I have a reputation to uphold."

Jack, remembering his father's old adage about time coming around again, waited patiently. Elliott's eyes glazed over, and Jack could see him running the possibilities through his mind, weighing the risks and rewards, calculating the profits to be made in the worldwide black market of Indian artifacts.

The waitress approached the table and with a nod at the menu asked, "Have you decided?"

"Just coffee," Elliott said without looking at her, his eyes still riveted on Jack's face. When she left, he asked, "What makes you think we can find the artifacts?"

Jack spoke in a low voice.

"The professor's daughter is here in Monument Valley. She said she's working on a project for her father, but I think she's looking for the artifacts that were in the van."

"Oh?" Elliott fell into silence, his face strained.

"I've been following her to see if she leads me to them." He paused significantly. "And, Elliott, you've been following her, too."

Elliott's mouth opened in protest, but Jack cut it short.

"Don't deny it. I've seen you. What are you, a stalker? A rejected lover?"

Jack watched the other man's reaction with delight. Elliott's face went white. A tiny tic began at the corner of his right eye and he put his hand to it. He had that look people get when they're hiding something, and it told Jack what he needed to know, that Elliott was acquainted with Amanda, maybe even knew why she was in Monument Valley. This was better than Jack had hoped for. Let *him* coax the information out of her. One way or another.

The waitress brought a cup and a carafe of coffee, and set them down on the table. "Anything else for you, Jack?"

"No, thanks, Louise. I'm just about to leave."

Elliott filled his cup from the carafe and waited until she was out of earshot. "Let's say Amanda leads me to those artifacts. What then?"

"Just make sure you get your hands on them before she does." He let a beat go by. "How you do that is up to you."

Elliott's brows slanted toward his high, fine nose as if he were considering the possibilities available to him. He fidgeted in his seat, shifting his weight like he'd been sitting a long time in an uncomfortable chair.

"Where are you staying?" Jack asked.

Elliott stood up and tossed a dollar bill on the table. "The

Recapture Lodge."

Jack took a business card out of his wallet and slid it across the table. "You can always reach me at the newspaper. Keep in touch. If I don't hear from you, you'll be reading about yourself in the paper."

Elliott picked up the business card and left without a backward glance.

Jack sat at the table a long time thinking about the conversation he'd just had. That was easy, he thought. Too easy.

Suddenly, he didn't trust the man. Misgivings set in, and he wondered if he was getting himself into something he hadn't counted on. All he wanted was to make some extra cash, fix up his trailer, buy a used printing press, maybe take a trip. He didn't want anyone to get hurt.

Thoughts of Sallie leaped into his mind, and he experienced a sudden stab of regret. He closed his eyes a moment until it passed. Maybe if he hadn't driven off before the storm hit . . . maybe Sallie would be alive . . . But, no. There was nothing he could have done to save her. He couldn't stop a rockslide. Accidents happen.

The jangle of the bell over the door announced the arrival of a busload of tourists carrying maps and tote bags. He pushed thoughts of Sallie away and looked at his watch. Almost time for lunch.

"Hey, Louise, honey. You got any of that apple pie? You know, with the cinnamon crunch on top?"

With the clipping about her father tucked safely in her purse, Amanda sped away from the *Desert Times Weekly*, in a hurry to get to her office. She picked up a fast-food lunch at the Texaco station in Mexican Hat, something she rarely did, and ate in the car.

At the Cultural Center, she parked in her usual spot, slung

the strap of her leather bag over her shoulder, gathered up the food bags and stepped out. The ripe scent of sagebrush after a rain meandered on a drift of air and she lifted her head to breathe it in. The sky was so blue and so deep, it looked as close as a suspended ceiling.

She was finishing her bean burrito and Diet Coke lunch when two high school girls came in to browse the bookshelves in her office. The mood at the high school was subdued, they told her, as news of what happened to Sallie was whispered in the classrooms and hallways. Students and faculty walked with downcast eyes, a football game was cancelled, and there was talk of postponing the upcoming Native Dance competition out of respect for Larry and Albert, even though they hadn't been in school for some days.

After the girls left and she was alone again, her thoughts went to Durango. He hadn't told her when he'd be returning with the children, but she supposed it wouldn't be for a day or two. Even so, a sense of waiting hung in the air, and it was only sheer willpower that kept her from glancing at the clock every few minutes. Though she was prepared to put him out of her life, she didn't know if she'd ever be able to put him out of her thoughts. Already loneliness was creeping in.

She set to work on the boxes containing eyewitness accounts of early life in the Four Corners, dragging them to within reaching distance of her desk. Her gaze fell on a carton labeled *Great Father Chronicles* and she opened that one first.

Inside were letters, journals and diaries of Winthrop Taylor, an Indian Agent in the beginning days of the Navajo Reservation. She sorted the contents and stacked them on her desk, putting all the letters together, separating the government records and reports from the journals and personal diaries.

She picked up an official-looking envelope stamped with the imprint of the Department of the Interior. Inside was a memo to Agent Taylor from the Bureau of Indian Affairs, dated October 15, 1868, appointing him to his position.

Mr. Taylor,

I should like to congratulate you for being selected Indian Agent for the soon to be annexed northern portion of the Navajo Indian Reservation effective January 1, 1869. This appointment is a very sensitive one. The area south of the San Juan River, known as Monument Valley, is dry, hot and isolated, and living conditions are harsh. You have assured us that you and your family are prepared to withstand the many hardships associated with wilderness living.

In order for you to adequately fulfill your duties, you will need to equip yourself with knowledge of past and present problems in the area, and the successful and unsuccessful approaches used by other agents.

You will be provided with housing and a salary as befits the position based on the remuneration of past Agents. Because of the comfortless conditions of your remote station, an incentive has been added to your compensation. You will be deeded a 160-acre plot of land adjacent to the reservation for your ownership and personal use if you remain in your position for at least one year.

The memo was signed by the Undersecretary of the Bureau of Indian Affairs, and as Amanda held it in her fingers, the man to whom it had been sent came alive in her mind. Feeling a little awestruck, she opened the diary to read the handwritten entries, and was soon transported into history to a landscape not much different from the one in which she currently resided.

January 10, 1869
Claudia and I have made the arduous journey to this

land of red earth and long horizons. I fear my wife is not much impressed with the Agent quarters as they can only be described as dilapidated. She immediately set to work arranging our sleeping room, and a curtained-off corner with a cot in the front room for our nine-year-old daughter, Bliss.

January 15, 1869

The earlier displaced Navajos began returning from Fort Sumner last August, but already trading posts have started to spring up along the banks of the San Juan River. Alas, the Indians have neither money nor anything to trade.

January 19, 1869

I was visited today by a young Navajo named Littlestar, at least I think that is what he is called as the Navajo system of names confuses me greatly. He said he was seventeen years and had lost his parents when the Navajos were moved to Bosque Redondo in 1864. He came back to Monument Valley with relatives when the tribe returned to Dinehtah last year.

"The Dineh have suffered much," Littlestar told me. "Now we hope for better times." I assured him that I would sleep on the ground, eat nothing but mutton, in fact do whatever the occasion demanded to make myself efficient in this position.

I have endured dark looks from Claudia for my remarks ever since.

March 3, 1869

I have come to realize that the Bureau does not expect much from its Agents. There is little made available to me to do my work, but I will do what I can in the interest of humanity. The Indians are forced to live in deplorable conditions. They call me Great Father and expect me to care for them, which I urgently want to do.

The sun slid from behind a lone cloud and slanted dusty rays across Amanda's desk and the reading material spread out in front of her. She glanced out the window. The last bell had rung, and students poured out of the high school.

They were wearing Guess jeans and Calvin Klein T-shirts and Nike sneakers. They climbed into school buses or drove away in their own cars. But Amanda knew that some of them went home to hogans, or to the sparest of living quarters with no electricity or running water. Such was the dichotomy of their lives. It hit her with a jolt that it was the ancestors of these kids she was reading about in Winthrop Taylor's journal. Quiet soon again descended, and she turned her eyes back to the diary.

Numerous entries described the hardships endured by the Navajos. Many fell ill and died. Whole families perished. Agent Winthrop decried the government's failure to honor one article of the treaty to the letter, and a year after the agreement was made, the Navajos were still waiting for the livestock promised them.

July 18, 1869

Despite the Navajos' hard work at planting, most crops are failing. An Illinois or Kansas or Iowa farmer would scorn the idea that anything at all could grow here. The Indians have endured great privation. I have hired Little-star to work for me as his last remaining relative has died.

September 2, 1869

I ordered blankets for the Navajos, and the government sent five hundred silk hats. I ordered flour for the Navajos and received fancy umbrellas. I ordered tinned foods and received boxes of overcoats with velvet collars. At least the Indians can wear the overcoats and be warm. Littlestar told me the previous Agent had been run off by Navajo headmen threatening to kill him. Claudia has fallen ill.

October 11, 1869

These are the best Indians on the continent, willing to work and not wanting to fight. The government has destroyed their living, taken their livestock, run off all the game, and shut them up on a reservation. Now their crops have failed. Damn it, they are starving to death in front of me.

A flash of sadness stabbed at Amanda. The plight of the Navajos was heartbreaking, and it was clear that Agent Taylor was becoming frustrated with his superiors. His numerous pleas for aid from the government did not penetrate the tangled web that had become the Bureau of Indian Affairs. The meticulous care with which he'd kept his agency records and private diaries underscored the devotion he'd originally brought to his post, but he was losing both patience and faith.

Her eyes misted at the thought of the hardships these people endured. These were Durango's predecessors, and she suddenly understood, really understood his compulsion to ensure that upcoming generations of Navajos cared enough about their heritage to safeguard it for posterity. The tribe had endured unbelievable travail, but through courage and an independent spirit had survived for hundreds of years.

A long sigh passed through her, a cascade of sorrow for them and for herself. She fixed her eyes on the pages of the diary.

November 14, 1869

Our darling daughter, Bliss, has been coughing for two weeks and is feverish hot. We have no medicine. The nearest doctor is hundreds of miles away. I fear for my family.

Footfalls scuffed softly outside on the wooden steps, and the door to the Cultural Center opened with a soft click. She was so engrossed in the diaries, the sounds were amorphous, only registering in a vague way at the back of her mind. She swung her gaze indifferently toward the shadow that fell across the doorway to her office.

A man stood there like he was waiting to be invited in. He was tall, with a beard, and smiling tentatively as if unsure of his welcome. Strangely, his presence did not alarm her. It was somehow familiar. It took a moment before she remembered the blue of the eyes, the lift of the chin.

"Elliott!"

Stupefied, she sat frozen in her chair. She didn't recognize him at first, had never seen him with a beard. She hadn't heard from him since she gave her engagement ring back to him. Thoughts of home wrapped around her like a big warm quilt, her comfortable, gracious rooms, things she recognized and had grown up with. Loneliness engulfed her and just like that, she slipped to the end of her emotional rope.

In a flash, she was throwing her arms around his neck and holding on to him for dear life. At last, something familiar, someone she could depend on.

"Oh, Elliott! I have so much to tell you!"

CHAPTER FOURTEEN

The view from the window tables at Goulding's Restaurant, a half mile down the road from the Cultural Center, looked toward the west where the sky glowed with color, golds and pinks and reds. Amanda sat in a booth across from Elliott, and had barely stopped talking since she laid eyes on him. She wanted to tell him everything that had happened to her since arriving in Monument Valley. Well, almost everything. She didn't plan to mention Durango.

A waitress brought menus and a heavy glazed pottery pitcher of water, then came back a few minutes later to take their orders. Elliott gave his order—and *hers*—while she appraised this new and different version of her former fiancé.

The beard gave him the craggy look of an unfinished sculpture. It didn't suit him, and she wondered what prompted his new look. She found herself studying his face. He wore a blank, passive look, but his eyes flashed with wariness reminding her of an animal forced by hunger to go on a hunt despite the presence of unseen predators.

Other diners came in; couples or families with children were being greeted by a pleasant Navajo hostess. Goulding's was as close to fine dining as could be found in Monument Valley, and was favored by tourists and locals alike. Since tourist season was nearly over, the clientele was now mostly local.

The soft cadence of conversation in the dining room was interrupted by the occasional too-loud voice of a child. Native

American music played somewhere in the background. She recognized the song as *Akua Tuta* from a Robbie Robertson CD Cammie had given her.

The sight of Elliott standing in the doorway of her office, appearing at the precise moment he did, as her senses were overwhelmed with emotion, had started a verbal outpouring she'd been powerless to stop. Words had spilled out of her mouth with an urgency that was foreign to her. It wasn't like her to want to confide in him. He'd never seemed much interested in what she was feeling inside.

But after the initial rush of warmth that came from thoughts of home, other memories crowded back like unwelcome guests, reminding her of how much she had not fit in there. Sometime during these past months, her old home had become nothing more than a place where if she had to go there, they'd have to take her in.

Now the shock of seeing him was wearing off, and she let silence fill the space between them while she masked her uneasiness behind a falsely cheerful smile. He'd been staring at her in a strange way. She noted his set face, his clamped mouth, and his fixed eyes. What was he thinking? What was he looking at? She began to feel combative toward him, an instinctive, almost protective, reaction as if the force of his will would take over hers if she didn't resist.

He reached out and covered her hand, gave it a squeeze and left it there. "It's good to see you, Amanda. I've missed you."

She didn't know what to say to that. His touch was unpleasant and she drew her hand away, letting it fall limply into her lap. If he was put off by that, he didn't let on.

"When did you start wearing your hair like that?"

She touched her thick braid. Is that why he was staring at her? He spoke again before she could answer.

"I like it down. Or piled up, you know, on top of your head.

Makes you look more sophisticated." He said it mildly, with a smile, but the sting was still there.

He moved his gaze over her, and she stirred self-consciously, suddenly tongue-tied, uncomfortable in her jeans, denim shirt and hiking boots. She'd forsaken makeup the day she arrived in Monument Valley, and her skin had since taken on a natural glow from fresh air and sunshine.

He quirked his eyebrows. "What happened to your face? You're all scratched up." Disapproval, more than any real concern, underscored each word.

Old habit forced her to drop her gaze to the floor, but she caught herself instantly and lifted her eyes, meeting his directly.

"It's nothing. Just a little accident in the backcountry." She suddenly wanted to be away from him.

"I noticed your Lexus wasn't parked out there. Just that Jeep Cherokee. Is that what you're driving now?" Reproach hung on him like mist.

"Yes, it is," she said, defenses rising. Somehow, this felt more like an interrogation than a conversation. "I traded in the Lexus. It's not my style anymore."

He snorted a laugh. "Oh, and this is?" The corners of his mouth were turned down, and he gestured in a sweeping motion with one arm taking in their immediate surroundings and everything as far as the eye could see. His gaze was cool, almost to the point of insolence, and there was rebuke in it.

"Yes," she said, tossing her head. "It is now."

A flash of anger brought fiery heat to her cheeks. Looking at him, she glimpsed the life she might have lived if she'd married him, the woman she might have been. She didn't like what she saw now any better than she did the day that she called off the wedding. It crossed her mind to get up and leave, but she remembered that she'd driven to the restaurant with him. Her car was still at the Cultural Center, but not too far away to walk if she had to. Or chose to.

Just then, the server brought their food and set the dishes on the table, fussing with the placement. "Can I get you anything else?" she asked.

"No, thank you," Amanda said politely. Elliott didn't reply. She glared at him and wagged her head at his boorishness. Sometimes he had the social graces of an ox.

He picked up his fork, but his gaze locked on her again. "Where'd you get that charmstone?"

Something in his voice struck her as unusual. His pale blue eyes turned spooky, making him look like some kind of a wolf. She pressed her fingers to the pendant she hadn't taken off since she was told it was for protection from enemies. Is that what he'd been staring at?

"I found it."

She began eating, hoping he'd change the subject. Remembering Albert's painting and her own questions about the pendant, she preferred not to discuss it with him.

"Where?" he pressed.

She stopped her fork midway to her mouth. His interest sounded more than casual and she answered warily.

"Actually, I think one of the students lost it. I'm wearing it until someone claims it."

He let it drop, and she made small talk while they ate, keeping the conversation turned away from herself after her initial outburst. Something told her she'd said too much already. It occurred to her that she hadn't asked what he was doing in Monument Valley and before she could, a flurry of activity drew her attention to the raised portion of the dining room near the salad bar.

Durango, shepherding three dark-haired children, two boys and a girl, was heading toward one of the family-sized tables on the mezzanine overlooking the window booths where she sat with Elliott. Pleasure alloyed with pain settled in a spot under her breastbone. Durango didn't see her, he was busy getting the children settled, but she had a clear view of him over Elliott's shoulder.

With much commotion and rearranging of chairs, placemats and silverware, everyone got seated except for the little tart-faced girl who was standing on her chair refusing to sit down. Her hair shown with coal-black luster and was tied in two pigtails that stuck out high above her ears, making her look a little bit like Minnie Mouse.

A boy about nine whose own eyes flashed with mischief was half-heartedly helping Durango coax her into her seat. The smaller boy who looked to be about six peered around the restaurant with a curious, intelligent gaze.

Elliott's voice penetrated her consciousness, and she shifted her eyes back to him. He was talking about something that happened at UCLA, something about his research grant, but Amanda missed the beginning of his remarks, so was a little lost. She refocused on his face, listening politely, trying to pick up the gist of his comments, but the magnetic pull of Durango was too much for her.

She slid an amused glance toward the big table where Durango was by this time looking quite frazzled. The little girl had finally taken her seat, but was squirming in the chair, knocking her napkin to the floor as she played with the salt and pepper shakers. Gently, Durango took them from her hands and spoke to her softly, pointing to something on the menu. As he retrieved the dropped napkin, he spotted Amanda and their gazes locked. His teeth were a gleam of white against the darkness of his skin as he flashed his wonderful smile at her.

She dipped her head in greeting and curved her lips returning his smile. Her heart did a little tap dance in her chest.

"Amanda? Are you listening to me?"

She jerked her attention back to Elliott. His face was tight with annoyance, the skin weathered by the elements. Squint lines around his eyes had deepened, making him look every one of his forty-five years.

"I'm sorry, Elliott. What did you say?"

"I was asking if you thought we could pick up where we left off."

This was so unexpected, she was too surprised to do more than stare at him. "Oh, Elliott, I don't think we—"

"I still have your engagement ring," he plowed on drowning out the end of her sentence. "Or I could buy you another one. We could start fresh. I'm taking a crew to Wyoming on a dig in a few months. You could come along. We could make it a honeymoon. Your stepfather said he'd be happy to pay for another wedding. What do you think?"

Aghast, she thought it was impossible. Frantically, she ran all the reasons why it wouldn't work through her head, trying to come up with one that wouldn't sound rude when she said it.

His eyes fixed on her, demanding an answer, but the sound of breaking glass coming from Durango's table drew her in that direction again.

Durango was hastily sopping up a spill with a napkin while a waitress rushed over with a towel. The restaurant manager pitched in, picking up the shards and replacing the broken water glass with a plastic one. The little girl started to cry and Durango, looking helpless, tried to comfort her.

The middle boy, ignoring his sibling, was turned around in his chair, apparently more fascinated with everything else going on in the room. His eyes met Amanda's, and he looked at her mildly. She offered him a tiny smile.

A hand gripped her arm and she snapped her eyes back, startled. Elliott had reached across the table to get her attention.

"What do you keep looking at?" he asked gruffly. "I'm talking to you."

She shook his hand off, and over his shoulder her gaze slipped back to Durango. Durango was watching them, his mouth grim, his dark eyes glittering. She knew he was wondering who she was having dinner with, who it was that had reached across the table to shake her arm roughly.

"Uncle Durango, why are you staring at that lady?"

Durango's head swung back to Eric, wondering as he always did at the boy's unchildlike powers of perception.

"What lady?" Doli chimed in loudly. Her three-year-old curiosity went into turbo mode, and she stood on her chair again to look where her brother was pointing. "Where, Uncle Dee? Who is she?"

"Not so loud, Doli," he shushed her. "She's a friend of mine. Her name's Amanda."

"She's pretteee," Doli exclaimed, emphasizing the end of the word, an attention-getting habit she had recently acquired. To Durango's dismay, it worked. Nearby diners looked briefly in her direction before continuing their meal. Only some of them smiled.

"Yes, she is pretty. Now, shhh. Sit down. Do you want a hamburger or pizza? James, I know you want pizza. Eric? Turn around here. Aren't you hungry? What do you want for dinner?"

Though he was attending to the children, his thoughts were on Amanda. He'd been surprised and happy to see her, but his chest had knotted painfully when he saw she wasn't alone. Who was she having dinner with? Strangely, he felt he had a right to know and kept casting glances at her, and his heart swelled when their gazes met.

He studied the man sitting across from her, sizing him up.

From where he sat, Durango could only catch glimpses of the man's face, but he appeared to be older than Amanda by more than a few years. They seemed to have a lot to talk about, and he wondered what it was. He found himself coming to grips with a sharp pang of jealousy. *Where had that come from?*

When he saw a swift shadow of anger sweep across her face, his temper rose. He didn't like the looks of that guy she was with, *and what the hell was he doing grabbing her like that?* Durango's muscles tensed, his body coiled ready to spring.

"Can I have ice cream?" Eric asked.

Durango swallowed his anger and settled back in his chair, letting his gaze linger as Amanda caught his eye again.

"No, you can't." He turned back to the menu. "Here, look. They have spaghetti. You like that."

Amanda rubbed her arm where Elliott had grabbed it, cleaving him with a look. "I was just saying hello to a friend," she said icily.

Elliott turned and threw a dismissive glance over his shoulder. "Who? That Indian?"

"He happens to be the director of the Navajo Cultural Center. My father was bringing his collection to the Center when he—" She stopped abruptly. Elliott had that look again, like he was being pierced with a sword.

"Look, it's late and I'm tired. I've got to go." She reached for her bag. More than annoyed with him, she was damn angry.

"Wait," he said. "Don't leave."

There was less command than usual in his voice. It had a pleading quality she was unused to. She tilted her head, studying his face. His eyebrows were pulled together in a frown. He had lines on his forehead and shadows under his eyes. He was definitely worried about something.

"Why are you here?" she asked. "Why did you come to

Monument Valley?"

He reached for her hand again, but she jerked it away. Their eyes connected and she saw the same expression on his face that she'd seen when she'd told him she was coming here. She hadn't been able to interpret his look then, but now it resembled fear, and while she was trying to figure out why that would be, he spoke again.

"I've come to bring you home," he said softly.

Astonished, she sat back in utter disbelief.

"I love you and want you to come home with me." His voice was inveigling, enticing, but when he smiled, she saw the brittle edge of it mirrored in his eyes.

She was speechless. She had expected anything but that, and something told her to be careful how she replied.

There was more hubbub at Durango's table. The waitress was taking orders, patiently enduring earnest questioning and frequent changing of minds. Amanda's eyes slipped away from Elliott, then back again in a flash.

"That's not possible," she said. "I have to . . ." She almost said she had to find her father, but a sixth sense stopped her. "I have to finish archiving my father's collection," she said instead.

His eyes began to lose their softness.

"And even then, I won't be going back . . . home." She faltered on the last word because its meaning had become so indistinct.

Elliott's expression behind his beard became grave as he launched into all the logical reasons she should do what he wanted. As he spoke, his words went from coaxing to desperation and not surprisingly ended with an insult.

"Forget about your father's collection. You always did have muddled thinking. Where did you get this stupid notion that you have to—"

That did it! She was through listening to him. She was

finished taking criticism without giving some back.

"Elliott?" she interrupted smoothly.

"Yes?" His voice was hopeful.

"I thought you'd like to know. That beard makes you look ridiculous."

He reared back in his seat, going cold and still, his blue eyes turned to ice. His mouth opened, then closed. No sound came out, but he gathered himself quickly. This time when he wrapped his fingers around her arm they dug in and it hurt.

"You listen to me," he growled, pulling her close, his face next to hers. "You don't belong here and I don't intend to let you stay."

His anger frightened her; it was a side of him she didn't know. He was egotistical and controlling and sometimes thoughtless and rude, but he had never before put his hands on her in a forceful manner.

She felt rather than saw movement. In a lightning fast motion, Durango appeared at their table and was lifting Elliott out of his seat, his fist scrunching the front of Elliott's shirt and jacket. Dishes rattled when Elliott's knees thumped the underside of the table as Durango hauled him into the aisle.

Durango's face, just inches from Elliott's, was a glowering mask of rage. "Take your hands off her," he demanded. With a little shove, he unclenched his fist from Elliott's shirt, but continued to glare at him. "And don't ever touch her like that again."

Nearby diners looked up in open-mouthed surprise, mimicking Amanda's stunned expression. She flicked a glance over to the mezzanine where the children had scrambled out of their seats and were standing, like stair steps, at the balustrade, watching. The little girl, her eyes like saucers, was stretched up on tiptoes so she could see better.

Elliott shrugged his clothes back on his shoulders, and

brushed his hand down his chest flattening the fabric. His expression changed from bewilderment to defiance. He stood his ground and threw a contemptuous look at Durango.

"And who the hell are you?" he demanded, not having the good sense to keep his mouth shut in the face of Durango's fury.

"I'm a friend of hers." Durango's voice was quiet and his lips were tight. "Who are you?"

"None of your business," Elliott replied and with that reached out and shoved Durango hard against a nearby table causing the stunned couple sitting there to scoot back in their booth.

Conversation in the room slowed and faltered, then was broken completely by the high pitched voice of a child.

"Ohhh, Uncle Deee! He hit you!"

Durango pulled his gaze away from Elliott and turned his head toward the mezzanine. "Go sit down, kids."

"Hit him, Uncle Durango," the older boy yelled.

"Let him have it," shouted the other.

Elliott took that moment to blindside a distracted Durango with a punch to the side of the face, knocking him back, scattering more dishes and diners. Other customers stopped eating immediately and those near the fracas jumped out of their seats and backed away.

Durango recovered instantly, and bracing against the edge of the table, pushed off, ramming his shoulder into Elliott's gut. Air whooshed out with a sickly sound, and they both fell to the floor swinging wildly.

When for a brief moment Elliott got the advantage, the two little boys who had been shouting encouragement to their Uncle Durango, clambered noisily down the mezzanine steps to join the fracas. The little girl followed, her pudgy legs pumping to keep up with her brothers. As the boys pummeled Elliott's head and shoulders, Amanda grabbed the little girl as she went by and pulled her away from the flying fists.

Elliott let go of Durango with one hand and began swinging behind his back trying to dislodge the boys as if he were swatting at mosquitoes. But the boys wouldn't give up.

"Let go of Uncle Durango. You leave him alone. I'll beat you up." Their voices, filled with the bravado of the young and indestructible, piled one on top of the other.

Onlookers abandoned their meals and formed a semi-circle around the fight. Some of the men laughed and cheered, egging Durango on, but didn't join in. Two others pulled the boys away and restrained them from re-entering the melee, but otherwise did nothing to stop it. Table legs scraped across the floor, chairs were toppled.

Finally, two husky waiters pushed through the crowd. "Break it up, break it up."

They hauled Elliott to his feet, and when Durango stood up, it was obvious that he had landed the worst of the blows rather than taking them. Elliott's right eye was swollen and his lip was cut and bleeding. He wiped his mouth with the back of his hand and glared hatefully at Durango.

Durango reached out, locked his hand on Elliott's shoulder, and pushed him toward the door.

"Get out of here."

Elliott, belligerent as ever, puffed himself up and challenged, "You can't throw me out. I'll speak to the manager."

"Go right ahead," Durango said with a sad laugh. "He's a friend of mine."

"I'll call the police!" Elliott returned.

"Go ahead," Durango said again. "They're friends of mine, too. Now leave!"

Elliott's jaw tightened and an explosion threatened in his expression. The waiters, still holding onto his arms, tightened their grasp.

"That's discrimination," Elliott spat. "This is a public restaurant, and you can't discriminate against me!"

At that, silence fell like all the air had been sucked out of the room. No one took a breath. After a moment, a Navajo man in back snickered quietly behind his hand. His two women dinner companions, also Navajo, giggled. Other Navajos joined in, their laugher growing louder until everyone in the place was roaring at Elliott's statement, even the manager, also a Navajo.

Amanda couldn't help laughing, too, and gales erupted from her as she looked at Elliott's chastened face.

"What's everybody laughing at, 'Manda?" the little girl wanted to know.

"I'll tell you later," said Amanda, her voice crumbling, her hands pressed over her mouth as she tried unsuccessfully to stop laughing.

"No, tell me n-o-o-o-w-w," insisted Doli, exasperated, leaning heavily on the last word.

Her brother spoke up loudly. "They're laughing because this white man says we're discriminating against him."

His explanation brought on renewed waves of laughter. Several customers, wiping tears from their cheeks, gasped for air before dissolving into laughter again, repeating and paraphrasing to each other what the little boy had said.

"We're discriminating against him!"

"Yeah, the Navajos aren't treating him right."

"The Indians aren't being *nice* to him."

Elliott, unused to being humiliated, scraped a spiteful glance around the room, stopping at Durango, who was not laughing. He shook off the hands holding his arms and stormed toward the door where he stopped before stepping out, and turned back once more to glare at Durango. The laughter in the room died at the unmistakable promise of retribution in his look.

As the mood in the restaurant grew subdued, everyone

returned to their tables. Amanda helped Durango round up the children, then joined him at his table on the mezzanine. Friends of his stopped by to shake his hand or give him a congratulatory whomp on the shoulder, and say a few words to Amanda, making sure she was all right.

The staff hustled around, uprighting chairs, cleaning up messes. The manager promised to replace any ruined dinners.

"And free dessert for everyone," he announced to the room as he approached Durango.

"Sorry about that, Joe," Durango said right away. "I'll pay for any damage."

"Don't worry about it, my friend." The manager jutted his chin toward the busboys who were sweeping up broken glass and crockery. "The laugh was worth the expense." He smiled. "How about if I fix your meals to go? It's getting late. I'm sure you'd like to get the kids home to bed."

Durango nodded. "Yeah, I would. Thanks."

The children, far from being ready to go to bed, leaned their elbows on the table and stared wide-eyed at Amanda while Durango did the introductions.

"This big boy is James, he's the oldest. And this is Eric."

"I'm the smartest," piped in Eric.

"And this . . ." Durango reached out and tugged one of the little girl's pigtails. "This is Doli."

"That means *bluebird* in Navajo," Doli said. She gaped openly at Amanda then reached out her hand and stroked Amanda's braid. "Can I touch your hair?" she asked belatedly, already doing it. "It's a pretty color."

Amanda smiled. "Of course, you can, sweetheart."

"Where's your Jeep?" Durango asked her. "I didn't see it parked outside."

"I left it at the Cultural Center."

"I'll drop you off to pick it up after we get our food."

Hiding her disappointment, Amanda nodded. She wanted to talk to him, spend some time with him, but refused to impose on his responsibilities to the children.

"I want to ride with 'Manda," Doli interrupted and began a chant. "Ride with 'Manda. Ride with 'Manda."

"No, you can't ride with her. You're coming with me."

Doli's bottom lip poked out and quivered. "I want to ride with 'Manda."

"It's okay," Amanda put in. "She can ride with me if she wants to. I'll drop her off at your house. It's not that far out of the way."

A grinning kitchen helper brought a stack of Styrofoam food containers and handed them to Durango, as if to a conquering hero. "Way to go," he said, referring to the fracas with Elliott. Durango nodded sheepishly, paid for the food, and they all left, Doli hanging onto Amanda's hand with both of hers.

Durango stopped at the Cultural Center parking lot to drop off Amanda and Doli. He switched the child safety seat into the back of the Jeep, boosted Doli into it, and fastened the harness around her middle.

"See you at the house," he called as he drove away, the boys waving wildly through the rear window.

Amanda leaned over the back of her seat, tucked her fingers under the buckle of Doli's seat restraint and gave it a tug to check the snugness, then slipped behind the wheel and started the engine.

"I have to go," said Doli.

Realizing too late that a stop at the restaurant restroom would have been a good idea, Amanda turned and looked meaningfully at the little girl.

Doli shook her head. "Can't wait."

"Okay."

Inside the Cultural Center, Amanda showed Doli the

bathroom, then sat at her desk, recalling that Elliott had interrupted her in the middle of reading Winthrop Taylor's diaries. While she waited for Doli, she read some more.

November 28, 1869

Littlestar sought my presence in private away from Claudia who is at Bliss's bedside every moment. He said his father was a Medicine Man and that Littlestar himself had been blessed with similar powers. He showed me his *jish*, his medicine bag, and asked for time with Bliss. When I discussed this with Claudia, she screamed at Littlestar and ran him out of the house.

December 1, 1869

Bliss is burning with fever. Her breath struggles in and out of her tiny chest.

December 3, 1869

I fear we are losing our child.

"Ready, 'Manda."

Amanda closed the diary, put it in her bag and in a minute, they were back in the car, on the highway heading for Durango's house. All that was left of the sunset was a faint peach-colored patch quickly being taken over by the night sky. On the horizon, distant clouds bubbled with dry lightning. Within seconds, darkness fell, unbroken except by a soaring dome of tiny stars and a fine sliver of moon.

In the back seat, Doli hummed quietly to herself, seemingly unperturbed at the scene just played out at the restaurant. At least Amanda hoped so, hoped nothing was being buried in a little-girl psyche that might manifest in some form of dysfunction later. From what Durango had told her about Sharron, Doli had been exposed to worse things than a fistfight.

Wondering what was really going on behind the cheeky expression, she glanced at the little girl in the rearview mirror, and caught sight of a tiny spot of light in the far distance. It split in two like a cell dividing as the fast-approaching car neared, and she absently flipped the mirror to night reflection, giving herself a mental shake in an attempt to fling off her own memories of what happened at the restaurant. Especially something Elliott had said that was replaying itself in her brain.

You don't belong here.

The note on her door at the trading post that first night had ordered her to *go back where you belong*. Different words, but the same meaning. Not a coincidence, and she held a growing misgiving at arm's length, twisting and turning it, trying to make sense of it, watching it morph into a ticking time bomb.

That Elliott had appeared at all was the real puzzle. He hadn't written or tried to get in touch with her after she left, not once. Why would he now show up with a new proposal of marriage? Well, a proposal of sorts.

No, you idiot, she scolded herself. It wasn't a proposal at all. He'd tried to bully her into going back with him.

Suddenly a flood of light filled the Jeep as high beams flashed on from the overtaking vehicle. Doli stopped humming and twisted around trying unsuccessfully to see over the high seatback. Amanda glanced at the rearview mirror and reflexively tightened her grip on the steering wheel, momentarily alarmed at a car coming up so fast from behind. Her eyes darted from rearview to side mirror, then widened as the car in back narrowed the distance even more, coming dangerously close, tailgating.

The glare from the car's headlights refracted through a layer of red dust covering the Jeep's hatchback window, making it impossible for her to see behind, and difficult to see ahead through the windshield. She raised a hand to cover the rearview mirror and ward off the blinding reflection, but a hard tap on her rear bumper forced her hand back to the steering wheel.

She sucked a breath and instinctively shoved her foot down on the gas pedal. Catching sight of Doli's wide, frightened eyes in the mirror, she mindfully suppressed the urge to panic.

Doli whimpered. "Who's that? Why did that car hit us?"

There was no time to answer, no time to comfort the frightened child. With fierce concentration on the road ahead, Amanda sped up and the pursuing vehicle fell back a little. In the dark, it was impossible for her to see the driver or tell what kind of car it was, but it was high-riding so had to be a pickup or some sort of sport utility vehicle. Suddenly it speeded up and bore down again.

"No! Don't!"

She gripped the steering wheel and braced for the bump. It was harder this time, and the Jeep swerved unsteadily toward the irrigation ditch that ran along the right shoulder. Fear surged through her body, the icy chill of it cutting to the bone. Jerking the steering wheel hard to the left, she regained purchase on the pavement, and with determined effort, pushed her speed up to eighty.

Her mind reeled as the other car gained on her and tracked in the Jeep's wake. *Dammit, who is that?* She pushed the gas pedal to the floor, trying to outdistance the phantom car, but it kept up, relentless in its pursuit. Doli was squirming in her seat, struggling against the harness restraints as she tried to look out the rear window. Her frightened whimpers had turned into throat-tearing sobs.

Amanda sensed rather than saw the pursuing car move into the other lane and pull alongside on the left. Frantically, she tried to outrun it, but it gained steadily, creeping forward until its passenger door was mere inches away. From the corner of her eye, she made out a vague shadowy hulk behind the wheel, but she dared not take her eyes off the road for a closer look. Gripped with helpless horror, she tightened her hands on the steering wheel as the other car edged nearer her door.

"Hey! Stop it!" The words burst stupidly from her lips.

Metal ground against metal and a spray of sparks arced into the night. Doli was crying hysterically now, loud, terrified half-screams, half-sobs. Fleetingly, Amanda wished she could give in to the same thing.

The Jeep raced forward, but the mystery car kept up, pushing and grinding, trying to force Amanda off the road. Her hands and forearms ached as she fought to keep control. She felt the dip as the Jeep slipped off the pavement on the right. The tug of tires in sand along the shoulder of the road told her she was losing ground. She knew she had to stay on the pavement, knew that if she hit the ditch at this speed, the Jeep might flip.

Calling on a reserve of strength she wasn't sure she had, and with muscles protesting in agony, she wrestled the Jeep back onto the blacktop. Fear knotted her chest and she gasped when her headlights picked up the cows on the road ahead.

With no time to think, she stomped on the brake, sending a pain from her injured ankle up to her knee. Tires screeched along the blacktop sending up a sickening smell of scorched rubber. She yanked the steering wheel hard to the right trying to avoid the animals, but the rear end of the Jeep cut sideways, skidding it in a forward motion toward a cow that was half on, half off the road.

A scream sprang from her throat, but it was quickly silenced by a jarring impact that struck the breath from her. Pain spiked through her head as it banged against the side window and she heard the awful bawling of the injured animal. She had a vague mental image of the pursuing car bouncing off the roadway on the other shoulder, then with tires spinning holes in the sand, roaring away into the darkness.

The Jeep spun off onto the sandy shoulder, throwing rocks and dirt clumps into the air, bounced heavily over the shallow ditch, then lurched to a stop about ten yards off the roadway. Rocks and sand rained down, clattering and pounding the roof of the Jeep. Then the ghostly quiet of the desert surrounded them. The engine had stalled out, but somehow the headlights still burned. Dusty sand drifted through yellow beams that bored a hole into the blackness.

"Mommy, Mommy, Mommy!" Doli's wail shattered the silence, and Amanda had the completely incongruous thought that sometimes, a bad mom was better than no mom at all. Instantly, she reached back, and with fumbling fingers, unfastened the safety seat harness. Doli dove over the console into the front seat, straddled Amanda's lap and squeezed her tiny arms around Amanda's neck, sobbing uncontrollably.

"Shhh, shhhh. Doli, it's all right. It's all right now. The bad car is gone. It's over. We're safe now."

No sooner were the words out of her mouth when two headlights appeared and moved along the highway from the direction she had just come. Brake lights flashed as the car slowed then stopped. Her breath caught as she staved off hysteria, unsure if help was arriving, or if evil had returned. The vehicle lurked motionless on the road, its engine chugging laboriously, producing a familiar *blup-blup-blup* rumble. She knew that car. She'd heard it before. But where? Her terrified mind couldn't remember, and she was too far away to see it in the dark.

She could feel unseen eyes inside the phantom car probe the Jeep where she sat with a terrified Doli. The child's arms and legs were clenched around Amanda's neck and hips. Despite her throbbing ankle and the liquid trickling down her cheek from the pain in her head, Amanda slowed her breathing, not wanting to further alarm the already stricken child.

High beams flashed from the idling vehicle, blinding her and she ducked her head to avoid the painful glare stabbing her eyes. Suddenly, the car sped away. She squinted through the darkness, willing her eyes to adjust in time to get a look at it, but to no avail. All she could see were tiny taillights disappearing into the distance though she had a sense the vehicle possessed a large profile. But tiny taillights meant an older model car. Unfortunately, there were plenty of those on the reservation.

She let out a shaky breath and turned the key in the ignition.

"Thank you, thank you, thank you," she whispered as the Jeep's engine roared to life. Doli had not loosened her grip, so Amanda let her be. Peering over Doli's head, she slowly steered the Jeep across the hard-packed desert floor, rolled down and up out of the drainage ditch back onto the road, and wasted no time getting to Durango's house.

CHAPTER FIFTEEN

"What did he say?" Amanda called to Durango from down the hall. She'd just had a shower in his guest bathroom.

"He said he'd write up the report."

"I heard that part. What else?"

"He said he'd go back and check on the cow."

Amanda walked slowly into the open-beamed living room, toweling her hair. The golden glow of reflected firelight on the stuccoed walls softened the strain pinching her features. She was wearing one of his T-shirts knotted at the waist. His drawstring pajama bottoms hung on her hipbones and billowed around her slender legs, puddling at her feet.

A gauze bandage, carefully applied by Cammie, covered the bloody scrape on the side of her head where it had hammered the car door window. The doctor, who had rushed over at Durango's call, had left thirty minutes ago after rewrapping the sprained ankle and prescribing ice and aspirin for the head bump. She'd also checked Doli and found her to be frightened but physically unharmed.

"No," Amanda persisted. "I mean what did he say to you in Navajo? That young one. The same one who came to Cammie's house the night my car was vandalized. What did he say when he was leaving?"

Durango knew what she meant, but didn't want to tell her, and busied himself at the fireplace, tending to an already blazing fire. Refusing to let it go, she came around to the front of the fire pit, settled herself next to him, curled her hand around his arm and tugged, forcing him to interrupt his busyness. Her expression held a wordless challenge.

How angry would she be if he told her that the Tribal cop had smirked and said, "The *bilagaana* seems to have lots of accidents." The subtle sarcasm of it had rung clearly in his Navajo ear, and he wondered if she'd picked up on the mockery in the officer's tone of voice. He hoped not.

"He said he was sorry for all your troubles," Durango lied.

She held his gaze a long while. Uncertainty flickered in and out of her eyes.

She's not sure she can trust me, he realized, she's remembering that I didn't show up to take her to Comb Ridge. He turned back to the fire, and she stood up and walked away. Her bare feet padded on the tiled hallway leading to the guest wing.

The fire was greedily consuming the chill that had crept into the house after the sun went down. The children were in bed, so only night sounds remained. Outside in the distance, a coyote barked. The last bark became a mournful drawn out howl, the familiar nocturnal desert serenade.

Durango lowered himself into the deep cushions of the sofa, ran a hand down his face and stared at the flames, his fear for Amanda and his anger at an unseen enemy vying for control. His fear edged out anger, but just barely. Someone had crossed the line from merely trying to scare Amanda to trying to harm her. Maybe kill her.

At that, anger surged again, and he slammed his fist into the palm of his hand. Who the hell was it?

When she and Doli hadn't appeared within a few minutes of his arrival from Goulding's with the boys, a sinking feeling had begun to gnaw in the pit of his stomach. A half-hour later, his apprehension had grown to full-blown worry. He turned the boys over to Nonni, a family friend who had moved in to help with the children, letting her complete the bath and bedtime ritual, and grabbed his car keys. He was outside headed for his truck when Amanda's Jeep raced up the driveway.

Doli's muffled screams from inside the car came to him first. Then, Amanda's bloodied, terrified face lit by the harsh security lamps flanking the drive materialized behind jagged cracks running through the windshield.

"Oh, my God! What happened?" His stomach burned with alarm.

Amanda braked sharply, tires skidding on the gravel, and that's when he caught sight of the bashed-in driver's side, crumpled from front fender to taillight. Before the Jeep stopped moving, his hands were on the door, trying to haul it open. It was bent, jammed, but he pulled and twisted until it wrung free.

"Christ, you're hurt!"

Doli was still clinging to Amanda like a kitten frozen with fear on a tree limb. Gently, he eased them both out of the damaged vehicle, prying the child away and holding her in one arm while sliding the other around Amanda's waist. Her knees buckled and she pitched forward, but he caught her and held her tight. Ashen-faced and trembling, she leaned heavily against him, wincing with pain as she limped to the house.

"Someone chased us . . . there were cows . . . a car came . . ." Stammering and sobbing, Amanda jumbled her words trying to tell him what happened. She started to slip from his grip, and he tightened his arm around her.

"Come on. Talk later. Let me get you both inside."

Fury had bubbled inside him as he listened to her tell the police what happened on the road. Durango didn't miss the significance of the hurried glance she threw at him when she described the mysterious appearance of a second car that sped away. She was making the connection with what happened at

Comb Ridge, hoping he got it, too. Either two people were following her, or someone was following the follower.

After the police left and they were alone, she had recounted what she'd discovered that morning—Jack's clipping file with the half-told story of a scandal, the witness who saw her father in a bar in Cortez, the freshly cut hole in a fifteen-year-old newspaper.

He was considering the implications of all that when Amanda, shoulders slumped, still shaken and unsmiling, came back into the living room and sat down next to him.

Her long hair was pulled up off her face and tied high on top of her head. The still damp ends hung down her back, long and glossy like the tail of a fine prize pony. She smelled like shampoo and soap, and he wanted to touch her skin to see if it was as soft and dewy as it looked.

"What's happening?" Her voice was a whisper, heavy with sorrow and unanswered questions.

"I don't know," he said. "But don't worry. We're going to find out."

She looked at him, the corners of her mouth turned down. He lost himself in the depths of those blue crystal eyes, then reached out and smoothed the line that dented the space between her eyebrows. Her breath slid out in a long, helpless sigh as she lowered her face to her hands. Her whole body seemed to fold in on itself. He pulled her close, tucked her head into his shoulder, and stroked her hair, offering comfort. That's all he had to offer right now. That, and one other thing.

"You're not going back to your apartment, you know."

"I know."

"Tomorrow morning we'll pick up your things . . ." He drew back, trying to catch her eye, wanting to be sure she understood. "Everything," he said, meaning it. "And move you out. You'll stay here. We'll bring whatever you need from your office, and you can finish your work here, too."

She nodded against his chest, and he caught the clean scent of her hair.

"Sallie's memorial is at two o'clock," he reminded.

She nodded again and sniffed. "Will Larry and Albert be at the funeral?"

He didn't answer right away. He never quite knew how to respond to white people's misconceptions of the Indians. The last thing most Navajos—the traditionalists, anyway—wanted to do was attend a function for the dead.

"It's a memorial, not a funeral," he said finally. "Death is handled differently on the reservation. There probably won't be many Indians there. Sallie's body has already been taken care of." He paused after he said that. "Some Navajo people cling to the old ways, others are more modern. Many are lost in between."

After some silent reflection, he spoke again. "No one has heard from Larry and Albert as far as I know."

"Are Larry and Albert lost in between?"

"Yes," he said. "I suspect they are."

More than silence, an undulating stillness seemed to hold them together in the moment. He became intensely aware of his breath in her hair, escaping strands of it brushing his lips as he circled both arms around her. He ran his hand over her shoulder and down her arm in a gentling motion, and felt the sensuous warmth of her skin increase in intensity. She stirred against him, moving closer, pushing against him as if seeking his warmth, causing a prolonged tug in his lower stomach.

He groaned inwardly.

A picture of his life flashed to mind. His work. The Cultural Center. His teaching and historic preservation activities. It had all been so simple and straightforward before, just the way he'd planned it. Taking in Sharron's kids presented a number of complications, but he could handle those.

It was different with Amanda.

Amanda's presence in his life had the power to change everything, and force him to take another look at some of his closely held convictions.

He tried to tell himself to back away from her, but he couldn't. Wouldn't. Something more powerful than common sense heated his blood and drew his mouth to the side of her face, moved his hand up her ribcage. She turned her head, and their mouths were close enough to breathe each other's breath. She was so darned soft.

He was sure that what he was feeling was love, but he didn't say it. Telling her he loved her implied the promise of a future together. He *couldn't* say it. But, damn, he wanted her—wanted to be with her—more than he'd ever wanted any woman.

Amanda took a deep quieting breath to still the leaping pulse beneath her ribs, and tension slid out of her body in a smooth fluid movement. She surrendered to the fascination of how his hand had moved up from her waist until his thumb was brushing the underside of her breast, stroking, soothing. There was no demand in it, only an offer of succor, there for her if she wanted it.

He radiated a heat she'd never felt from Elliott. Part of her wanted to retreat from it, her rational mind told her she should. But she pressed into it instead, taking it in. Taking him in.

He lifted her hand with exquisite tenderness and placed it in the center of his chest. She felt the thunder of his heartbeat, and shuddered with longing.

He drew back slightly and raised her chin, turning it up so he could capture her gaze. When he spoke his voice was soothing as the desert wind.

"Will you stay with me tonight?"

The question set her pulses dancing with excitement, but she hesitated, torn by conflicting emotions. She'd thought about this moment, hoped it would come even though she hadn't known where it would lead. But now? Like this? She wasn't sure this was the time. Was it wrong to make love for reasons of comfort and need? It might not be entirely right, but she couldn't make herself feel it was entirely wrong, either.

She let her fingers linger over his heart as if to persuade herself, the warming sensation under her fingertips helping her to decide. Never had she had such powerful feelings.

"I want you so damn bad," he said. The invitation smoldered in the depths of his eyes, his gaze demanding an answer. Her body ached, yearning for his touch.

"Yes," she answered, drinking in the comfort of his nearness. Her body ached for his touch.

He gathered her hands in his, lifting them to his lips. She hadn't known that her palms could be so responsive, that his lips kissing her there could be so arousing.

He led her to his bed and gently laid her down. Kneeling over her, he slid his hands under her T-shirt, letting his fingers brush her breasts, and she raised her arms. It was his shirt, and she smelled him in the fibers when he slipped it off over her head. When he tugged the drawstring of the pajama bottoms, she lifted her hips so he could slide them off, too. The chill that caressed her skin was instantly warmed as she watched him removed his own clothes, not as slowly as he'd removed hers, but rather with an urgent need.

He caressed her, his touch light but bringing fire to her skin. He lowered his mouth to hers, and their lips met in a deep kiss that grew in passion. His hand drifted to her stomach, then lower, and she responded to it, intensifying the undulating sensations throbbing inside her.

He moved on top of her, and the feel of his body covering

hers was so exciting, she closed her eyes and concentrated on it. When he drew himself up slightly, she opened her legs, and he gently lowered himself into her, filling her up, jolting her consciousness into oblivion.

"Open your eyes," he whispered, hoarse and breathless.

But she couldn't, she was taken up by the sensations of his touch, by the heat spiraling in that place where he was buried into her.

"I want you to look at me when—" He didn't finish, breaking off quickly and taking a breath as the muscles of his buttocks tightened and he stopped moving against her. After a moment, he began again, slowly. "I want you to look in my eyes," he said.

She did as he asked, locking onto his intense gaze, seeking the message in its depth. All at once, her heart was hammering, and they moved together, finding a rhythm. At first, he went slowly. The desire that surged through her body where it pressed against Durango's was so overwhelming, it made her feel faint. She wrapped her legs around him, clasping him to her, straining toward him. She was drowning in heat as intense as that in the desert, and like the desert, it was wonderful and terrifying at the same time.

His black eyes glittered as he watched her face and she realized he was holding himself back, waiting for her to climax, and that was enough to release it. Her pulses pounded in her ears as she gave into it, making her forget everything else except what she was feeling right there in that place.

Durango's hard breathing raced, then a groan burst from him, and he held her so tight that for a moment she couldn't take in air. Afterward, he lay on her, not moving, the weight of his spent body pressing her into the soft mattress.

At last, he released a deep breath and a long sigh of surrender, then rolled to the side, and lay back, bringing his arm up to rest the back of his hand on his forehead. He lay that way in total repose, his profile sharply defined by moonlight coming in through the window, his lips curved in a small, contented smile.

She snuggled against him, and laid the side of her face on his stomach, breathing in the smell of their lovemaking there. After a while, he lifted her gently, stroked the hair off her face, and pressed her head into the hollow of his shoulder. He dragged the sheet over them and they slept that way, naked against each other.

Next day, the wretched sadness of the memorial service, and Amanda's unshakable feelings of guilt over Sallie's death tore at her throat and she wept bitter tears. Durango, sneaking worried glances at her from the corner of his eye, held her hand protectively. When it was over, he braced an arm around her waist, but she'd gently pushed it away and walked tall and straight down the aisle out of the tiny mission to the car.

He seemed to sense her need to be alone with her thoughts, so they rode most of the miles home in silence. She couldn't help casting a nervous eye at passing cars as the terror of being chased on the highway the previous night threatened to shatter her fragile control. Durango placed a reassuring hand on her knee.

"You're with me now. You're safe. I won't let anyone hurt you."

She welcomed his words, accepted them with genuine gratitude, but they didn't lessen the reality of what had happened. She hadn't come to grips with the fact that someone had tried to kill her.

Would she ever? Could anyone?

Thinking about it in the stark light of day swept her emotions from shock to disbelief and back again.

Returning to Durango's house after the service, he led her

into the guest room, partially drew the blinds against the piercing glare of midday sun, and threw back the Navajo blanket on her bed.

"Try to get some rest," he said, kissing her gently before leaving her alone. His kiss was sweet. She put her fingers to the warmth still lingering on her lips.

A soft desert breeze drifted through the double doors leading in from the shaded patio. Durango had moved her belongings here into the guest wing, which was large and comfortable with a high ceiling that added to its feeling of spaciousness. Her computer was set up on a long, rectangular library table. Floor to ceiling windows framed a view of russet-hued monuments standing in relief against a backdrop of hazy mountains. Adjoining the bedroom was a satillo-tiled bathroom with a step-down shower stall as large as a walk-in closet and a door that opened onto a private outdoor garden and hot tub.

She was grateful for Durango's understanding and indulgent attention. And his protection, too. Memories of their lovemaking the night before brought a heat that tugged low down in her belly. The feeling of his body on hers, in hers, remained in her thoughts, vivid and imposing.

The unreality of recent events sent waves of weariness and despair washing over her, and she swallowed the lump that lingered in her throat. She caught her reflection in the mirror over the dresser. Fatigue had settled in pockets under her eyes, and her hands shook when her fingers weren't locked into a tense clasp. The charmstone at her neck gleamed softly, offering a modicum of comfort.

Though she'd promised Durango she would take a nap, she sat instead at the window, watching how the golden light of late afternoon climbed the eastern rock face as the sun went down behind the western ridge. Her thoughts drifted back over the past week. She struggled to make sense of all that had happened to bring her to this time and place, but she was too tired to remember much past yesterday.

She heard a knock and Nonni appeared in the doorway, worry written in the lines of her face. "You didn't have lunch. Can I fix you something?"

"No, Nonni. Thank you."

"Durango said dinner at seven. Okay? I'll feed the children earlier."

"Yes, that's fine. Thank you."

Nonni and her husband Hitathli occupied a small, furnished suite of rooms off the kitchen, servants' quarters from an earlier time though Nonni was more family than servant. Her attentions were soothing and restorative, bringing comfort and solace to Amanda. She had fleeting visions of burying her head on Nonni's wide bosom and crying her heart out.

When exhaustion and confusion threatened to overwhelm her, she got up, walked to the bed and lay down fully clothed on top of the sheets. Through the deepening fog of sleep, she checked off the next few days.

Tomorrow, Saturday, was Jeremiah's fortieth birthday, and Judy had planned a family gathering at their house in Bluff. Durango's family would be there. Amanda didn't feel much like celebrating, but she liked Jeremiah, adored Judy, and looked forward to meeting Durango's mother and grandmother.

She'd take Sunday to read more of Agent Winthrop's diaries, a big step toward completing the project that had brought her to the reservation.

Then, first thing Monday, she and Durango would go to Cortez to search more old newspaper files, track down the witness who saw her father in a bar, and try to figure out what the hell was going on.

On Saturday, James, Eric, and Doli ran ahead of Amanda and

Durango as they rounded the house into the Moons' backyard. Birthday balloons tugging at the end of string tethers were tied to limbs of cottonwood trees lining the perimeter. Pastel-colored streamers were swagged along the roofline of the house and wrapped loosely around the deck railings. Rock music beat out from loudspeakers brought outside for the party.

Amanda was aware of the picture they presented as they joined the others in the backyard, a pseudo family consisting of mom, dad and the kids, arriving at a birthday gathering. Her heart squeezed a little at the thought of it.

Jeremiah, wearing a backyard barbecue apron over a fringed leather vest and his ever present ropes of beads, was standing at a fired-up grill fashioned out of a half-barrel set on metal legs. Steaks, hotdogs, and chicken breasts sizzled as he placed them one by one on the cooking grate. He turned, a smile breaking on his lips, and greeted Durango in Navajo. The two men exchanged a masculine hug complete with the requisite mutual back slapping.

"Ah, thank you for coming," Jeremiah said heartily.

"How could I miss the birthday celebration of my brother-in-law and favorite Navajo *wannabe?*" Durango replied with a teasing grin.

Jeremiah laughed uproariously at this, and the good-natured male back pounding began anew. When it was over, Jeremiah brushed a kiss across Amanda's cheek, rested his hands on her shoulders, and looked at her, his face suddenly serious.

"I'm so sorry about what happened to Sallie. She will be missed. It must have been a horrible experience up on that mesa. Storms can come in so fast here." He shook his head. "And you. Let me look at you. Are you all right?"

"Yes, thank you for asking, Jeremiah. I'm fine."

Reluctant to mention what happened on the highway three nights ago, not wanting to stir up dire conjecture on what was supposed to be a day of celebration, she quickly directed the conversation away from herself.

"I'm a little concerned about Larry and Albert, though. No one has seen them."

"Oh, I wouldn't worry. They're used to spending time in the desert. That's where they get their best ideas for their paintings. I'm sure they honored the memory of their mother in a traditional way. A way we might not understand, but who understands the young Navajo men today, anyway?" He threw a glance at Durango. "Ah, but that's a topic for another day."

At Durango's prompting, Eric and James stepped forward to say hello. Doli peeked out from behind Amanda's legs and was greeted with a playful pigtail tug by Jeremiah.

"Hello, little one," he said.

After the children were sent off to play with the other kids, Jeremiah turned to Durango. "How long will they be with you?"

Durango shook his head. "I don't know. Officially, they're in my foster care now. If Sharron won't give them up, Social Services could terminate her parental rights. It has to go through the courts, of course."

Jeremiah nodded, his face thoughtful.

"I'd like to keep them," Durango said, after a moment.

"You'd give them a wonderful home," Jeremiah replied. "And a future. I hope it works out."

Durango briefly met Amanda's eyes, then looked away. She followed his gaze and watched as the boys ran to join up with Jeremiah's three rowdy sons. Doli, running behind on short little legs, gamely struggled to keep up. Amanda was sure that despite the boys' devotion to their little sister, Doli would be chased off to play with the girls in short order.

Judy approached, hugged her brother, smiled at Amanda, and cocked an inquisitive eye at the casserole dish Amanda was holding.

"You cooked?"

Amanda smiled back and shook her head.

"I'm afraid not. It's Nonni's tortilla chicken casserole. She couldn't come. She and Hitathli were waiting for a phone call from her family in Tuba City. A relative is ill."

Judy nodded and took the dish. "Come, both of you. Mother and Grandmother are already here."

"I told them I'd pick them up," Durango began by way of explanation, sounding like a child afraid of being blamed for something that wasn't his fault. "But they didn't want me to." His voice trailed off.

"Yes, well, you know Mother. She will drive Father's pickup until the wheels fall off. They practically are now."

Judy turned and tossed her head in a come-along motion. Leaving Jeremiah to tend the grill, the three of them headed for the house. Durango draped a loose arm around Amanda as she walked at his side. The weight of it felt good on her shoulder, natural and comfortable, and something fluttered in her chest. After last night, there would never come a time when she could feel his touch and not want to wrap herself around him.

"*Ya at eeh*, Durango." Friends called as they walked to the house, nodding to Amanda, slapping Durango on his shoulder in a gesture of camaraderie, the younger ones, his students, raising their hands for a hearty high-five.

There were lots of people she didn't know. Most of the women were in the midst of meal preparation or childcare. The men, some wearing black reservation hats trimmed with silver hatbands, were off to one side speaking Navajo. She heard a car pull up in front, and saw Noah and Cammie get out. They waved.

The screen door slapped open and shut as people went in and out of the kitchen, women carrying trays to an already laden buffet table, children tagging along hoping for a snack before the meal. Inside, Judy set Nonni's dish on the drain-board next to a middle-aged Indian woman shelling peas at the sink.

Durango walked to the woman and gave her a warm hug, which she returned.

"Mother, I'd like you to meet someone. This is Amanda Bell. I've told you about her." The woman turned to Amanda.

"This is my mother, Millie Yazzie," said Durango.

It was plain to see where Durango got his good looks. Amanda studied the high cheekbones and angular features of the still-handsome woman. Millie Yazzie carried the youthful remnants of classic American Indian beauty, a beauty that would last a lifetime. She was wearing jeans, well fitting on her slender frame, and a white blouse. A turquoise and silver choker circled her elegant neck. Shiny, black hair was twisted and coiled at the back of her head, held in place with an ornate turquoise hair ornament.

"Hello," said Amanda. "I'm pleased to meet you."

The older woman's warm smile reached her eyes, and she looked at Amanda with open but friendly curiosity. "Ah," she said. "At last I meet the light-haired *bilagaana*. The lemonade lady. That's what some of the Indians call you. Because you are tall and have long, yellow hair."

Amanda laughed. "Thank you, I think," she said, accepting what she hoped was a compliment.

Millie Yazzie laughed, too, and her smile lingered.

Next to her was an old woman in traditional Indian dress working methodically at a flour board on the counter. Her gnarled hands were dusted with flour and looked too frail to be kneading dough. Millie spoke to her in Navajo, and the old woman turned to look at Amanda with the ever present reticence that seemed to be preprogrammed into the DNA of the Navajos, especially the older ones.

The old woman's features were less angular though the family resemblance was there. Except for the eyes. They were dark gray, faintly streaked with hints of blue, a stunning contrast to her bronzed, wrinkled skin. Amanda peered down at the upturned face, a softer version of Durango's.

"This is *my* mother," said Millie. "Durango's grandmother. Bernice Littlestar."

As Amanda greeted the old woman, the name stirred in her memory then rose like a bubble to the surface of her mind. *Littlestar—the Indian boy in Agent Winthrop's diary!*

"Littlestar?" Amanda smiled. "I've come across that name in my research," she said to Durango's mother. "Might it be a relative?"

Millie Yazzie shrugged. "It's a common name. Many Navajo families, including ours, have been on the reservation since the return of their ancestors from Bosque Redondo."

Amanda nodded, but said nothing further. It wasn't a name she recognized as common, but maybe it was to the Indians. She made a mental note to ask Durango about it later.

The screen door banged open and three children scrambled in, their eager faces flushed with a rascally glow.

"When can we eat?" Judy's littlest boy wrapped his arm around her leg at the knee, put his fist in his mouth, and looked up at her expectantly.

"I'm hungry," said a blond girl. Amanda recognized her from the Presbyterian Mission. She was the minister's daughter.

"Me, too," the son of one of the high school teachers piped in excitedly. "Me, too. Me, too," he chanted, jumping up and down.

"Yes, yes. We can eat soon. Go wash your hands," Judy instructed. "And tell the other kids."

The children ran off as the women turned back to a flurry of last-minute meal preparation. Judy picked up a basket of bread, handed another to Amanda, and they walked outside to a buffet table that had been set up in the shade.

Wonderful aromas hovered over the table. Homemade tortillas, Navajo tacos, potato salad, green salad, green beans, corn relish, scalloped potatoes, fragrant floury loaves of bread, and crocks of Anasazi beans. There were chips, dips, pretzels, and dozens of cookies for the kids. Not only was there enough food for the day, but, Amanda suspected, there would be plenty left over so everyone could take a plate home.

Conversation faltered and everyone's attention was redirected to the food table. Guests ambled over, but no one approached the buffet.

Durango came forward with his grandmother and helped her fill her plate. Five or six other elders joined them. The rest of the guests stood back out of respect until all the senior family members were served, then they moved forward to help themselves.

Amanda watched Durango escort his grandmother to a picnic table where other family members were seated. He spoke softly to her in Navajo, fussing over her, settling her into a seat, and when he was sure she was comfortable, looked up to catch Amanda's eye. He met and held her gaze, his mouth curving in a smile. His glance set something loose in her chest. He looked so damn sexy standing there.

She admired the way he carried himself. Even his smallest movement held the grace of a mountain lion. As he came near her and took her arm, his smile grew wider.

"You look beautiful," he said.

Night was settling beneath a silvered moon. The last of the guests had gone home. Durango sat at a picnic table with his sister, watching Amanda bid goodnight to Cammie and Noah. Amanda broke into a wide open smile at something Cammie said, then Noah spoke, and she threw back her head and laughed. God, she was pretty.

Judy's voice broke into his thoughts

"I saw Buck the other day. Ran into him at the trading post." When Durango didn't answer, she inquired, "Have you been able to find a deed or title transfer to that property?"

"Not yet. I'm still working on it."

He didn't want to tell her there wasn't much hope left. The court deadline was fast approaching, and nothing had turned up in the archives at Tribal Headquarters or at the land registry.

"Mother would hate to lose that land. She'd especially hate to see condos built on it."

"Condos?" This was something new. And unthinkable.

"Yes. I heard Buck has been talking to a developer."

Durango stared in disbelief. "But there are pueblo ruins out there. He can't destroy them."

"He can if he owns the property. He can do anything he wants with them then."

"Well, he doesn't own the property and he's not going to." During the long silence that followed, his eyes drifted back to Amanda.

"Mother asked me about you and Amanda."

He stirred uncomfortably and his gaze, which had been devouring Amanda, faltered.

"There is no me and Amanda," he said.

Appearing to concentrate on the tabletop, she used the tip of her finger to absently scoop some loose crumbs into a tiny pile on the checkered cloth.

"Hmmm." Her tone became deliberately mild and curious. "Then I guess that's why you've been touching each other with your eyes all day? When you're not using your hands, that is."

At that, he turned to his sister, surprised that she'd noticed, and wondered if anyone else had. He didn't want how much he cared to show.

"You see too much," he said.

"I see everything," she replied. "You don't see enough." Judy smiled at her brother. "Mother likes her. Said she seems like a nice person."

"She is a nice person."

Durango kept his reply neutral. He knew where Judy was going with this, and he didn't want to think about it, let alone talk about it. Somehow talking about it, saying the words out loud made it something that had to be faced, decided on. He wasn't ready for that.

His sister started to speak again, but he stopped her.

"Judy, please. Don't. I told you. She's not Navajo. And I have work to do. And now I've got Sharron's kids to take care of." He looked away again.

Brusquely, she swept the crumbs off the tablecloth. "Hey." She put her hand on his forearm and squeezed hard, using the pressure of her fingers to make sure she had his attention. "You don't have to prove anything to Father anymore. He's gone now."

Durango tried to move his arm away, but she held on. Her voice was hard, but sad.

"He meant well. He did what he thought best. It was his way to follow tradition. It was the only way he knew. You turned your back on the old ways when you left. Don't use those same traditions now as a shield. Navajo custom has always been a blending of cultures."

Judy released her grip, and Durango connected with her intense gaze as she went on.

"Sharron wasn't right for you, but not for the reasons you think. Not because of what our father said she was, but because of what she really was." Judy touched her fingertips between her breasts. "In here."

In the distance, something was agitating the coyotes. The echo of their mournful howls drifted faintly on the desert breeze.

"Sharron was always a wild child. The name Running Girl suited her perfectly. She would never have stuck with you. You were ambitious and high-minded. Drugs and alcohol were tempting her even then. You just didn't know it."

No, he hadn't known for sure, but he'd suspected. He said nothing as she went on.

"You didn't cause the situation she's in now, and you're not responsible for anything leading up to it. She was already heading down that path in high school."

Judy's words struck him full force on and he reeled. He knew she was saying the things he'd stopped her from saying in the past during the rare occasions he'd allowed any conversation about Sharron at all. Now it was said, and the words hung in the air, ugly as three-day-old road kill.

He tried not to look, but couldn't stop himself. He was forced to see what others had known all along. Sharron careening down the highway in an old pickup with the older boys, their drunken yahoos and catcalls shattering the dark desert night. Sharron coming to school bleary-eyed and sick from overuse of some substance, if she came to school at all. Sharron hurrying to meet him in the moonlight, stripping off her clothes as she neared, her cheeks flushed and lips already swollen from some other boy's kisses.

He'd blocked his mind to it, built and rebuilt the walls that had kept the memories out, but now his chest burned with an inner pain as they crashed through the imperfect barriers. He pulled in a long breath, then blew it out in a forceful stream, releasing the ache.

Judy put her hand on the side of his face, a gentle touch, her fingers at his temple. Her face was serene and he found comfort in it. She looked like their father only younger, softer. Strangely, there was comfort in that, too.

"You have her children now," Judy said. "Give them a real home, the kind of home you would have given them if things had turned out differently and they had been yours."

Durango nodded and hugged his sister in a fierce but fond embrace. "Thank you. I will."

When he released her, she took his hand.

"Come, my brother. Come inside and let me show you my birthday gift to Jeremiah. Did I tell you I bought a painting by his favorite artist when I went to Santa Fe last month? I drove a hard bargain with the dealer, of course. How else could we afford anything by J. D. Challenger?"

Chapter Sixteen

On Sunday morning, outside the Recapture Lodge in Bluff, Elliott Sheffield unlocked his SUV, opened the hatchback, and reached inside. A canvas satchel coated with the permanently embedded dust of countless archaeological digs was stashed next to a box of shovels, trowels, buckets, maps, tape measures, and string, the accoutrements of a dig site. Impatiently, he unbuckled the bag, took out a pair of binoculars, and tossed them on the passenger seat. Then he went into the motel office, paid for another week, strode back out, and climbed behind the wheel of the 4×4.

The memory of being humiliated by Durango at the restaurant burned a hole in his chest. He'd spent three nights thinking about it. Three nights feeling the heat of embarrassment scorch his face. Three nights making a plan. He hadn't worked out all the details yet, but he would. There was still time for payback.

He cranked the key in the ignition, and the engine roared to life. Tilting the rearview mirror to look at his reflection, he gingerly fingered the still puffy lump over his eye and the wash of purple under it.

A swift shadow of anger swept his face and narrowed his eyes. Amanda's rejection of his proposal was far less painful than the fact that she had chosen Durango Yazzie over him. After a moment, he swallowed the bitter taste of his fury, shifted into gear and drove out of the parking lot, turned left on the blacktop and headed toward Monument Valley.

"Doli, sit over here, okay?"

Amanda helped the little girl move to the other end of the library table and arrange a coloring book and new box of crayons just so. After much deliberation, the child picked the red one out of the box and held it in her hand. She turned her eyes on Amanda who was settling herself at the other end.

She was aware of the child's gaze and returned it with a smile. After the terrifying experience on the highway, Doli had rarely let Amanda out of her sight. She was apprehensive and clingy, startled easily and was sometimes whiny. Amanda indulged her, letting Doli sit nearby while she worked.

"What are you doing, 'Manda?" Doli stared curiously, holding the still-unused crayon in her hand.

"I'm reading a diary."

"What's a *dyree?*"

"Di-a-ry," Amanda corrected. "It's a daybook, a journal." How do you explain a diary to a child? "It's sort of a story, about a person's life. People write down what happened to them that day."

Doli nodded in solemn understanding. "Like when Nonni made pancakes for breakfast today?"

"Yes," Amanda answered.

"Like when Uncle Dee took Eric and James hiking today?"

"Yes."

Doli thought a minute.

"Like when that car chased us yesterday?"

Amanda cringed inwardly. She hoped Doli would eventually forget that. "Yes, but it wasn't yesterday. Look, why don't you color that picture for me, and Nonni will stick it on the refrigerator."

"Okay."

216

Doli opened her coloring book, but curiosity had her in its grip and wouldn't let go. She watched Amanda reading.

"Who wrote in that di-a-ry?" she wanted to know, pronouncing the word carefully, mimicking Amanda.

"This one belonged to Mr. Winthrop Taylor. He was an Indian Agent."

Doli nodded again, then rubbed the red crayon on a line drawing of a horse. Amanda turned back to the journal she'd been reading the night Elliott showed up.

"What's a Indian Agent?" Doli's head was tilted to the side, her chocolate-colored eyes big and round and inquisitive.

It occurred to Amanda to wonder how much Doli had been exposed to her cultural history. She didn't attend school yet, and no one may have ever talked to her about her ancestors or her family ties.

Yesterday at Jeremiah's birthday party, Doli and her brothers, though strangers, had been instantly accepted by the other children just as Amanda had been welcomed by the grownups. They were all made to feel like part of the family. There was no disapproval. No one criticized, no one judged. They just loved. Regrettably, she wouldn't continue to be a part of that, but Doli and her brothers would if the adoption went through, and even if it didn't.

"You know what, Doli? Your Uncle Durango will explain that all to you when you're older."

The little girl nodded, her attention already turned back to the red horse.

Amanda found her place on the page and picked up the story of Agent Taylor and his family.

December 4, 1869

Claudia has taken to her bed distraught and overwhelmed with our dying child. I told her Littlestar had learned medicine and chants from his father. She screamed at me to keep him away from our precious girl. When Claudia was asleep, I brought Littlestar to Bliss's cot. I did not need to beg his help. He gave it gladly and sang and prayed softly through the night.

December 5, 1869

Thanks be to the Lord, we have our darling Bliss back. Her fever is gone and she is breathing normally, asking for food. Claudia is weeping with happiness. I embraced my Navajo friend in a bear hug and promised to repay him before he shyly ducked away.

Christmas Day 1869

Our gift giving was meager as we celebrated this day of Jesus' birth. Claudia had made a rag doll for Bliss for which she was most grateful. Littlestar presented Claudia with a piñon nut bracelet he had made for her. I fear she was most ungracious in her acceptance. I very much wanted to give Littlestar a gift for saving my daughter's life, but have nothing of value to spare.

Amanda looked up at a sound in the hall. Nonni came in carrying a tray with a turkey sandwich on a plate and a glass of iced tea in which floated a slice of lemon. She set the tray in front of Amanda, then smiled at Doli.

"Come, bluebird, it's time for lunch. Then a nap."

"Do I have to now?" Doli looked at Amanda for confirmation, but with hope of amnesty in her eyes.

Amanda nodded. "Yes, sweetheart. You go along." She thanked Nonni for the lunch, then asked, "Is Durango back yet?"

"No, but I expect them any time."

Nonni left and Amanda gazed through the sliding doors at

the sun-rinsed desert, her mind on the tall dark man whose hands did the most wondrous things to her body. He was in her thoughts all the time, vibrant and electrifying.

Sighing, she turned the page of the diary and read on.

March 1870

Today is Bliss's birthday. She is ten years old. A teacher comes from the Presbyterian Mission with lessons once a week, but I fear Bliss is missing out. This is not much of a life for her. Claudia is angry every day.

June 1871

The government has failed to provide aid for the sick, indigent and helpless Indians. It has failed to fulfill its obligations to them. I am compelled to see them suffer and close my ears to their pleas. Claudia, Bliss and I have been constantly ill because of the leaky house furnished us by the government. Everything is lacking and I cannot do my job. Tomorrow I must resign my post.

August 1871

The Indian Commissioner has refused my resignation. I must stay on. Indian leaders offered me $1000 a year from their treaty money to supplement my salary. Of course, I cannot accept. It's doubtful they will ever see a penny of it themselves.

Amanda read the last page and closed the journal. A folded piece of paper that had been stuck between the last page and the back cover fell in her lap. On paper yellowed and stiff with age was a copy of Agent Taylor's resignation in which he detailed the atrocities only mentioned in his log. She read it, then refolded and replaced it, set the volume aside, and opened another.

From the terraced bench of land above a tumble of easy-chair–sized boulders where Elliott sat, he had a clear view of the patio, the swimming pool, and the grounds surrounding Durango's house. Nothing else intruded on the desolate expanse of sagebrush and cactus desert land except a khaki colored streak of road that snaked its way south toward the Arizona state line.

Hidden from the house behind a scramble of gray-green brush that fronted his narrow ledge, Elliott lifted binoculars and zoomed in on one of a pair of glass patio doors, adjusting the lenses until he could see inside the room. Amanda came into view, bent over her books and papers, reading. Idly she lifted a hand and draped a drift of silky hair behind her ear. She was wearing it loose, the way he liked it. The little girl he'd seen with Durango at the restaurant was busy at the other end of the table, swinging ankle-crossed legs that were too short to touch the floor.

From his vantage point, Elliott was able to capture the layout of the house and watch the people inside. He was close enough to hear bits of conversation when anyone was outside, and sometimes voices drifted up to him from an open door or window.

Durango had left with the boys at mid-morning, the three of them headed out across the sandy tableland with backpacks and water bottles. In the house with Amanda and the little girl were an old Indian woman, probably the housekeeper, and an aged man, her husband.

A low stucco wall ringed the tiled courtyard. Potted yucca, brittlebush, prickly pear, agave, and barrel cactus blended with other desert plants to form a natural garden that stretched seamlessly over the wall onto the desert floor. There was enough white-cushioned patio furniture to seat several guests, but from what he'd seen so far, Durango had no visitors. Except for that movie director, Noah what's-his-name, who was staying in the guesthouse at the end of the driveway by the road. It was rumored that Noah spent most of his nights at the hippie doctor's house.

The only discordant note to the scene below were the dogs. Four Rhodesian Ridgebacks, long-legged, steel-jawed, and now, apparently having caught Elliott's scent, sniffing the air, beginning to pace nervously. He shuddered at the sight of them. He didn't like dogs, was afraid of them.

He concentrated on Amanda, his broad, sturdy fingers twisting and coordinating the focus and viewing rings of the telescopes until her neck and chin filled the lenses. She was still wearing that damn pendant. He'd recognized it right away as an amulet from her father's collection. The collection Jack had his sights set on.

At the thought of Jack, Elliott couldn't hold back a snort of derision. Who did that old fool think he was, trying to make a deal on something that didn't even belong to him? Jack said the professor was dead, so there was no need to worry about that, but where did the shipment go? Maybe Amanda knew after all, since she was wearing something from it.

Elliott suspected Jack knew more than he'd let on, so he might be useful, at least. If he wasn't so stupid, that is. Elliott looked toward the dirt road in the front of the house. Jack was driving by in that ancient, ridiculous-looking psychedelic van, slowing down, craning his neck to peer up the long driveway. Christ, it's broad daylight. He might as well walk up to the front door and ring the bell.

Intolerant of ignorance, Elliott blew a disgusted breath, a faint noise inaudible to the humans below, but the dogs caught it and stirred again. He glanced at them nervously and shifted position, stretching his cramped legs.

Jack's face across the table at the Turquoise Café drifted into his memory, the way the newspaperman had smirked as he flattened the faded clipping on the sticky table. Remembering, Elliott's gut knotted just as it had that day, and sweat broke out on his forehead. He knew he risked bringing that nasty business back to light by coming here. But he'd had no choice.

His mind pulled back to the present at the sound of voices from below, coming closer. Durango and the boys were returning from their hike. They walked through the flimsy ocotillo cane gate onto the patio and all three of them dropped their backpacks, stripped out of their clothing, and jumped into the pool.

Elliott's anger simmered to the surface at the sight of Durango, his muscular arms and powerful shoulders pulling him fluidly through the water. After several laps, Durango swam to the side of the pool, braced his hands on the edge, and effortlessly straight-armed himself onto the deck as water ran in rivulets down his back and buttocks.

Elliott's eyes raked Durango's naked body, and his anger became a scalding fury at the thought of Amanda being naked with him. Of Durango touching her. Or her touching him. Such thoughts were almost more than Elliott could bear, but he forced himself to take some deep breaths and slow the fury that was painfully overtaking him.

Durango toweled himself off, wrapped it around his middle and called to the boys splashing and yelling in the pool.

"Come on, Eric. James. Let's see what Nonni's making for dinner. It smells good to me."

Elliott lowered the binoculars and swallowed hard, wrenching back his jealous rage. With considerable force of will, he brought his breathing under control, calming himself. A plan was taking shape in his mind.

Amanda opened the next of Winthrop Taylor's diaries. She'd heard Durango in the pool with the boys, but was now only vaguely aware of muffled sounds coming from another part of the house. Late afternoon quiet shrouded the desert like a blanket as she read of the tragedies befalling the Taylor family, and the Indians.

February 1872
   Claudia has been ill in the head since Christmas.

A breeze tinkled the wind chimes near the gate, and the click-click-clicking of the dogs' nails as they pattered around the patio momentarily broke Amanda's concentration. After a brief glance outside, she turned back to the diary and was quickly absorbed, heedless of time passing.

March 1872
   Last night Claudia wandered into the desert. This morning she was found dead.

She felt a gentle hand tug at the spill of hair down her back. She turned to see Durango, the corners of his mouth lifted in a smile. He'd put on jeans and a shirt, but his hair was still wet from the shower and hung black and sleek to his shoulders. He bent and moved his arms around her. She relaxed into them, but quirked an eyebrow in question.

His smile grew. "Are you at a stopping place?"

"Why?"

"I have something to show you. Can you take a break?"

"What is it?"

"It's a surprise. You'll have to come with me. But I promise you'll like it."

She marked her place in the volume, set the diary on the table and started for the closet.

"No," he said. "You don't need to change clothes. What you're wearing is fine."

She looked down at her khaki twill pants and peach silk tank top. Scuffed black-and-tan day-hikers were on her feet. She held out her arms, turned her hands palms up, doubtful.

"Are you sure?"

"I'm sure."

"Where are we going?"

"To a place the boys and I went to in the desert today. Come on." She caught a faint glow of mischief in his flashing eyes.

On their way, Durango pulled two blankets from a hall linen closet and tucked them under his arm. In the kitchen, Nonni smiled knowingly, and handed him a picnic basket out of which poked the long narrow neck of a wine bottle. He nodded his thanks, and offered his free hand to Amanda. She took it, noticing its strength, and the hardness of his fingers, then followed in his wake as he strode across the patio into the desert.

The golden sun was almost touching the western ridge, and coolness was settling into the shadows cast by tall sage and desert willow. Soon they were out of sight of the house, but Durango walked with purpose. Still holding his hand, she followed secure in the knowledge that he knew every inch of this desert even in the dark.

Moments later, they climbed the shallow slope of a sculpted sandstone mesa, picking an easy path over boulders that had broken off and fallen to the ground centuries before. At the top, the ground leveled off, and Durango dropped the blankets and set down the picnic basket. He led her up a winding trail to a wide plateau swept smooth by thousands of years of wind and rain. The edge dropped off in a steep cliff that fell sharply to a deep canyon below.

"Look," he said and held out his arm majestically, as if presenting royalty.

The whole of Monument Valley spread before them, glorious and mysterious, stretching past Moki Dugway, beyond Muley Point to Comb Ridge, a misty blue rise in the distance. Sleeping Ute Mountain presented a jagged silhouette on the eastern horizon.

Fiery sunset bathed a seemingly endless million miles of red, ocher, and vermilion, the color of blood, the life force of the earth. The scent of sage, carried on a warm wind, caressed her skin like an exhaled breath. Amanda was sure that if she put her ear to the ground, she'd hear a heartbeat.

"Oh!" That was all she could say, spellbound at the panorama unfolding to infinity in front of her. "It's so beautiful."

They spread the blankets on the ground together, positioning them for the best view of the lingering sunset. Durango poured wine and handed her a glass. They sat close together, and he slid his arm to snuggle around her neck, bending it as if to protect her throat. He put his other arm around her waist and pulled her back against him, her rump between his thighs, his arms circling her from behind. She rested her chin on his forearm and yielded to his warmth. Nighthawks swooped and spun in and out of the canyon depths, their occasional sharp dives sounding like miniature jet airplanes.

They sat that way without speaking until the sun glided beneath the western horizon, casting surreal shadows over the convoluted ridges and canyons and upthrust monuments. Rose-colored streaks washed the darkening sky; and soon a full moon took over the job of lighting the desert, drenching it with liquid silver. She stared at the nearly solid canopy of stars, letting herself be transported into their depths.

"What are you thinking about?" he whispered.

She could feel his breath on her cheek. It was warm and moist, and smelled of mint and cloves, and that's what she was thinking about. That, and the warm hardness of his body.

"Tomorrow," she answered. "I'm wondering what we'll find in Cortez. If there really was a witness who saw my father in a bar there."

He squeezed her in a little hug. "If there was, we'll find him. I promise." He dropped a tiny kiss on the tip of her ear.

"I need to talk to whoever it is."

"I know."

"I want to go to the newspaper office there, and look in their archives, see what they wrote about what happened to my father. And try to find out what was clipped out of that old paper." She had a sudden thought and tilted her head back to look at Durango. "Do you think there's a connection?"

"I don't know. We'll find out."

There was silence as they sipped their wine and fell into private thoughts. The pressure of his arm was warm and strong, making her feel comforted, safe. She relaxed again, letting her mind drift, then remembered.

"Oh, I've been meaning to tell you something." She turned sideways in the circle of his arms. "I came across the name Littlestar in my research. That's your grandmother's name."

"Mmm hmm," he hummed. His lips skimmed her hair, and she wished he'd kiss her in that spot where her neck and shoulder met. Her heart jammed in her throat when he did just that, and for a moment, she forgot what she'd been talking about.

"Durango?" she said, breathless.

"Mmmm?" he crooned against her skin.

"Could it be your family's ancestor?"

He trailed his mouth up her neck, over her jaw and across

her cheek. Sensuously, he closed her eyes with his lips.

"You're not listening," she croaked. She was finding it hard to think, hard to catch a breath.

He lifted his head, his eyes half-closed, his gaze reaching into her. "No," he purred, "I'm not. Can we talk about it tomorrow?" He stroked her hair, watching it glide through his fingers. "Right now I'm concentrating on how your hair glistens like gold silk thread." He lowered his mouth to lick her lips. "And how you taste." His arms tightened and his hands caressed her breasts. "And how you feel."

She moved her body against him, slid her arms over his muscled shoulders. She shoved her fingers up his neck into his hair and tangled her fists in it. Her lips, hungry with desire, sought his.

He lowered her to the blanket and pressed his body along the length of hers, heating her through her clothes. The bare skin of his arms touching hers burned like a blaze in a stone fireplace. She trembled, but not from cold, and he pulled the blanket over, cocooning them in each other's body heat.

Then his hands were in her hair and his lips were everywhere, and she begged him not to stop and he didn't, not for hours.

The high ridge across the wide sandy expanse was being backlit by the first hint of dawn when Elliott roused from sleep with a jerk. Below in the distance, barely discernible through the dim light, Durango and Amanda walked arm-in-arm toward the house, carrying blankets and their shoes. Up the stucco steps, halfway across the tiled patio, they stopped and kissed. Their lips parted and they smiled, then they went inside.

Elliott honed his anger on the sight of them.

CHAPTER SEVENTEEN

Durango wheeled his rig to the curb in front of the *Cortez Sentinel*. The newspaper occupied space on Main Street in a row of low one-story buildings. Its façade, sporting a new paint job, had spread over into an adjoining building, a precursor to the expected growth that would take Cortez out of the small town category.

Amanda stepped out of the truck, and drew in a deep breath of the gorgeous day. To the southwest, Sleeping Ute Mountain pushed its rounded profile into an undisturbed expanse of blue. The jagged teeth of the snowcapped San Juans bit into the sky at the northeast edge of town. Across the street and down half a block was the Museum of Southwestern History where she'd talked to Sarah Hardy about the charmstone. No one had yet claimed it and she continued to wear it. She was beginning to suspect no one would claim it, that it had been meant for her all along.

In the lobby of the newspaper office, a receptionist showed them to a large folding worktable where back issues of the paper were kept in broadsheet-sized ring binders.

"These only go back a year," she pointed out. "If you want to look at issues older than that, you'll have to go to the library. They have them on microfilm." She left and went back to her duties up front.

Amanda pulled a chair up to the table and sat down. She thumbed the corners of the pages looking at the dates.

"Here it is," she said.

Durango leaned over to look.

Under the headline, *"CU Professor Dies in Fiery Crash"* was a story that basically reiterated what Jack had written in his paper. Except for one thing.

"Look," Amanda said, her heart kicking up a notch. "The name of the witness who said he saw my father."

"Joseph Tsosie," read Durango.

"It says he saw my father at the Little Bear Saloon. Do you know where that is?"

"No, but it shouldn't be hard to find. Come on. Let's go talk to the bartender. Joseph Tsosie might be a regular customer."

The receptionist made a copy of the article, and gave them directions to the Little Bear.

"Go east towards Mancos. It'll be on your left, but it's not open now. It doesn't open until noon."

Durango thanked her and looked at his watch.

"That'll give us time to check out the newspaper archives at the library," he said to Amanda.

The library was off the main drag, a big, newly expanded building in the final stages of completion. Wooden barricades blocked the entrance to the parking lot, which was filled with construction trucks and hard-hatted workers, so they parked on the street.

The microfilm room wasn't yet open to the public, but when Durango told the librarian they were doing a project for the Navajo Reservation, she let them use it.

"We're still getting organized in here," the librarian said, unlocking the door. "The painters are scheduled for tomorrow."

Microfilm cases were neatly arranged in boxes that had been moved to the middle of the floor, leaving space around the perimeter for the painters to do their work.

"The dates are written on each film case. Month, day and

year. Next year we hope to have these on the computer," she said apologetically. "Good luck. If you need copies of anything, just push this button. It's ten cents a copy. Just keep track of how many you make and pay at the desk on your way out. Honor system." She smiled and left them alone, closing the door.

Amanda sat down at the machine while Durango looked through the film cases.

"What date did you say we're looking for?"

She told him. "But any dates on either side of that will do."

He pulled out a film case and handed it to her. She threaded the film over the gear wheels, and under the viewing lens of the microfilm machine, then turned it on. The viewing screen illuminated, and she scrolled the pages.

The stories about the University of Colorado Archaeology Department's excavation repeated what she'd already read in Jack's old newspapers, general information about the expected start date, but little else.

Durango read the viewing screen over her shoulder as she scrolled pages across the screen.

"There's your father's name," he said. "Looks like he was the lead archaeologist on the project."

Amanda knew nothing about her father's work back then. Her mother had already married Daniel Broadmoor and they were living a world away from the dusty little town of Bluff in southeastern Utah, and light years away from her last visit with her father.

Images of printed newspaper pages moved up and down on the screen as she worked the directional lever. When she got to the end of the film reel, she removed the spool.

"Here's the one for the week of May twenty-second," Durango said and handed it to her.

She inserted the reel on the spindle, threaded the film, and turned the focusing knob. A gasp jammed in her throat as a photograph came sharply into view. She spun the sizing wheel, and a face filled the screen.

"It's Elliott," she said, gaping in disbelief.

The headline over the picture ran across three columns: *Student Arrested for Pilfering Indian Antiquities.*

"*Elliott Sheffield, a University of Colorado student in Boulder was arrested on Wednesday when he was caught illegally digging Indian artifacts. Sheffield, who had no permit to dig on Indian land, will face federal charges in connection with disturbing the sanctity of human remains.*"

Amanda wanted to say something, but no words came and she merely stared, not even blinking.

A deep line dug into Durango's forehead as he skimmed the rest of the article, reading parts of it out loud.

"... was caught after dark ... stolen items included potsherds as well as intact pots, primitive jewelry, stone weapon points, burial objects ... Sheffield was part of a team of archaeologists working on a university-sponsored excavation at an Anasazi site in the town of Bluff, Utah, but had gone off on his own after dark to illegally pilfer in the desert south of town ...

"Investigators from the San Juan County Sheriff's office, the Bureau of Land Management, and the Federal Bureau of Investigation found clear evidence of human remains on the surface of the site ..."

Something wrenched inside her chest. Durango's face was a grim mask as he read on.

"The university team was led by professor Maynard Bell who was not charged in the theft. Sheffield was not a student of Dr. Bell, but had applied for and been accepted as a guest on Dr. Bell's team of archaeologists."

Amanda read along in bewilderment. Elliott was a lot of things, but a grave robber? The thought brought a sick hollow feeling to her stomach. Questions chased each other around in her brain, but all she could think to say was, "He never mentioned that he knew my father."

Durango, scowling blackly, pushed the copy button. "Keep going," he said, indicating the other film spools. "See if there's anything else."

With trembling fingers, she manipulated the controls, her eyes scanning the screen for other stories on the theft. There were a few follow-up articles, but no new information. An item dated the following year indicated that all charges against Elliott Sheffield had been dropped in exchange for his promise never to return to the area. No further details were given.

There was no listing in the phone book for a Joseph Tsosie, so they headed out Highway 160 to find the Little Bear Saloon. Amanda, still shaken from the blow of discovering Elliott's nefarious activities at a dig site, stared silently at the passing scenery. The revelation was both distressing and disturbing.

As he drove, Durango watched her furtively.

"I'm fine," she assured him, seeing his worried face out of the corner of her eye.

He took her hand and gave it a small squeeze anyway.

"You're a terrible liar," he said.

The Little Bear Saloon was outside the Cortez city limits, set back off the highway a few miles past the Mesa Verde National Park entrance. It was an old building with weathered wood siding, a low-slung roof, small windows, and a big parking lot. According to a large banner out front, it served as a combination campground, trading post, and café specializing in barbecue. A few vehicles were already parked nose-in close to the entrance.

Inside, they stopped to let their eyes adjust to the dimness of the room. Tables near the entrance were empty, but a few patrons sat in the fake leather booths lining the walls right and left. A U-shaped bar took up most of the space in the middle.

Inside the U, a bartender wearing a T-shirt that said *Go tell somebody who gives a damn* was drawing drafts. He looked up when they came in and nodded. "Be right with you folks." He wiped his hands on a towel, put the drinks on a tray and carried it to a group in the corner booth.

The Little Bear was obviously a seat yourself kind of place, so Amanda followed Durango to the bar and hiked up on a barstool. She looked around, trying to imagine her father coming into a place like this. The image wouldn't come together in her mind.

Two other people sat at the bar, a woman who looked like she'd been there a week, and at the other end, a lone Navajo man hunched over a glass of beer. A spread of coins lay in wet overlapping circles on the surface of the bar in front of him.

Someone had cranked the jukebox, and Willie Nelson lamented being on the road again. The woman sitting at the bar moved her shoulders in time to the music. The man at the end stared at his glass.

Durango laid some bills on the bar as the bartender approached.

"Howdy, folks. My name's Rico. What'll you have?" The bartender was big with broad shoulders and a chest as solid as a side of beef. His face was jovial, his smile genuine.

Durango's hand hovered over his stack of bills. A fifty-dollar bill tented lengthwise was pinched between his first two fingers. He straightened his fingers pointing the bill toward Rico who lowered his eyes to look at it, but didn't touch it.

"Information, friend," said Durango with a smile.

Rico's eyes flashed and his smile broadened. "If it's worth a fifty, it might be worth a hundred."

"It might be worth two hundred," said Durango, his voice

hushed and serious. "Depends on how much information you give us."

Rico shifted his substantial weight from one foot to the other, and leaned with his elbows on the bar.

"Sure. What do you need to know?"

"We're looking for a man named Joseph Tsosie. Do you know him?"

"Why are you looking for him?" The question sprang more from curiosity than challenge, but Durango didn't answer.

"Are you a relative?" Rico asked, still inquisitive.

"Maybe."

Rico slid the bill from between Durango's fingers.

"Yeah, I know him."

"Does he come in here often?"

"Yeah, pretty often."

"Where does he live?"

Rico lowered his eyes to Durango's hand. Durango picked up another bill and extended it. Rico took it and folded it in his palm.

"He lives on County Road 21, out near Arriola."

Amanda listened in anxious silence.

"What's the address?" Durango asked.

Rico shrugged. "Don't know."

The weight of disappointment slumped Amanda's shoulders, and she released the expectant breath she'd been holding. Durango was flexing a muscle in his jaw and staring at Rico, waiting for him to go on, his hand hovering over the bills on the bar.

"But you could ask Rosie," Rico offered. "She dates him sometimes. She's off now. Works nights."

Rico fell silent and seemed to be deliberating a private dilemma behind his eyes. Still Durango waited.

"You got any more of those fifties?" Rico asked after a moment, his tone deliberately nonchalant as if he didn't really care.

Durango picked one up and held it out.

Rico took it, put it with the others, and tossed a nod over his shoulder.

"That's him there. Sitting at the end of the bar."

Amanda shot an uneasy glance at the man who was down to his last three inches of beer, eyeing the bartender, looking like he was ready for another one.

"Draw two of whatever he's drinking," Durango told Rico. "Wait ten minutes, then bring them to the table in the corner."

Amanda took a seat at the table. Durango sat down across from her, took out his cell phone, and dialed a number. While he spoke to someone in hushed tones, Amanda's attention was drawn back to Joseph Tsosie. His hair was dull black and looked like it hadn't seen a comb in days. His wide nose broadened his face, but didn't hide the gaunt look of too much booze and not enough food.

Durango ended the conversation, snapped his phone shut, and put it back in his pocket. Rico brought their drinks, stopping on the way to whisper in Joseph's ear after which Joseph turned to look curiously at Amanda and Durango. Mistrust rolled off him in waves, but eyes on the two beers, Joseph Tsosie slid off his stool and walked over,

The worn down heels of his beat up cowboy boots tilted his feet at an unnatural angle, giving him an exaggerated bowlegged gait. He was wearing stiff new blue jeans with the bottoms rolled up into cuffs, and a dirty sheepskin-lined leather jacket. He stopped next to the table and peered at Durango.

"*Ya'at'eeh*," Durango said, pushing the beer glasses an inch in his direction.

Joseph sat down. "*Ya'at'eeh*," he returned, regarding Amanda with a mild glance, then fixing a stare on Durango, his black eyes full of questions.

Durango introduced himself and Amanda. Joseph nodded, but said nothing. Tense and suspicious, poised to run, the toe of one booted foot pointed toward the door, he reached out and pulled the glasses closer to his side of the table.

"What do you want with me?" he asked, his eyes on Durango. "Why the . . ." he looked at the beer glasses. "Why buy me drinks?"

He had the voice of someone who spoke mostly Navajo, the words clipped and guttural. Amanda opened her leather bag, pulled out the article about her father's accident, and laid it on the table, turning it toward him. Joseph lowered his eyes to look at it.

"This article says you saw Dr. Bell in this bar with someone the night he was killed. I'd like to know more about that."

Joseph glared at the piece of paper, pressing his lips, and heaving a sigh, his heavy brows pulled together in a frown. He looked like he was sorry he'd left the safe harbor of his seat at the bar.

Durango spoke a few words in Navajo, and Joseph's body relaxed a little. "It's all right," Durango said, reassuringly. "We're not the police. This is Dr. Bell's daughter. I'm her friend. We want you to tell us what you know."

Joseph nodded, took a swallow, set his glass down, and wrapped fidgety fingers around it.

"They got it wrong."

"Who?" Amanda asked. "Got what wrong?"

"The paper got it wrong. I didn't see them in the bar."

Amanda exhaled a disappointed breath, but Durango didn't give up, wouldn't let the man's reticence get the better of him.

"Where *did* you see them?" Durango pressed, leaning closer.

Joseph picked up on the urgency in Durango's tone and seemed to develop a sudden sense of self-importance as the possessor of sought-after knowledge. He sat back in a casual pose, a corner of his mouth tilted in a shiftless smile. "*Outside the bar.*"

Durango glowered and spoke to him in Navajo again, only this time using a tone that suggested to Amanda he was swearing at the man.

"Don't play games with me," he said in English. "You tell me everything you know about this even if I don't ask the question. Get it? I just called and found out who your parole officer is. I think he'd be mighty be interested to know that you're spending your free time in a bar. Now talk."

Joseph slashed his eyebrows and moved from his indolent position, suddenly eager to share.

"I was in the parking lot." He pointed toward the door with his chin. "Waiting for Rosie. She's my girlfriend."

At the mention of Rosie, his lips opened in a smile, showing a broken front tooth. "She works here. I was waiting to drive her home."

"Go on."

"A van pulled up next to me. There was an old man slumped down in the passenger seat. He had white hair and his eyes were closed. I thought he was passed out."

His words made Amanda shiver inside. "Who was driving?" she asked.

Joseph shrugged. "A young guy. White. He got out and went inside. It's dark out there, so I couldn't see his face real good, but he was tall. Wearing a sweatshirt with a college on it."

"What college?" Anxiety crept into her tone and she made an effort to rein in her emotions. She didn't want to frighten Joseph into evading their questions again, or openly refusing to tell them anything.

"I'm thinking," he said, appearing to be annoyed at her impatience. He pursed his lips and looked at something in his memory. "I don't remember," he said at last. "Anyway, he came out a few minutes later and drove away. The old man hadn't moved. I forgot about it."

Silence stretched and Durango's glare across the table intensified until Joseph went on.

"Rosie's shift was over, she came out a few minutes later. I was gonna stay at her house that night, so I stopped at the liquor store across from City Market to get something to take. She never has anything in the house," he complained in an aside to Durango before continuing. "The same van I saw was parked at the liquor store."

Amanda moved to the edge of her seat.

"How did you know it was the same van?" Durango asked the question that was on the tip of her tongue.

Joseph reared back, taking offense at being thought a liar. Or stupid.

"I could tell. I got eyes." He pointed to them in case Durango hadn't noticed. "It was coated with mud and some kid wrote 'wash me' on the back. The old man was still slumped against the door. Hadn't moved. That made me wonder. Even passed out drunks move once in a while."

Amanda closed her eyes against the picture Joseph was painting. Remorse struck her like a fist in the stomach, but she hung on his words.

"When I parked, the driver was coming out with a paper bag. I got a better look at him in the light. Same white guy. Same sweatshirt. I started to get out, but he looked at me and there was something about him that made me stay in the truck."

Conversation in the room had picked up as more people came in for the lunchtime barbecue. Rico now had a helper behind the bar. Someone had put more money in the jukebox, and Garth Brooks's voice poured out of speakers on the ceiling.

Amanda clutched her hands in her lap, waiting for Joseph to go on.

Joseph lifted his glass, took a thoughtful swallow, and licked his lips lightly before replying. He narrowed his eyes and directed his answer to Durango as if Durango were the only one who would really understand the meaning of what he was about to say.

"He had mean-looking *bilagaana* blue eyes," he said. "Like a lake, but frozen over."

The chilling way he said it tightened the knot in Amanda's stomach.

"Then what happened?" Durango probed.

Joseph shrugged. "Then he got in and drove away."

Amanda sat stock still, trying to assimilate what she'd just heard. The rumored second occupant of the van was real, not a rumor after all. Someone had been with her father. There was someone out there who knew something. Her thoughts checked, and she remembered the second note left on her door. Whoever wrote it had information about her father, too, yet no one had come forward, and she'd never seen that old woman in Twin Rocks Canyon again.

Durango was speaking again, his eyes burning into Joseph's.

"How did you know the van you saw in Cortez was the same one that burned up on the reservation?"

"I didn't right away. But the van I saw had a University of Colorado parking sticker on the back window. My cousin, she works for the Tribal Police, and she told me the burned up van had a sticker like that on it. It was black and scorched, but they could still read it. That got me thinking it was the same one."

"Did you tell any of this to the authorities?"

When Joseph didn't answer, Durango repeated the question.

"Did you?"

Joseph, eyes lowered, lips shut tight, didn't reply. Durango spoke to him in Navajo again, and Joseph shook his head.

"Not at first," he said. "Rosie didn't want me to. Didn't think I should get involved. But later I did. Guess the story got screwed up. The paper said I saw them in the bar. I didn't. I saw them in the parking lot."

Joseph drank his second beer in one long pull and set his glass down with a thunk. He wiped his mouth with his sleeve and started to get up. Durango wrapped a hand around his arm and pulled him gently back into his seat. He slipped two of the fifty-dollar bills into the pocket of Joseph's grimy jacket.

"Thank you," Durango said, and Joseph grunted.

Amanda dug in her purse for a pen and something to write on. "If you remember anything else, I want you to call me. I'll write down our names and the phone number. Okay?"

Joseph nodded.

Her hands were shaking as she dug through the items in her big leather bag. Impatiently, she pulled out her makeup case and laid it on the table, then her car keys and her wallet, followed by her daily planner, which she opened. She slipped a silver pen from its holder and ripped out a planner page. As she began jotting the phone numbers, something made her look up. Joseph was staring at the things she'd taken from her purse with stunning disbelief.

"What's wrong?" she asked, a little frightened by his expression.

His confused eyes shifted to her face, then dropped back. She followed his gaze to the table.

Along with keys and a turquoise good luck charm, she'd clipped a small plastic-encased picture on the key ring. Familiarity and force of habit had clouded her awareness of the novelty, and she'd forgotten it was even there. Now she looked at it. The picture had been taken a year ago, she and Elliott sitting arm in arm on the edge of a hotel pool in Palm Springs.

Pursing his lips, Joseph tilted his chin indicating the laminated photo.

"That's the man. The one driving the van. With the frozen-lake eyes."

The drive back to Monument Valley was a blur. She felt empty inside. Threads of thought began to unravel and she let her mind drift. Every thought led to Elliott. Elliott arrested for grave robbing. Elliott knew her father. Elliott had been with him on his trip to Monument Valley, and she had to slam her brain shut on where those thoughts led.

Elliott had argued with her about coming to Monument Valley, then showed up expecting to take her back home. His rage when he left the restaurant bordered on madness, showing a side of him she had never known. Her gut burned with disbelief and fear and she shuddered.

Oh, Elliott! What did you do to my father?

Questions swirled in her head until she thought it would explode. A hollow unsettled feeling swelled beneath her breastbone, and she blinked rapidly a couple of times before calming her pounding heart. Her thoughts trailed off into a sigh of frustration and confusion.

Durango turned from the road a moment to look at her, and she met his gaze. Dusky shadows moved across his face as the car sped along the two-lane blacktop. He offered her a smile of reassurance, and she drew strength from it, beating back the fear storming inside her, allowing some of the disappointment to ebb away. His smile lingered a moment longer, then he turned back to the road.

She stared out the window at the darkness creeping across the washes and into the folds of the deep purple mountains in the distance.

"Elliott's not at all the man I thought he was," she said sadly.

"He's exactly the man I thought he was," Durango replied, making no attempt to hide his disdain.

CHAPTER EIGHTEEN

Tangerine mists hovering over the monuments disappeared as night rolled through Monument Valley.

The hippie van, barely visible under low-hanging cottonwood branches down the road from Durango's house, had been there for hours. In the driver's seat, Jack Rice stared at the sprawling adobe house illuminated like a princely oasis in a vast black expanse.

Durango and Amanda had returned hours ago, but still Jack didn't move. The resolve he'd made earlier in the day had ebbed and flowed all afternoon and evening, and now he was losing what was left of his nerve.

Durango wasn't going to like what Jack had to tell him about Dr. Bell's accident. About Elliott. Especially about Elliott. And he won't like Jack's part in any of it, either. Hell, his part in it could get him a jail cell.

Christ, Jack old boy, this is some fine mess you've got yourself into.

All he'd wanted was to make a little extra money selling Indian stuff. Hell, everybody did it. Mistrust of Elliott had seeped in the day they made their deal at the Turquoise Café, but how was he supposed to know Elliott was insane?

He wasn't sure just how insane Elliott was, but guessed it was insane enough that someone was going to get hurt. Maybe even him. And that eventuality weighed heavily in his decision to tell Durango what he knew.

Reluctantly, he uncurled his fingers from around the steering wheel and edged a hand to the door. Screwing up his courage, he pushed the handle, shoved the door open, and slid off the seat.

The click of the door when he closed it made more noise than he'd expected, and the dogs out back must have heard it because they barked a few times, then trotted to the perimeter of the electronic barrier. Jack stood still and waited until they calmed down.

A wave of guilt made his gut wrench. He reached into his pocket, took out a quick-dissolve antacid, and popped it in his mouth. He closed his eyes and breathed shallowly until the wintergreen-flavored tablet did its work. He should have stopped to help when Elliott ran Amanda off the road with the little girl in the car.

Sighing heavily, he pulled a hand down his face, stretching the loose skin under his eyes and on his cheeks. Fatigue was taking control of his muscles, making his arms and legs twitch. He hadn't slept a full night since . . . He counted back the days, and regret surged. Not since Sallie died.

Sallie had been coming to him each night in a dream. Her face was bloody from cuts where the rocks had smashed into it, and she was standing at the bottom of Comb Ridge, but looking right at him. She stood there crying, tears running down her face, mingling with the blood, and she spoke to him.

"Tell," she pleaded. "Tell what you know." She said it over and over, and he'd jerk awake, drenched in sweat, saliva filling his mouth, making him feel like he was going to throw up. Then he couldn't go back to sleep. Each time he wondered how Sallie knew he had anything to tell. It always amazed him how often the Indians seemed to know things they couldn't possibly have knowledge of. Private things like what was in someone's head. Or his heart.

This morning he'd made up his mind to tell Durango,

because Durango would know what to do.

But also, so Sallie would leave him alone and he could get some sleep.

Jack took slow shuffling steps down the dusty road to the end of Durango's driveway. Then his courage took a holiday. He ducked into the shadows cast by the gourd house and waited for it to return.

Inside the house, nighttime quiet drifted through the rooms. The boys were in bed as were Nonni and Hitathli. Doli's sobs had subsided when she was allowed to sleep in Amanda's bed.

Durango sat hunched over, his arms resting on his thighs. A letter stamped with an official seal and signed by the court clerk dangled from his hand; with his other hand, he massaged his temples.

He had one week to present proof of ownership or lose Wild Horse Mesa, the land on which his mother and grandmother had lived all their lives. He shook his head at the mockery of it. Yazzie land had been Yazzie land for over a hundred years, and no one had ever questioned it. Until now. Until Buck Powell.

Condominiums. *Jesus.*

Frustration pushed him to his feet, and he tossed the letter aside. He wouldn't allow them to be turned out of their home. Nor would he allow the destruction of the cliff dwellings in the outback of the property. The primitive castles, towers and pueblos of an ancient community had survived for centuries. He wouldn't let a bulldozer raze them now. Ownership of the land wasn't the important thing. Stewardship was.

He cursed as anger seared the edges of his self-control. He'd have to figure something out, maybe get the deadline extended until he had more time to search for a deed. Right now, his thoughts were on finding Elliott Sheffield and throttling answers out of him if he had to.

Or maybe just throttling him for the satisfaction of doing it.

Durango went down on one knee in front of the fire and stirred the coals to a low flame, mentally reviewing the events of the day. Joseph Tsosie's story and his identification of Elliott as the driver of Dr. Bell's van were staggering. The shock of hearing it had hit Amanda full force, taking a physical as well as emotional toll on her. He hated what it was doing to her, hated seeing the pain and confusion flooding her eyes, her mouth drawn in a tight sad line. He didn't know how much more she could take, didn't know if he'd be able to protect her from more.

Doli was having a delayed reaction to the terror of being run off the road with Amanda. Her initial resiliency had morphed into whimpering and petulance, and she argued over everything from what to eat to what to wear. She clung to Amanda, trailing her through the house with big sad eyes, screaming in fright if Amanda went out of sight. Even Nonni couldn't comfort her.

The dogs set up a racket and drew his attention. He wondered what was bothering them. They'd been anxious and agitated for days, pacing and sniffing the air. That usually meant a coyote or some other wild animal had ventured too near the house, but he hadn't seen any animal tracks other than those belonging to the dogs.

Their high-pitched barks and throaty moans intensified, and he went to the window to investigate; his footsteps soundless on the thick carpet. Moving to the door, he went outside and peered into the darkness beyond the perimeter of the security lights.

With a hand motion he stilled the dogs, and stepped off the deck. His truck was parked where he'd left it on his return from Cortez. Amanda's Jeep was angled off a few yards away. Nonni and Hitathli's old pickup was beyond that. There were no lights in the gourd house and Noah's Mercedes wasn't parked there.

He must still be at Cammie's.

Durango walked down the driveway, looking right and left, then turned to look back at the house. The lights in the guest suite were off. Amanda must have gotten Doli settled for the night. Except for the living room where he'd been sitting, the rest of the rooms were dark.

He took one final look around, his eyes boring holes into the night, then went back in the house and turned off the lamps in the living room.

His heart thundering, Jack slipped into the shadows behind the hanging gourd trestle as Durango came out the door of the main house. Through the vines, he watched Durango walk down the driveway, then stop and look around. That would have been the time for Jack to step out of the shadows and let his presence be known, call out a greeting, ask to be invited in because he had something important to say.

But Durango went back inside, the windows went dark and the opportunity was lost. A combination of relief and disappointment settled over Jack. Relief because he'd earned a reprieve, disappointment because he'd have to endure another visit from Sallie tonight.

He waited a few minutes for his heart to slow down, then started toward his van, rehearsing for the umpteenth time what he was going to say to Durango. His fingers probed his pocket and pulled out another wintergreen tablet. He slipped it on his tongue, and it was instantly propelled out of his mouth on a gust of air as an arm clenched his neck and squeezed from behind. Then his left arm was roughly pushed up between his shoulder blades, and he went down on his knees from the pain.

Amanda bolted upright in bed at the sound of the dogs barking furiously outside. She cast an anxious glance at Doli curled up next to her. The child stirred and whimpered softly but thankfully didn't open her eyes.

Durango's voice, swearing and shouting, joined the uproar of the dogs, and footsteps pounded on the deck at the other end of the house. She swung her legs to the floor and grabbed her robe, slinging it over her shoulders, her arms searching madly for the sleeves. In the hallway, she closed the bedroom door quietly, holding the doorknob to deaden the snap of the latch, and hurried to the front of the house, arriving in time to see Durango haul Jack Rice in the front door.

"Jack!"

He grimaced with pain as Durango's grip dug fiercely into his upper arm. Durango's other hand was wound in the back of Jack's collar.

Scowling mercilessly, Durango pushed him roughly into a chair.

"I found him hiding behind the gourd house. He was spying on us."

"No, I wasn't, honest," Jack protested. "I can explain."

Durango glowered. "Well then, you'd better start before I call the police. I was just about to call them anyway."

Jack's face went white. "No, don't. Let me talk to you first. I'll tell you everything."

Breathing heavily, Durango stood over Jack, his fists clenched, waiting for the newspaperman to begin.

Jack's features crumpled as he clasped his left shoulder and rocked forward in pain. The red marks on his neck grew more crimson. His expression when he looked up at Durango was a mixture of contrition and fear.

"You're not going to like it," he said, and glanced at Amanda. "Either of you."

Jack's story poured out. His voice was plaintive, his expression ashamed and afraid. When he finished, he put his head in his hands and kept it there as if waiting for the executioner to come and put him out of his misery.

The room was silent except for the crackle of the fire. Questions hammered Amanda, but she felt dazed, wrung out, unable to concentrate. Durango sat next to her, his face clouded. She could feel his thigh, warm and hard against the length of hers through her thin robe, and she was thankful for his steadying presence.

Though her brain was in tumult, she was able to put some of the facts together without knowing the why of any of it.

Elliott had come to Monument Valley with her father, or intercepted him on the way, then killed him, making it look like an accident, apparently intending to steal the collection of art and artifacts destined for the Navajo Cultural Center. But a group of unidentified Indians had taken the collection and her father's body. That was the crazy part.

Hell, it was all crazy. Her mind wouldn't wrap around any of it.

Then Elliott had returned to Monument Valley, followed her, vandalized her car, and ran her off the road. He must have had a good reason to risk coming back. Part of the agreement for dropping the federal charges against him was that he never return. It must have been something more important than merely patching up their relationship. Something more serious than grave robbing even. Like the fear that she might discover what he'd done to her father. She shuddered.

But Jack had followed her, too. He'd wanted the artifacts, and had made a deal with Elliott to find them and split the profits. She cast a dubious glance in Jack's direction. She wasn't sure how much of what he said she could believe.

He said he'd followed her and Sallie to Comb Ridge, but left before the storm hit. That much was probably true. He couldn't have been who Sallie was talking to, because she knew Jack. She wouldn't have asked, "Who are you?"

But she didn't know Elliott.

Had Elliott been out there, too?

With horror, she recalled the terror in Sallie's voice. Someone was doing something that frightened her. What was it? Loosening rocks and starting a landslide? Kicking them down on top of her?

Oh, Sallie. I'm so sorry. Tears clogged her throat, and she had to swallow them back before she could speak.

"Someone left a threatening note on the door of my room at the trading post in Mexican Hat," she said to Jack. "Was that you?"

Jack lifted his head and looked at her shamefaced, his eyes swimming with repentance. "No. I saw someone do that the first night. It was dark and I didn't recognize him then, but looking back on it now, I think it was Elliott." Sweat beaded his forehead. "It didn't seem important at the time. I forgot about it."

Amanda absorbed that. That fit, too. Elliott was trying to scare her into going back home on her own without having to make his presence known. That was probably the reason for the spray paint and tire slashing.

Who left the note telling her to come to Twin Rocks Canyon? Was that Elliott, too? No, probably not. It was an old Navajo woman she'd seen out there, not Elliott.

But the old woman had seen something before she ran away.

Amanda's mind was wandering into vague and shadowy territory, and she quickly pulled it back. She glanced at Durango who looked equally perplexed. He hadn't moved and had barely said a word, but his face had changed, the features less sharply defined. He seemed thoughtful, but she could tell his anger still simmered just under the surface.

He drew a breath and his brows knitted. "How badly do you

think Elliott wants those artifacts?" he asked Jack.

"Pretty bad, and I don't think my offer of a deal meant anything to him. I think he was after them in the first place."

"What do you think he'd say if you told him you knew where they are?"

"But I *don't* know where they are," Jack protested.

Durango got up to use the phone, and when he returned outlined his plan.

Elliott returned to his hidey hole overlooking the Yazzie spread before daylight. He'd had to make a trip to the Wal-Mart in Cortez late yesterday for some rat poison, then before heading back stopped to hit some slots, and play a little Blackjack at the Ute Mountain Casino in Towaoc. Later, after one too many beers in the hotel bar, he'd decided to get a room and sleep it off, make an early start this morning instead of driving through twisting McElmo Canyon in an impaired condition, reeking of alcohol.

He wasn't stupid.

In fact, he firmly believed that superior intelligence won out every time. He credited his own success, both personal and professional, in part to his extremely keen intellect.

But academic intelligence alone wasn't enough and that's why he was able to best his colleagues, both the teaching staff at the university, and his fellow researchers out in the field, at every juncture. For Elliott had been blessed with a street fighter's sense of survival layered under a façade of good looks, grace and charm. Having a father with money didn't hurt either.

It was now 8:00 a.m., and he crouched in the shade behind his sagebrush shelter, watching the house. The sun hadn't yet touched his ledge, but when it did later in the day, its rays would reflect off the rock rise behind him, making it unbearably hot.

It was already hot below where the dogs were stretched out on the patio, their big mouths hanging open, letting their tongues loll and drip on the tiles. Every once in a while one of them got up, paced the grounds, then plopped down for another nap.

The little Indian boys who had jumped on his back and pounded him at Goulding's were out there. The older one was throwing coins in the pool, then diving in to retrieve them. The younger boy sat on a pool chair at the umbrella table, studiously playing a hand-held video game, his face intense in absolute concentration.

The housekeeper and her husband had been talking on the phone and arguing in Navajo all morning, their voices drifting up through the open windows.

The doors opened now and his body tensed slightly in that involuntary response to the unexpected. Amanda stepped out, and he felt a stirring halfway between his gut and his groin. He studied her face, his eyes tracing her hair that was woven into a fat golden braid. He wished she wouldn't wear her hair that way.

She said something to the boys, who answered politely, then she ducked back in and pulled the doors closed. Elliott eyed the dogs who had looked up at her intrusion, then settled back into somnolence. He stared at them, thinking about how big they were, wondering how well trained they were, wondering what it would take for them to venture beyond their electronic barrier.

He shook himself out of his ponderings about the dogs and let his thoughts drift to Jack Rice. Jack was a threat and a problem, but he was ignorant, so it evened out. Elliott smiled at the thought of the man actually expecting to split the proceeds of the sale of those ceremonial pieces when instead, after Elliott found out exactly where they were, Jack was simply going to split. Permanently.

Elliott's black vengeful thoughts were interrupted by the faint chiming of his cell phone. Cursing himself for forgetting to turn it off, he grabbed it quickly, silencing it, already knowing who was calling.

"Yes."

"Is she coming back with you?"

Elliott paused before answering. "No."

"Where is she now?"

"She's probably eating breakfast with the Indian. She moved in with him."

A string of curses came from the other end, then the silence of thinking.

"Does she know what happened at Comb Ridge?"

"Nah. But someone else does. The local newspaper guy. He was there when I took the professor in and set the fire."

"What?" The sound erupted from the tiny cell phone.

"He said he saw the whole thing."

"Did he recognize you?" The other voice was agitated, slightly panicked.

Elliott almost recounted Jack's blackmail threat and offer of a deal at the Turquoise Café, but after a beat of silence, he lied. "No. But I think he knows what happened to the stuff."

Another curse. "Are you sure the old man's dead?"

A snort of derision from Elliott. "What do you think? An old man can live in the desert for five months? Of course he's dead."

Elliott could hear breathing, the clunk of a coffee cup. "Then forget about her. Concentrate on the newspaper guy. I don't care what you do or how you do it, just get those ceremonial pieces back."

"Don't worry. I know what to do." Elliott's voice was cool and smooth, but he gritted his teeth and his eyes narrowed in anger. He hated taking orders, especially hated having to continually placate and pander to Daniel Broadmoor, a man to whom he was inexorably indebted.

"You'd better if you ever hope to finance any more research." Daniel laughed a sound with no mirth. "Or your digging days are over, boy."

This had the intended effect on Elliott and the hand holding the cell phone shook.

"I said I knew what to do."

"Forget my stepdaughter," Daniel repeated. "Go after the newspaper guy."

The connection broke off from the other end and Elliott fumed. The hell he'd forget Amanda. Not a chance. He'd find those pots and beads, and get back at her and that arrogant Indian all at the same time.

He leaned against the rock and let his brain poke at the germ of an idea he'd planted there. He'd already set the wheels in motion by buying the rat poison. Now it was the timing that would be crucial. Timing, and the patience to work out the details, and wait for the opportunity.

At nine, Elliott saw Durango leave in his truck. He shifted his eyes to the big windows of the guest suite. Amanda was back at her worktable with the little girl.

Travis Dance was reed thin, tree tall, with dark inquisitive eyes in a baby-smooth face. Except maybe for those eyes that missed nothing, no one meeting him for the first time would suspect that he was really Special Agent T. R. Dance assigned to the Monticello office of the Federal Bureau of Investigation. Especially dressed as he was now in western boots, wide-brimmed hat and jeans, he was often mistaken for a rodeo cowboy.

Durango arrived in Monticello at ten-thirty, and when he stepped into the coffee shop found those black snapping eyes peering over the top of a booth back in the corner. The two men greeted each other with the firm four-handed handshake of trusted friends who hadn't seen each other in a long time, right hands clasped tightly, left hands placed on top of the handclasp, adding an extra measure of affability to the gesture. Durango slid into the bench across from Travis, and for a moment the years melted away, and Durango was a boy again at running practice on the track behind the high school with his close friend.

"Thanks for meeting me, Trav. I need your help."

"I'm already on it. After you called last night, I got the okay to move ahead like we discussed. It's all set up. An agent will be standing watch in the gourd house while you and I and Rice wait out at Wild Horse Mesa for this Sheffield character. We'll nail the bastard. Don't worry."

"Any chance you could go easy on Rice? From what he says, he got caught up in more than he bargained for."

"I can't make any promises, but we might be able to work something out since he's helping us. He's small-time, not even a blip on the screen of the antiquities black market. But we've been watching Sheffield off and on for years. Had no idea he was connected to that incident at Comb Ridge, though."

"No one did, but there'd been rumors of a second person in the van. Of course, those rumors got back to Amanda."

Travis's eyes softened as he observed his friend. "Your girlfriend still think law enforcement dropped the ball on that?"

Durango nodded. "Yeah. She's pretty upset."

"Those boys sure have it rough lately with budget cuts and hiring freezes, and all. Their investigators are stretched to the limit. I guess it looked like plain and simple drunk driving. They wrote it up, closed the case and went on to something else that seemed more pressing."

A waitress brought menus, then walked away saying she'd be right back. Travis picked up a menu and handed one to Durango. "What are you having? I'm buying."

"Just coffee. I have to get back. Nonni's sister is sick, and she and Hitathli might have to go to Tuba City for the day. I've got Sharron's kids there now and they're a handful. I don't want to leave them alone too long."

Travis nodded in understanding. "Don't worry, friend. We'll keep them all safe."

CHAPTER NINETEEN

"Elliott Sheffield?" Helen Benally looked at Jack with a perplexed expression from behind the registration desk at the Recapture Lodge. "We don't have anyone here by that name."

Jack's heart took a tight beat of disappointment. "Did he check out?"

Helen punched the computer, her round face crumpled in concentration, then she thumbed through a printout in a wire basket on the desk. "No. Nobody by that name has checked in."

For a moment, Jack's mind went blank, and then it came to him. Of course. Elliott would use a phony name.

He pressed, trying not to let his uneasiness show. "Tall, curly hair. Drives a green truck. I saw his truck parked out here last week."

Helen's face lit with recognition. "Oh, you mean Gene Butler. Has all that digging equipment in the back. He's still here. I haven't seen him in a day or two, but he's paid through next week."

Hiding his relief with a casual smile, Jack handed her a sealed envelope. "Guess I got the name wrong," he mumbled as if it were of no consequence. "I'd like to leave him a message. Will you see that he gets this? It's important."

Helen took the envelope with no expression. If she wondered about the confusion in names, she didn't show it.

"Sure," she said. "If I see him."

Jack drove back to his office to wait for the phone call.

At the first ring, Jack thrust forward in his chair and grabbed the phone.

"Desert Times Weekly."

"Your message says you know where the stuff is," Elliott said without preamble.

"Yeah. But I need help getting it out. There's a lot of it and I can't carry it myself. It's at the back of Wild Horse Mesa."

There was a moment of silence, then a surprised question. "How did it get there?"

"Dunno. Those Indians that took it must have dumped it."

"How did you find it?" Elliott's voice was agitated, his tone slightly suspicious.

Without missing a beat, Jack bluffed.

"Never mind how. Do you want it or not?" He tried to sound tough and implacable. "If it's too much trouble for you, I know someone else who can help me." He tensed waiting for Elliott's reaction, his heart pounding in his ears.

"Look, old man, I'm just being careful."

Then Jack heard paper crinkling. Elliott was unfolding the note, and Jack let out a relieved breath.

"How do I get there? I can't read your damn map."

Jack gave directions, sending Elliott by way of the northern, most difficult access road.

"Turn right at the jeep road and go another mile. When you come to a pile of rocks that look like a bear watching TV, park there. I'll be waiting. We'll have to walk in another half mile to get it. It'll only take about an hour to carry it out."

Elliott hesitated so long, Jack wondered if he'd hung up the phone.

"I'll be there," Elliott said at last. "If I'm late, wait for me."

The line buzzed with a broken connection. Jack replaced the

receiver, then after a moment, dialed a number. It rang three times before Durango answered.

"Hello."

"Tonight at ten."

"Okay." Then, "Are you all right, Jack? You're okay with wearing a wire?"

"Yes," Jack replied, even though he wasn't.

Elliott parked his truck in the wide wash behind The Three Sisters, three identical rocks balanced on the edge of a stacked landform. Keeping to the cover of tall sage and desert grasses, he climbed to his ledge overlooking the Yazzie house.

Anxiety made his nerves jump. His mind was spinning. It was too soon. He hadn't worked out all the details of his plan, wasn't yet ready to leave Monument Valley. But after tonight, he'd have to. He wouldn't be able to stick around.

He unwrapped the burrito he'd just purchased from the Taco Bell at the gas station in Mexican Hat, and chewed thoughtfully. Except for the phone ringing in the house, it was quiet down below. All three vehicles were parked out front, but no one was about. The dogs were outside, but he hadn't seen the kids. Amanda was still working on those damn papers. Durango hadn't shown his face.

Elliott finished his burrito, quietly folded the greasy paper and put it in his pocket, then leaned lazily against the rocks. He might be a little late meeting Jack tonight, but so what? Jack would wait.

He watched the house through narrowed eyes, turning over and rejecting ideas one by one as the hours dragged by. He had a goal of sorts. The difficulty was executing the steps to reach it. There were a number of obstacles in his path, not the least of which was Durango Yazzie.

The sun beat down and Elliott retreated from the oppressive

heat of midday. Hunger rumblings in his stomach turned his thoughts to food again. He looked at his watch. Only four. Just then, Durango came out, threw a backpack and a liter water bottle in the back seat and drove away.

Elliott sat forward, all senses on alert. This was unexpected. Where was the Indian going? How long would he be gone?

An hour later, Elliott was still contemplating Durango's departure when he heard voices coming from the front of the house. The housekeeper came out carrying a fat burlap tote bag, and climbed into the cab of the pickup. She looked like she was crying. The husband brought suitcases, tossed them in the truck bed, then got behind the wheel, fired the engine and drove away, leaving a cloud of dust as he bumped down the road toward the paved highway.

Well now, that was interesting. And convenient. It looked like the old Indians would be gone for a few days.

Elliott smiled, then uncapped his bottle of water and drank deeply, his mind doing rapid calculations. After a while, he sneaked back to his truck, and drove to Goulding's Grocery to buy four pounds of hamburger and another burrito.

Amanda glanced out the kitchen window at the sun sliding down in the sky, bathing the desert with a violet glow. The quiet that was settling in could easily deceive someone into believing that nothing at all had happened in the world that day.

But she knew that wasn't true.

After Jack had called that morning, Durango had spent most of the day on the phone with Travis, finalizing their plans for tonight. He'd been tense and edgy, his face tight with apprehension. Without being told, the boys sensed something was up and thankfully played quietly in their room. Doli stayed with Amanda at the worktable.

Before Durango left the house, he'd wrapped an arm around

her waist, crushed her to his chest, and kissed her long and deep.

"Elliott will pay for what he did," he said, his face against hers. "And he'll never hurt you again." When he looked at her, his beautiful dark eyes swam with heat, and she searched for an unspoken I love you in them. "Tonight it will be over," he said.

Tonight it will be over.

She felt a tightening in the vicinity of her heart and blinked hard. After tonight, it would be over, and she'd have the answers to all the questions about Elliott and her father. But tomorrow, she'd say good-bye.

The house still smelled yeasty from the bread Nonni had baked that morning. Lacing through the pleasant aroma was the savory scent of the stew Amanda was stirring in the big black pot on the stove. Nonni had been making it when the call came telling her that her sister had died. She'd begun packing immediately, apologizing profusely for having to leave Amanda with the children.

Amanda's heart ached for the old woman, and she had given her a hug and slipped some money in Nonni's tote bag, curling Nonni's fingers over the bills when she tried to give them back.

"Just in case, for an emergency," Amanda had insisted, and Nonni had reluctantly accepted them.

Amanda's attention was pulled to the dogs on the patio. Cooking smells had reached them, and they were standing at the sliding door, looking in, ears pricked, their noses making smudges on the glass. She'd have to remember to feed them, too.

"James! Eric! Wash your hands. Dinner is ready."

Doli was already sitting at the table waiting, her big eyes following Amanda, a look of quiet seriousness on her face. The boys came in, showed their hands front and back, then sat down.

"No video games at the table, Eric." Amanda smiled at the

earnest little boy.

He rolled his eyes in childish exasperation, slid off his chair, and took the game off the table and to his room. When he returned, she filled their bowls with stew, gave them each a thick slice of buttered bread, and they began to eat. A stab of longing pierced her chest. She would miss the children so much.

Durango pulled off the two-track and followed a roadless course through the desert toward a light flickering in the distance. Travis, in the passenger seat, wearing a windbreaker with FBI in big white letters on the back, handed Durango a two-way police radio.

"Here. Clip this on your belt. Push this button to talk and I'll hear you. Let up on it and you can hear me."

Durango took it and glanced at it. "What about Jack? Can we hear him?" He shifted his weight, hitched his hip and clipped the small hand-held radio to the waistband of his jeans.

"Yes. He's rigged with a voice-activated recorder. We'll be able to monitor any conversation from his end, but he won't hear us."

Travis held out a gun, offering it to Durango. "Do you know how to use this?"

Durango tucked it in his waistband at the small of his back. "It'll come to me," he said lazily, his tone wry and too innocent.

Travis turned to look out the windshield, smiling at Durango's sarcasm.

The distant flickering bloomed into a yard light attached to the corner of Millie Yazzie's house next to the satellite dish. Durango parked in the shadow of the pole barn, and the two men walked across the yard and up the steps into Millie's kitchen. It smelled of fry bread and tomato sauce.

After a warm greeting, Durango's mother and grandmother left the kitchen, went into the living room, and turned on the television. Through the doorway, Durango could see the light from the television screen pulsating over the walls and furniture.

Chair legs scudded on the floor as Durango and Travis settled themselves at the kitchen table. The volume on the TV went down slightly, and Durango smiled to himself as he realized that his mother wanted to listen to what they were going to talk about. *Just like the old days,* Durango thought fondly, remembering other nights at this table with Travis when his over-protective mother pretended to be busy in another room while they plotted adolescent adventures. He lifted his eyes to his friend who was smiling back, sharing the unspoken memory.

Durango unfolded a piece of paper on which he'd drawn a diagram and flattened it on the tabletop. He leaned forward, his eyes studying the familiar outlines of the ancient cliff dwelling that he hadn't seen since he was a teenager, but remembered in detail. Travis joined him, his smooth-skinned face grave, the corners of his mouth turned down, his brow bunched in concentration.

"The cliff dwelling faces southwest and there are forty-five rooms on two levels. There are three ceremonial *kivas* and four defensive towers," Durango explained. "It's virtually untouched. No excavation has been done out there that I know of."

Travis's intelligent eyes traveled over the diagram, taking in the layout. He nodded and Durango went on.

"It's about a mile hike from where we are now. We'll split up at Soda Lookout." Durango's finger tapped the paper. "Here. Then I'll take the western ridge to Coyote Cliff Tower, this way." His finger moved, tracing a line. "You go east to just above the Great Kiva. Right here."

They inspected the sketched diagram.

"There used to be an old timber ladder to get up there," Durango remembered, and looked at Travis. "If it's not there,

263

you'll need to climb over the fallen rocks. It's steep, but you can make it.

"From our locations up there, we'll be able to see Jack down below at Bear Rock. It's the only access to the cliff dwellings from the north. We're high enough that we'll be able to see Elliott when he turns off the jeep road, too. No surprises."

Travis narrowed his eyes, giving close attention. "No surprises," he repeated.

"Jack will bring Sheffield in through the plaza and lead him to this small kiva, right here where it joins this wall. He thinks Jack needs help carrying the pieces out. I'm here." Durango tapped the map. "You're here." Another tap. "When you give the word, we come down this easy slope and make the arrest. He'll be boxed in, nowhere to run."

"Do you know if he carries a weapon?" Travis asked. "Archaeologists sometimes carry a gun with their tools for protection against wild animals when they're digging in an isolated area."

Durango shook his head. "I don't know."

Travis straightened and zipped his windbreaker, but not before Durango caught a glimpse of a .45 in a shoulder holster underneath.

"Let's go," Travis said.

It was so still outside, not even the wind chimes moved.

The boys were in bed in their room at the end of the hall. Doli was snuggled in a quilt on the sofa next to Amanda, still refusing to sleep in her own bed, still refusing to leave Amanda's side.

Amanda ran the back of her fingers lightly over the child's soft cheek and brushed a tousle of hair off her forehead. The little girl didn't stir, her peaceful breathing kept its steady rhythm. The room was dim, lit only by the flames flickering in the fireplace, and the glow of a lamp next to the sofa. Amanda turned the brightness up a notch, and opened the last of Agent Taylor's diaries.

But concentration didn't come. Thoughts of Elliott intruded. Elliott, and the chaos of the past few days. She shook her head at the unreality of it.

It seemed a lifetime ago, but even when they were engaged, she had known little about the details of his work. He had guest lectured at the university, presented papers at academic conferences, and was often out of town on research excavations after which his findings were written up in professional publications. Though she'd never gone along on a dig, she had occasionally accompanied him to a conference when he was presenting. He was very impressive, respected by peers, and admired by students. But by tomorrow, he would be in police custody. He would be ruined.

Doli made a tiny mewling sound in her sleep, and Amanda glanced over. The child's eyelids fluttered, but she didn't waken. Amanda turned back to the diary.

The years following Agent Taylor's unsuccessful attempt to resign his post were no better than his early years on the reservation. Conditions of the Navajos continued to decline. Taylor felt powerless to help them. Government agents had begun to exploit the Navajos in a new way—taking the rugs woven by the women and marketing them to buyers back East. A rumor began that the military had forced some of the Navajo women into prostitution. In addition, there were threats from other tribes.

1875—Many of the Navajos are being kidnapped into slavery by tribes from New Mexico. In retaliation, the Navajos have kidnapped New Mexicans. But when I rescue them and try to return them to their families, they escape and run back to their Navajo homes where they are taken in as adopted family members, not slaves.

All of a sudden Amanda's skin prickled, and she looked up as if someone had called her name. She sat still a moment, listening, then put the diary on the end table, and walked down the hall to the boys' bedroom. They were asleep, arms and legs akimbo, bare feet poking out from under the blankets. She straightened their bedcovers, tucked them in, and stood a moment, looking at their faces.

The tiniest whisper of unease brushed the skin on the back of her neck, and she shivered slightly as if someone had imperceptibly stroked a hand down the hair on the back of her head. With a final glance at the sleeping boys, she withdrew to the living room.

Her eyes were on the diary, but her brain wasn't taking in the words, struggling instead to catch a memory. There was something she had to remember, something she was supposed to do. A vague disquiet pressed down on her as she turned the page.

1876—Bitter quarrels between the Navajos and white settlers cause daily disruption. Whites do not want to settle next to the reservation. The government is considering moving some of the Navajos and appropriating some of the best grazing land for the railroad, and to satisfy the white settlers.

Two years later, Taylor had had enough.

1878—My efforts have come to nothing and my health is failing. I gave Littlestar the deed to the plot of land awarded me by the government and have tendered my resignation from my post.

Amanda stared at the words, her thoughts churning. *He gave Littlestar his land.* She wondered where it was. Agent Taylor had never mentioned its exact location except to say it adjoined the reservation boundary. Could the Littlestar in the diary be related to Durango's grandmother? Anticipation grew as she read on.

This time, the government accepted Taylor's resignation, but did not appreciate his comments and suggestions on how to improve the lot and living conditions of the Navajos. Taylor left with a reprimand and a blemish on his record.

*1879—*My days as agent are at an end. With a sense of failure and loss, I leave for California next week. Bliss refuses to leave with me as she has fallen in love with Littlestar and they wish to marry. I have been unsuccessful in changing her mind, so gave my blessing to the marriage since it is the only way to keep her safe in these unstable days of white and Indian unrest. I know Littlestar will protect her.

After reading the final entry, she gazed into the fire. Waves of hope washed over her. Could it be Durango's property that Agent Taylor was writing about? If so, would the court accept the diary as proof of ownership?

And there was something else, something that brought excitement to her heart. If this was Durango's land, then it appeared that one of his ancestors had married a white woman.

The face of Bernice Littlestar came quickly to mind, her gray eyes signifying the likelihood of an Anglo ancestor somewhere in her lineage. Amanda let a thread of possibility unravel, then closed her mind to it, afraid to project the implications of such a union and what it might mean to Durango.

The remaining pages of the diary were blank, but letters and papers were stuffed in the cloth pocket on the inside back cover. Letters from Bliss to her father, creased and yellowed with age, told of the birth of Bliss and Littlestar's son, the home they'd built on the property Taylor had given them, the trading post they'd opened on the road leading to the reservation. Life had improved for them, but very little for the Navajos living inside the boundaries.

A copy of Taylor's final resignation letter and the government's mean-spirited acceptance, as well as a hand drawn map was mixed in with the personal letters. Someone had sketched a rudimentary Taylor-Littlestar genealogy on a piece of parchment. Some of it was written in Navajo and she couldn't read it.

She put it aside and unfolded the map, being careful not to let it fall apart under her fingers where the folds had cracked with age. The lines drawn on the page were smudged and faded, but she could make out the San Juan River and a single road. The mesas were marked with Xs, and some of the monuments were named. A dotted line defined an irregular plot of land, but she couldn't make sense of it, couldn't read the words, and couldn't place the landmarks.

Her thoughts suddenly redirected to the dogs. Something about the dogs was bothering her, and she realized with a start that she had forgotten to feed them.

But there was something else. They were too quiet. She hadn't heard a sound from them, not even the tick-tick-tick of their nails on the patio tile.

Setting the diary aside, she went to the sliding doors and opened the drapes, expecting to see four hungry dogs, but they weren't there.

She put her face to the glass and cupped her hands around her eyes to block the reflection from the inside light. Her eyes scanned the patio, but saw nothing. She slid the door open and stepped outside. The air was cool, soothing on her skin. Beyond the low patio wall, she saw one of the dogs stretched out on the sand. Moving closer, she realized it was Diamond, the young female.

Alarmed, she knelt in the sand next to the animal and discovered the dog wasn't breathing. Its head was thrown back, and foam and vomit coated its mouth and seeped into the sand. Amanda's eyes swept the ground near the dog, and when she saw the partially eaten raw hamburger, the hair on her arms came alive.

She stood and stared into the cavernous darkness, then walked hesitantly to the edge of the light. She saw three more dark forms lying several yards away, the other dogs and they were dead, too. Hunger had persuaded them to breech the electronic barrier when someone tempted them with poisoned meat.

Comprehension exploded in her brain, and she felt a hot flash of terror. For what seemed like an ungodly long moment, she was frozen in place. Then she turned and raced back to the house just as Doli's scream split the night.

Jack Rice stood at the base of the rock shaped like a bear watching TV, shifting his weight back and forth. He was uncomfortable. The tape securing the recording equipment under his clothing made the skin of his chest and back itch. He tried to ignore the irritation, but it was too much for him and he scratched, fully aware that he dare not do so in front of Elliott.

He pulled back his sleeve and read his watch by the light of the moon. Another half-hour to wait. As desperate as Elliott was to get his hands on those artifacts, Jack had expected him to be early.

Startled, Jack spun when something snapped behind him. He thought he saw a shadow moving in the rocks, but when he narrowed his eyes and looked hard, he didn't see anything.

God, he was jumpy. He wished he could get this over with,

yet at the same time dreaded what would happen to him later. That little detail was open to question. Agent Dance hadn't exactly offered him immunity, and the idea of going to prison made Jack's stomach roll. The thought that he might die there made him want to get in his van and take off.

But, no, he wouldn't do that. He couldn't let Elliott get away with killing that professor. If he did, the daughter might end up dead, too. He didn't want that on his conscience. He had a lot on his conscience as it was, but he never killed anyone.

Jack shuffled his feet, impatient for this to be over. Durango and Travis were somewhere up there in the darkness. All Jack had to do was take Elliott to the kiva. Durango and Travis would do the rest.

He tensed and jerked his head at a rustling in the shadows. Nothing. Jeez, he was jumpy.

Amanda stood in the doorway, staring into the living room, too frightened to move, too sick to cry. Elliott was clutching Doli against his chest, one arm around her waist, pinning her arms, his other hand pressed tightly over the little girl's mouth, smothering her muffled cries. Doli's eyes, snapping with fear, locked on Amanda and pleaded for help as she squirmed and kicked wildly.

"Put her down," Amanda said, her voice quaking. "Please don't hurt her."

"Tell her not to scream," he said. His eyes were hard as he glared at her. A chill shock held her immobile.

"For God's sake, Elliott. She's only a child. You're scaring her!"

The hand over Doli's face tightened, and panic flicked into his eyes. "I said tell her not to scream!"

Amanda cast an anxious glance at the hallway leading to the boys' room. She didn't want to wake them. Taking slow careful breaths to quell her own fear, she held out a soothing hand to Doli.

"Don't cry, sweetheart, okay? If you don't cry, you can come to me."

At that, a dark scowl crossed Elliott's face, and he backed up a step. Doli renewed her squirming.

"It's the only way," insisted Amanda. Rising terror fractured her voice. "Please let me have her."

Reluctantly, Elliott set the child on the floor. When he removed his hand from her mouth, she flew into Amanda's outstretched arms, her eyes and mouth scrunched up with the effort of not screaming.

"There, there, baby," crooned Amanda, hugging her and stroking her head. "I've got you now. You're safe." She glowered at Elliott. "No one is going to hurt you."

She faced Elliott with an angry stare. Something was wrong with his face. None of his features fit right. The flesh looked haggard, lines were visible around his icy eyes. His skin was ashy with tension. She thought she was looking at a stranger, and in a way, she was. This was not the Elliott she knew.

"What do you want, Elliott? Why are you here?"

The sound of her voice was enticing. It excited Elliott and started an insistent tug in his groin.

Invading Durango's private territory had seemed just as important to Elliott as keeping his secrets, just as important as getting his hands on Bell's southwestern artifacts collection, but now that he was here, he wasn't sure what he was going to do.

He looked around the room at the stucco walls and open beam ceiling. Hanging on the wall were rugs he recognized as Navajo. His gaze moved to Amanda. Her eyes were glossy with fear, and she was holding the little girl as if the child were her own. Amanda was part of Durango's territory now, and that presented a wide range of possibilities that he'd first begun thinking about during the long hours in his hideout.

But right now, something bothered him. He didn't remember coming here. Sometimes it seemed as though his body and mind functioned independently. He'd come back to himself feeling as though he'd been asleep when he knew he hadn't. Sometimes only seconds would have passed, sometimes whole minutes. These episodes of blank memory were becoming increasingly more frequent, and they terrified him.

Amanda was looking at him, waiting for him to say something, and he shook himself out of a near stupor.

"I want you to come back with me," he answered. "We can still get married, pick up where we left off."

His hand went into his pocket and pulled out the .45 he usually carried in the truck. He didn't remember putting it in his pocket, and now it was in his hand. "I'm prepared to use force, if necessary."

He realized immediately that was a stupid thing to say. If he forced her to come with him, the first thing she'd do when they got back to California was tell everyone. Her stepfather would pitch a fit and say he'd screwed up. Again. Her mother would call the police. The police would ask a lot of questions and then . . .

His thoughts whirled out of control and panic gripped him. The hand holding the gun began to shake, and with a sickening twist in his gut, he realized there was no way he could take her back to California with him.

A sinking feeling started in the pit of Amanda's stomach. The quiet menace in his voice took her breath away.

My God, he's crazy. Only sheer effort of will allowed her to keep the fear from showing on her face.

She was still standing in the open patio door, half in and half out. It entered her mind to turn and flee, and her body flexed to take the first step, but James and Eric were asleep down the hall. She couldn't leave them.

Elliott's hand trembled, and he waved the gun. "Get away from the doorway," he said. "Sit down so we can talk."

She walked to the sofa, picked up the quilt and wrapped it around Doli, then sat down holding the child close.

Elliott moved around in front of the fireplace and stood staring at her with an unreadable expression. Gritty silence dragged on.

She thought of Durango and Travis out at the ruins. They were expecting Elliott to be there with Jack. She wondered how long they would wait for him to show up.

She knew she had to respond to Elliott, but didn't want to say anything to set him off. She had to keep the children safe. She should probably try to make a deal with him. Agree to go along with him if he'd let the children stay here. Maybe if she kept talking, she could stall for time until she figured something out.

A reply was forming on her lips when Elliott's eyes widened and his gaze jumped over her shoulder. With dread tightening her stomach, she turned around to see James and Eric standing in the hallway. James was holding a shotgun and it was pointed right at Elliott.

The moon slid behind a stray cloud and high on top of Coyote Cliff Tower two men peered over the rampart to the trail that headed toward the ruins from the south.

"Here comes Durango," whispered Larry.

"Oh, jeez," Albert croaked. "He's got Travis with him."

"We're busted," said Larry.

Albert thought a moment, then pushed away from the sandstone block wall, and headed for the ladder that led to the lower levels.

"Come on, let's try and head him off."

Durango tensed, his ears alert, then a soft sound behind him made him freeze. He reached for the .45 and pulled it out, pointing it skyward as he dove into the shadows.

The soft sound became soft footsteps, coming closer. His muscles went taut with anticipation, his heart thundered. Every cell and fiber of his body coiled to spring. Two dark figures emerged from the other side of the boulder.

He leaped onto the path, his legs braced, his gun pointed forward.

"Freeze! Stop right there."

The two figures stopped instantly. "Durango, don't shoot. It's me, Larry."

"What the—"

"And me, Albert."

Durango lowered the gun and his mouth fell open. Blinking with bafflement, he stared stupidly. They were similarly dressed in black cotton shirts with red bands around their heads. His eyes looked them over from top to bottom, taking in their apparel.

"What the hell are you two doing here?"

Just then, the radio on Durango's belt scratched to life and Travis's voice crackled in an urgent whisper.

"Durango? You'd better get over here to the Great Kiva. Right away."

Durango saw the knowing look pass between Albert and Larry as resignation filled their eyes.

"We're busted," said Albert.

"Looks that way," said Larry.

CHAPTER TWENTY

Durango took off down the path and loped across the ridge toward the Great Kiva, Larry and Albert following behind. His feet slipped in the scree mantling the slope, but he used his hands and the toes of his boots to scrabble up the incline to the second level of the cliff dwelling.

"What is it? What happened?" he asked, breathing hard as he joined Travis on top of the wall of the Great Kiva.

The cedar log roof that had once covered the kiva and the pilasters supporting it had rotted away long ago, and Durango followed Travis's gaze down to the floor of the ceremonial space. Flames dancing in a huge firepit dug into the earth bathed the faces of the people gathered around the fire in a golden glow. Fifteen or twenty of them, teens to elders, peered up at them in blank though unafraid silence.

Astonishment kicked the air from Durango's lungs and briefly numbed his mind, and for a moment, what he was seeing didn't make any sense. He continued to stare, dumbfounded, as Larry and Albert descended the handmade wooden ladder leading to the kiva floor.

"Come," Larry said to Durango, motioning for him to follow. "Meet our people."

The words *our people* sent genuine disquiet to Durango's brain, and his long legs took the crossbars of the ladder two at a time down to the kiva floor. Travis, looking equally mystified, clattered down behind him.

Durango's eyes traveled over the faces of the assemblage. They weren't all men as he had first thought. Some of them were women and girls. He recognized Jeleeda, the singer from the Rainwater boys' band.

"Hello, Durango," she said. She held her head high, lips parted in a confident smile.

The drummer from the band, seated next to her, waved a salute. He was wearing a black shirt and red headband just like Larry and Albert. Then Durango noticed they were all dressed in similar fashion. Black shirts, red headbands. A sort of uniform. Some of them wore hats.

Through the shadowy gloom, he could distinguish the faces of his students from the cultural preservation club. A teacher from the high school dipped his head in greeting. Two grandmotherly elders he'd seen at Goulding's Grocery sat silent and stone-faced, next to Sani, the old one, a powerful Navajo Medicine Man who gazed back at Durango, stoic and proud as always. And there were others he recognized but didn't know by name.

Bewildered, he turned to Larry and Albert for explanation. The boys looked at each other as if each one wished the other would speak up.

Durango wished someone would speak up and tell him what the hell was going on.

"What is this? Who are these people?"

Albert stepped forward with the air of a proud warrior, and swept his arm, taking in the gathering.

"This is our preservation posse. We are the *Ndaakaaigii*."

Those that walk about, Durango interpreted the Navajo word to himself, but stared at Albert, still not understanding.

"Walk about where? And why? What's a preservation posse?"

"We're doing what you taught us," Albert replied, his tone slightly defensive. "We're protecting our heritage. We walk the desert looking for those who disturb the places where our ancestors lived. And where they died."

It took a moment for that to sink in, then suspicion slithered into Durango's gut, and he narrowed his eyes.

"And what do you do with these people when you find them?" he asked, afraid he wasn't going to like the answer.

Larry spoke up. "We run them off. We take back what they've excavated—"

"Stolen!" interjected Albert.

"And we return the artifacts to their rightful place. If we know who they are, we report the illegal pothunters—"

"Thieves!" Albert corrected.

"We report the thieves to the authorities," Larry conceded, then took a determined stance, his keen eyes searching Durango's face.

Albert straightened his shoulders and lifted his chin defiantly as if he expected someone to argue with what he was about to say. "We're the leaders," he announced proudly.

"I figured that," Durango replied in a droll deadpan.

While he was trying to get a handle on the idea of a secret Navajo traditionalist political action conservancy group, a man separated himself from the gathering and came forward. He was dressed the same as the others, except for the black reservation hat on his head. Coarse, shoulder-length gray hair spiked out from under the wide brim. Firelight glinted off the wide silver band circling the crown.

The man's face was deeply creased and cinnamon brown, but as he got closer, Durango realized the man wasn't Navajo. The flesh around his eyes was wrinkled and leathery, but the eyes themselves were blue, and the deep color of his skin came from too much time in the sun. When the old man smiled, Durango was reminded of Amanda.

"Allow me to introduce myself," the man said. "I'm Dr. Maynard Bell."

An expectant hush blanketed the kiva. Not one person moved. In the light cast by the leaping flames of the fire, they looked like sacred ceremonial statuary.

"Hello? Hello?" The raspy voice coming from the police radio startled everyone, and Durango shook off his shock and darted a look at Travis.

"Hello?" Radio static grated the air.

"That's Noah," Durango blurted. His hand flew to his radio and he keyed the mike and spoke into it.

"Noah? This is Durango."

When there was no reply, he spoke again, his tone urgent, imploring. "Where are you?"

A long pause.

"Noah?"

"Yeah. I'm here. In the gourd house."

An unsettling tremor raced through Durango's body, and he locked eyes with Travis who looked stricken, the color draining from his face.

"Where's Agent Miller?" Travis shouted into the radio, his voice tight with dread.

Noah's words came back shaky and barely discernable.

"He's here in the gourd house. It looks like he's . . . dead."

Amanda froze. The fear in the room became tangible, the air thick and fetid. She could breathe it, taste it on her tongue.

James's grip on the shotgun was steady, but fear danced in his black eyes like bright flames.

"Leave Amanda and my sister alone," he demanded in a voice that despite his best efforts to sound grown up was that of a frightened little boy.

Time stopped. Elliott's eyes were riveted to the shotgun in the boy's hands, and he nervously licked his lips. His own hand, the one holding the gun, trembled.

Headlights burst in through the windows at the front of the house, washing the room, arcing on the walls, then quickly disappearing from sight. Elliott's panic-filled eyes darted around, seeking the source of the intrusion.

Amanda's heart jolted, instantly recognizing the headlights of Noah's car turning into the driveway, then veering off to park next to the gourd house. She opened her mouth to scream, her body gathering itself to make a dash for the front door when a shotgun blast exploded the reading lamp on the table beside her, pitching the room into darkness.

Then, Elliott's gun discharged in an earsplitting roar, and she felt something hot pierce her side. Pain bloomed in a white fog inside her brain, and she tumbled off the sofa to the floor. Doli, yelling at the top of her lungs, spun out of her arms and rolled away, still wrapped in the quilt.

Amanda's head hit the floor with a crack, and a kaleidoscope burst behind her eyes. The noise was deafening. The children were screaming, but she had no idea where anybody was. She wanted to shout at them to run away, but the words jammed up in her throat. In the pandemonium, she wasn't sure they would have heard her.

Ceramic pots shattered to the floor as Elliott thrashed around in the dark, trying to get his hands on her. Furniture was up-ended and knocked across the room, sending framed photographs and potted plants flying. His fingers grazed her ankle as she struggled to pull her pain-riddled body toward the front door. She kicked out wildly at him, her heel connecting with something hard. She guessed—*hoped*—it was his head.

Searing daggers of pain sliced through her ribs into her chest. Just enough illumination drifted in through the windows from the yard lights for her to see the outline of the front door. She dragged her agonized body toward it and reached for the doorknob, just as Elliott fell on top of her.

She wanted to scream, but his hand clamped over her face, crushing her cheeks and nostrils together. Why is he doing this? He couldn't possibly hope to get away with it.

He was crazy.

The children! Where were the children? She tried to look, but all of Elliott's weight pressed down on her and her strength began to give out.

A ceramic bowl shattered against the back of Elliott's head, the shards raining down on her face. One of the boys had hit him with it, yelling at him to let her go. She had a vague awareness of Eric straddling Elliott's back, pulling the hair at the back of his head.

In his attempt to fend off the little boy, Elliott's weight shifted just enough for her to bend her knee and ram it between his legs. Howling with pain, he rolled off her, cupping his crotch with one hand, and swinging a backhanded fist at Eric.

The little boy was sent crashing against a glass-fronted curio case that tilted and threatened to topple over. The glass panes splintered, pieces falling down in slow motion, while Doli renewed her hysterical screaming. James, his wide eyes locked on his brother crumpled on the floor, pressed against the wall, immobilized with terror.

Elliott was writhing on the floor, moaning. Amanda, unable to do more, rolled her head toward the children.

"James," she started, but choked on the blood filling her mouth. "Take Eric and Doli and go get Noah," she said when she could speak.

Paralyzed with fear, the children didn't move, and through a fit of coughing, Amanda pleaded with her eyes for them to run.

Suddenly, Elliott was on her again, and the pain in her ribs seared down to her pelvis, raking her insides with fire as she tried to wrench away. His breath gusted out harsh and hot on her face. One of his hands was twisted in her hair, the other was over her face, preventing her from breathing. She gasped, desperately trying to take in air. The pain in her side was driving her insane, and the room swirled around her.

It took only minutes for them to reach Durango's truck. He flung open the door on the driver's side as if to tear it from its hinges. Travis, yelling into his hand-held radio, threw himself into the passenger seat. Larry and Albert dove into the back as the engine roared to life, and Durango rammed the accelerator to the floor, spinning the tires in the gravel. Travis keyed the radio, calling frantically for his standby agents to go to the Yazzie household to get Amanda and the children.

Durango drove blindly over the bumps and gullies, cursing himself for underestimating Sheffield, and praying he'd get back to the house in time. His heart went dead in his chest at the thought of losing the woman he loved. He tried to remember if he'd told her he loved her before he left. Stupid, stubborn idiot that he was, he probably hadn't. He would personally tear Elliott limb from limb if anything happened to her or the children.

In the back seat, Albert opened his fingers to reveal the handful of red dirt he'd managed to scoop up during the race back to the truck. He spit into his hand, mixing saliva with the dirt. Larry and Travis watched as Albert dragged his forefinger through the mixture, and deliberately drew ocher colored lines over his face, striping his cheeks and forehead.

"Navajos didn't wear war paint," Larry said, scoffing.

Albert snorted derisively. "*Bilagaana* don't know that." When he finished, he turned for Larry's inspection. "How do I look?"

"Scary," Larry conceded.

Strangely, Amanda was aware of a pinprick on her arm even though the cacophony in her head had reached a crescendo.

When the dissonance mellowed into a mere ten thousand church steeples chiming all at once, she thought she heard someone calling her name through a pillow. She supposed that was a funny thing, but couldn't make herself laugh, or even talk. Gradually, she felt like she was floating, oddly disembodied as if her arms and legs had gone hollow.

When the voice got closer, she opened her eyes and stared at Durango. The sight of him warmed and comforted her, but when she tried to move, something stabbed under her ribs and she winced. He winced, too, as if he were the one in pain. His face showed anguish, pale and taut, his dark eyes swimming with tears. His mouth quivered when he said her name.

"Stay with me, Amanda," he mumbled, leaning over her, stroking her hair back from her face. "Oh, baby, please stay with me."

They were the words she'd been waiting to hear, soul affirming words, life changing words, but then she wondered if he meant now, or later. She wanted to ask him what he meant, but couldn't.

Turning her head slightly, she realized Durango was not the only one kneeling beside her. Men and women were tending to her, EMTs or the rescue squad, she couldn't tell which. One of them turned to look at her, and she saw that it was Cammie.

"You're going to be fine," Cammie assured her. "The ambulance is here. I'll go with you. I gave you something for the pain. It should kick in any time."

That was the pinprick she had felt, and what was responsible for this feeling of euphoria sweeping her body.

"Durango?" she whispered. "There's a diary in the living room. I hope it's still there . . ."

"Hush," he said, the word came out thick from his constricted throat. "Don't talk."

A burning sensation raced through her torso, and she held a

breath until it subsided. "You have to read the diary, be-cause . . ."

"Shhh," he said. "We'll talk about it later."

"You always say that," she mumbled, slurring her words.

Just then, gentle hands lifted her onto a gurney. As she was being wheeled away, Durango walked alongside holding her hand, watching her face, his own face twisted with pain. Police cars were parked at all angles on and off the driveway, doors left ajar. Flashing lights painted the trees and the house in washes of red and blue. Policemen were everywhere, rushing in and out of the house.

As the gurney neared the ambulance, she caught a glimpse of Elliott in the back seat of an unmarked car. His head was bent, his hands cuffed behind his back, his shoulders shaking miser-ably. Then she was lifted into the ambulance and couldn't see him anymore.

"How are the kids?" she asked.

"They're mostly okay. A few cuts and bruises, but they're coming to the hospital, too."

Cammie's face appeared next to Durango's. "I'm going to check them over. Don't worry about them, okay? I'll see that they're taken care of."

The ambulance sped out of the driveway, the eerie wail of the siren splitting the night. Durango squeezed her hand and she closed her eyes again. As she was falling into a deep bed of feathers and air, he lifted her hand and brushed his lips across her fingers.

"I love you," he whispered.

Chapter Twenty-One

The sky over the eastern mountains was just beginning to glow as Durango prepared to leave Monument Valley for a ten o'clock meeting with Judge Luke Benson. Amanda, still recovering from her injuries, was going with him, but Durango worried the trip might be too much for her.

"Are you sure you can ride that far?" he asked. "It's a three-hour drive to Monticello. Maybe you should stay here with Nonni."

"No," Amanda replied, straightening her spine as much as the tightly wrapped bandages around her ribs would allow. "I'm fine. Really."

But she moved gingerly, taking shallow breaths, and grimaced a little as he helped her into the pickup. When he reached in to buckle her seatbelt, she gently batted his hands away and did it herself.

He chuckled obligingly at her resolute show of self-reliance. Or was it stubbornness, he considered affectionately, giving her two quick kisses on the lips.

Her eyes were soft when she slid the leather cord holding the charmstone from around her neck, and slipped it over his head. "For protection from your enemy," she said, and kissed him a third time.

Durango climbed behind the wheel, moved the gearshift into first, and drove slowly over the rutted dirt road until he reached the pavement and could pick up speed without fear of jostling her.

Monticello, located near the Old West hideout of Butch Cassidy's Hole in the Wall Gang, was now the seat of government for San Juan County. All the county services as well as the justice center and the jail were housed in a brand new set of pink-and-tan–stuccoed buildings at the foot of Blue Mountain. Included in the complex was the Seventh District Court where land ownership disputes were resolved.

Judge Benson had called an informal preliminary hearing in his chambers prior to scheduling formal courtroom proceedings to review Buck Powell's claim and Durango's counterclaim of ownership of Wild Horse Mesa. He'd been a judge in San Juan County for thirty-five years and was familiar with nearly every square foot of land in the county, both on and off the reservation. And, as he'd explained to Durango over the phone, in all his years on the bench, he'd found that questions of ownership could often be resolved during a good, old-fashioned sit down of the parties involved.

"No need to drag in high-paid, time-wasting lawyers, and tie up a courtroom if it isn't necessary," he'd declared.

When they arrived, Buck was already there. Judge Benson's clerk led them into the judge's private chambers where they took seats at a large round conference table.

In a moment, a door on the far wall opened and Judge Benson hustled in wearing a cowboy hat, cowboy boots, a heavily fringed leather jacket, and a stunning malachite bolo tie. There was enough pure white hair on his head to curl around his ears and lie against his neck. The smile on his deeply tanned face was big and genuine. He greeted them with cheer, hung his hat on a hook by the door, and after introductions were made and small talk dispensed with, got right down to business.

"Now about the question of who owns that land out on Wild

Horse Mesa," he said. "Why don't you tell me what's going on. You can start, Mr. Yazzie."

Durango was aware of the nearly weightless charmstone where it lay on his chest, smooth and cool against his skin. He imagined he could feel it pulsing, surrounding him with protective energy.

He nudged away a flicker of apprehension, sat forward and began, summarizing his family's history in Monument Valley, offering Agent Taylor's personal papers and diaries as evidence in support of his claim. As he spoke, he pointed out passages that expressed Taylor's gratefulness for Littlestar's healing and the subsequent transfer of land to him. He unfolded Taylor's hand-drawn map, interpreted the notations written in Navajo, and identified the sketched landmarks.

"These are pueblo walls. Some are crumbled, but many are still standing. This is a ceremonial structure. Beyond that, here, is a burial ground. On the south acreage, my grandfather built a house and grazed sheep."

Judge Benson peered at the map through gold wire-rimmed glasses, his face set in concentration, listening intently, nodding at intervals.

"Thank you," the judge said when Durango finished. "How about you, Buck. What have you got?"

"I'll keep this brief," Buck replied, exuding self-importance. He outlined his position in a few words, spread blueprints out on the table, and explained his plans for developing the land.

"This land belongs to me, and I can prove it," Buck said. With a screw-you look in Durango's direction, he opened a file folder and took out an official-looking sheet of paper.

From where Durango sat, he couldn't make out the small print, but a whipsnake of dread coiled in his chest when he read the words at the top. *Deed of Trust.* Beside him, Amanda tensed, and flicked him a dark look of worry.

"I believe this speaks for itself," Buck concluded, handing the deed over to the judge.

"Well," Judge Benson said, leaning back from the table with a surprised expression. He took a moment to examine the document. "If you don't mind, I'd like you to leave this with me," he said to Buck. He turned to Durango. "And these diaries and papers, too. I'm going to need a little more time to review them before I give you my decision. You can wait in the anteroom. I shouldn't be long."

After the court clerk's offer of refreshment was declined, Buck fitted himself into a wingchair in the corner, a look of satisfaction on his face. Amanda took a seat next to Durango on a long cowhide sofa, but she was uneasy and her fingers fidgeted in her lap. Durango caught one of her hands, stilling it, and laced his fingers through hers. She was clearly distressed, and so was he. It had never occurred to him that Buck would actually have a deed, and he wondered why Buck hadn't mentioned it before.

When Durango's gaze drifted across the room, Buck intercepted it and held on, refusing to back down. Buck's patronizing expression was bold and insulting, and Durango had to resist the urge to boot his pompous butt out into the lobby.

Minutes went by. A half hour, then an hour, as Durango beat back the despair that tried to settle in his gut. He couldn't imagine telling his mother and grandmother they would have to move off their land. He glanced sidelong at Amanda who, in her effort to avoid Buck's smug look, was staring at a magazine with such intensity she might have burned a hole in the page.

Finally, the court clerk returned. "Judge Benson will see you now."

The judge was waiting for them behind his paper-strewn desk. Several agonizing moments went by while he finished jotting notes on a pad of paper, and when at last he looked up, his expression was unreadable.

After thanking them for waiting, the judge directed his gaze to the corner of the room, his eyes losing focus as if moving back into memory.

"I've been out to Monument Valley many times," he began. "More so when I was younger and could hike a bit. Back then the land was pristine wilderness. Less so now, but we can't escape growth or stop progress, can we? Nor would we want to," he said, answering his own question. "Sometimes we have to suck it up and give the developers their way."

Durango felt Amanda's eyes on him, but he didn't look at her. He was frozen in place, hanging on the judge's words, dread gathering.

"Take this new municipal complex," the judge went on conversationally, stringing his story out. "Too modern according to some folks, too citified and overdone," he said. But then he went on to name some of the amenities that had not been available in the old falling-down brick courthouse.

"Coffee shop in the lobby, restaurant with outdoor seating, music on the plaza, retail shops on the main floor. And public art everywhere." At this last, the judge waved his hand grandly, indicating the lobby and everything else outside his door that was decorated in the familiar Southwest color scheme of pinks, tans, and turquoise.

"But I don't mind it," the judge continued. "I like parking my car in a covered garage out of the sun. I like having a bathroom in my office.

"But beyond that, this new facility is convenient for the townspeople. Why, folks can pay their taxes, renew their driver's license, apply for a marriage license, pay a parking ticket all in one central location. That's the way they do things these days. It's called progress." He looked searchingly at Durango and then at Buck.

Durango pulled in a steadying breath, pummeling down the anger and disappointment building in his chest. Beside him, Amanda's shoulders slumped. A small grin was forming on Buck's face.

Judge Benson rested his elbows on his desk, steepled his fingers, and regarded Buck appraisingly, his gaze an intense laser beam of a stare.

"But that doesn't mean we should build condominiums in the middle of the desert in Monument Valley, and certainly not on an historic site. And especially not on land that doesn't belong to us. There are laws against that."

Buck's self-satisfied smirk fell as the judge continued.

"You have a deed. May I ask where you came up with it after all these years?"

"I found it in my father's belongings after he died. It was tucked in his Bible," Buck huffed in a show of indignation.

Judge Benson shook his head in gentle derision, his face solemn. Then he looked at Durango.

"I understand your mother and grandmother are still living out there."

"Yes, they were born there, as were generations of Yazzies before them. My sister and I were both born and raised in that house. There was never any question of ownership. No one ever challenged us before."

"Of course not," said the judge as if Durango had just stated the obvious. "Because clearly it's your land."

Utter confusion washed Buck's startled features. "Just a minute, Judge. I've got a deed—"

Buck's protest faltered as Judge Benson's stern voice cut him off.

"That land was given to an ancestor of the Yazzie family more than a hundred and twenty-five years ago. They've had continuous possession. There's no question about the chain of title.

Based on this diary, the Yazzie family has superior right. I've ordered a new deed drawn up and recorded backdated to 1878."

Durango eased out a breath that had backed up in his throat, relief replacing the disappointment constricting his chest.

Buck started to argue again, but Judge Benson interrupted, speaking sadly. "Buck, I remember your daddy as an honest man. What the hell happened to you?"

Buck's jaw dropped. "What?"

"That deed you gave me is a fake."

"No, it's not. I—"

"I've been looking at deeds since before you were born. Did you think I wouldn't know a fake when I saw one?"

"I . . . I . . ." Buck stammered.

Judge Benson pressed a button on his telephone console and spoke to his clerk. "Send 'em in, Mary Lee."

Two San Juan County deputies came in, walked directly to Buck and addressed him politely. Paralyzed by shock, Buck didn't resist when they put his hands behind his back, snapped handcuffs around his wrists, and led him out the door.

After they were gone, Judge Benson shook his head in mild consternation, the glint in his eye hinting of a private joke in his mind. "Well, that was a slam dunk," he said, half to himself, his lips quirked in amusement.

Then, "Sorry, Durango. Didn't mean to worry you none. I knew what my decision was going to be. I just couldn't help stringin' ole Buck along. He always was a pain in the ass, even as a little squirt. His granddad and I were friends," the judge added by way of explanation.

Judge Benson shook hands with Durango, then turned to Amanda and took her hand. "It was nice meeting you, my dear. Good luck to you both." His eyes glittered with good wishes. "And, Durango. Give my regards to your mother, will you?"

Judge Benson removed his hat from the hook by the door,

settled it firmly on his head, and promptly left the room.

Elation was erasing the anxiety from Amanda's heart as she headed with Durango across the satillo-tiled courtyard of the municipal complex toward the tables on the restaurant patio that Judge Benson had referred to.

Offices and shops lined the edge of the plaza, and in the center of the courtyard near the fountain, glass cases and display tables held Native American baskets, rugs, pottery, and jewelry, all handmade work fashioned by local artists. Paintings and sculptures hung from temporary walls erected and angled for best viewing. Some of the artists stood next to their work, answering questions or helping customers make a selection.

"Where do you suppose Buck got that deed of trust?" Amanda asked as they claimed a table in the shade of an umbrella.

"That's what I'd like to know," Durango answered, accepting a menu from a waiter and immediately becoming engrossed.

Amanda was about to comment further when a familiar face out on the plaza caught her eye. Quickly she stood, and leaving Durango at the table, hurried out to a display of handwoven baskets and glazed pottery. Reeling, she stared into the face of the artist, the woman she'd seen at Twin Rocks Canyon so many months before.

"*Ya at eeh,* Amanda," the old woman said, a smile crinkling her aged face.

Amanda's heart gave a leap. "It's you!"

"What is it? What's wrong?" Durango came rushing after her, and as he approached, acknowledged the woman standing beside her display table. "Oh, hello, Mary."

Openmouthed, Amanda turned and stared at him in astonishment. "You know her?"

"Yes," he said, and greeted the old woman with a gentle hug.

"Amanda, this is Mary Cly. She's a member of *Ndaakaaigii*."

Amanda looked back at the elder, remembering the day she'd been summoned to Twin Rocks Canyon by a note left on the door of her new apartment.

Mary Cly looked at Amanda, but spoke to Durango in Navajo. When she finished, he repeated her words in English.

"She said she's sorry she ran away that day. She'd asked you to meet her because she wanted to set your mind at ease about your father. But someone was watching you from the ridge, and she became frightened. She tried to warn you."

"Please tell her thank you," Amanda said, talking around the lump in her throat.

Durango did as she asked, and the old woman smiled and spoke again. Amanda could hear the warmth in the words.

"She said she is happy you are reunited with your father," Durango told her.

"Thank you," Amanda said again, her heart swelling with emotion.

Mary spoke again and Durango tilted his head, listening. Then he smiled at Amanda. "She has a present for us."

Mary selected a vase from the collection on her table, and held it out, offering it to Amanda. The vase, embossed with ears of corn, had a handle on each side and two spouts. Again, Mary spoke in Navajo, looking at Amanda, but directing her words to Durango so he could interpret.

"It's a wedding vase," he explained to Amanda. "In Navajo sacred tradition, the vase is filled with water or herbal tea, and the bride and groom drink from it to toast their union. First, they each sip from one side, then the vase is turned, and they each sip from the other side. She wants us to have it. And, oh," he added. "The corn is a fertility symbol."

As Amanda took the vase, a rush of happiness quickened her heart. She put her arm around the old woman's shoulders and held her in a loving hug. "Thank you so much," she said to Mary. "I'll treasure it forever." Then, "Tell her, Durango."

Durango interpreted, and Amanda held the woman's gaze a moment longer. A customer who had been admiring Mary's work approached with credit card in hand, so Amanda and Durango bid Mary good-bye and took their leave.

Amanda turned toward the patio and the umbrella table they had just vacated, but Durango took her arm.

"Come on," he said. "This way."

"What's this way?" she asked, letting him lead her across the plaza.

"Didn't you hear Judge Benson say we can get a marriage license here?"

Amanda stopped in her tracks so suddenly a twinge of pain poked her ribs.

"Durango Yazzie! Is that your idea of a marriage proposal?" Her tone was scolding, but a wild fluttering began in the region of her heart.

Durango stopped, looking shamefaced. "No," he replied, reining in his enthusiasm. "No, it's not a proper proposal. I'm sorry."

He reached for her hand, and led her to one of the marble benches near the Spanish fountain and settled her on the edge of it. Deliberately, he took the vase and set it on the bench between them. When he put her hand to his lips, his eyes shone like moonlight in crystal water.

"Will you marry me?" he asked.

Exhilaration surged through Amanda and she was filled with joy. "Oh, yes, I certainly will marry you!"

He wrapped his arms around her and she winced as he squeezed a little too hard, but she didn't pull away. In the middle of their embrace, a light smattering of applause broke out from a few smiling passersby who had overhead Durango's marriage proposal.

"Now, let's go get that marriage license," Durango said, "before we draw a real crowd."

EPILOGUE

Two Years Later

Amanda had never been happier. All the people she loved would be in her home today. Her heart swelled with joy as she cuddled the newest member of the family and stroked the raven-black hair fringing the tiny face that, except for the cornflower blue eyes, was a miniature duplicate of Durango's.

"Hello, Taylor Littlestar Yazzie. You've made my world complete."

Francina tiptoed into the nursery and sat on the loveseat next to Amanda and the baby. Love spilled from her eyes as she admired her four-week-old grandson.

Amanda smiled at her mother. "Do you want to hold him?"

Francina's face lit. "Of course, I do." Amanda slipped the blanketed bundle into Francina's arms. Francina cradled the baby against her breast and whispered, "He's so beautiful."

"Yes, he is."

Amanda tried to remember the last time she had felt this close to her mother. Not since she was a little girl, and she gloried in this shared moment. There had been way too few of them, but she planned to make up for that.

New mother and new grandmother, side by side, each in their own thoughts, gazed adoringly at the baby. His eyelids fluttered, and he peered back at them for a moment, then closed his eyes and dropped off again.

"Your father is happy to be back," Francina said after a moment. "It was wonderful of Durango to ask him to be curator of the Cultural Center. He's very grateful to be able to stay on to work with the two of you."

"I'm grateful he's here," Amanda replied.

Miraculously, it seemed, she had her father back, too. Thanks to Larry and Albert Rainwater. After they'd witnessed Elliott's attempted murder of her father at Comb Ridge, they risked their own lives to pull him from the flaming wreck and take him to safety. Her father had suffered weeks of amnesia, and they called on Sani's powerful medicine to heal him. It was Sani who had suggested they keep him safe until Elliott was no longer a threat, and it was Sani who'd spoken to her in Navajo when she found him stranded on the side of the road. He couldn't resist trying to ease her mind about her father's safety, while at the same time keeping *Ndaakaaigii* secret.

She smiled remembering how furious Durango had been when he discovered what the boys had been up to with *Ndaakaaigii*. But later, after he thought about it, he realized their intentions though ill-advised, were admirable. He'd been the one, after all, to teach them the importance of preserving their heritage. The boys just took their dedication to an unexpected level. And, in the end, no harm had been done.

In fact, a great deal of good had come of it. Hundreds of artifacts had been salvaged and returned to their places of origin, or failing that, displayed in the new Navajo Cultural Center she had designed. When her father agreed to take the job as curator, it had freed Durango to combine filmmaking and teaching into a satisfying career. His first historical documentary, *Ndaakaaigii,* the story of Larry and Albert's preservation posse, was being featured on PBS tonight. After dinner, they would all watch it together.

At the sound of an audible sigh from Francina, Amanda lifted her gaze and saw a flicker of sadness cross her mother's face.

She laid a gentle hand on her mother's arm.

"What is it?" she asked.

A line creased the fine brow and Francina sighed again. "I was just thinking . . ." Her voice floated off.

"About Daniel?"

Francina nodded, tears threatening. Though her mother had immediately filed for divorce from her stepfather when the nature of his business venture with Elliott was revealed, Amanda knew she harbored some regret at the pain that had been inflicted.

"How could I not have known what he and Elliott were up to?" Francina's voice was constricted in her throat, and she sniffed.

"But you couldn't have known, Mother. Don't blame yourself. I didn't know either. They went to great pains to hide their secrets from both of us."

She slid her arm around her mother's shoulders and kissed her lightly on the cheek. "It's all over now. Please don't think about it anymore. Daniel and Elliott are in jail paying for their crimes."

Though Daniel had been calling the shots, Elliott had done the dirty work, and they'd both raked in hundreds of thousands of dollars from the Native American antiquities black market.

After his arrest, Elliott confessed everything. That's when she found out he had followed her and Sallie to Comb Ridge. He claimed that his foot had slipped and knocked a rock loose, accidentally setting off the rockslide that killed Sallie. Nevertheless, they charged him with her death as well as looting and the attempted murder of her father.

She hugged her mother again. "Let's not think about the past. Let's only think about today and the future. I have my father back in my life, I have you, and I have an adorable baby . . ."

Her voice drifted off as she looked at the circle of diamonds in the wedding ring on her finger. "I have a wonderful man who loves me . . ." And a place to belong, she added silently, a place where I fit in.

Francina nodded thoughtfully. "When will the adoption be final?" she asked.

"That's the other reason to celebrate," said Amanda, her eyes shining. "Sharron voluntarily relinquished her parental rights, and the judge will sign the papers tomorrow. James, Eric, and Doli will be ours, though I feel they already are."

"Oh, Amanda, I'm so happy for all of you."

"Thank you, Mother. My family is now complete." An overwhelming surge of emotion washed over her, and she wondered if it was possible to be too happy.

At that moment, she heard voices coming from downstairs. The others were arriving.

Noah and Cammie were married now, Cammie plump with a new life growing inside her, Noah beside himself with happiness about being a father. But he was also glowing with the success of his new film for which Larry and Albert had written the music, and in which their band, Harmony, had played the soundtrack. The CD of the soundtrack was topping the musical charts, and there was talk of Harmony going on tour in the fall.

The boys were making a lot of money now and spending most of their time in Los Angeles because of their work, but their hearts remained in Monument Valley. They'd made a major contribution to the Cultural Center and were financing a community desert patrol to continue the work they'd begun with *Ndaakaaigii.*

A burst of childish enthusiasm announced the arrival of Judy and Jeremiah Moon, followed by increased splashing in the pool as the Moon children joined James, Eric, and Doli in the water.

Amanda heard Durango welcome his mother and his grand-mother.

"Let's go down and greet the guests," Amanda said. Her mother nodded and laid the baby on his back in the bassinet. Amanda checked the baby monitor, then mother and daughter slipped out to join the others in the living room of Amanda's new home on Wild Horse Mesa.

After an exchange of kisses and hugs, everyone moved onto the deck to admire the view of the cliff dwellings.

Judy put an arm around Amanda and squeezed lightly. "Thank you for helping us keep our land, Amanda. If you hadn't found proof of the Yazzie family ownership during your research, Buck Powell would have destroyed the ruins, and there would be condominiums out there now."

Jeremiah cocked his leg, braced a foot on a low crossbar of the deck railing and gave Durango a comradely pat on the shoulder. "Yeah," he agreed, looking at Amanda with a teasing gleam in his eye. "And it's a good thing Durango read those diaries and found out he had a white ancestor, so you could be part of our family."

Everyone roared with laughter as Durango exchanged a long-suffering look with Jeremiah and reached for Amanda. He drew her close and nuzzled her hair.

"I would have married her anyway," he told them, slipping a hand down to pat her rear. His gaze veered off toward the cliff dwellings.

"Has Jack ever forgiven you for leaving him there that night?" asked Jeremiah after a brief silence. In all the excitement, no one had remembered that Jack was waiting at the north canyon under the rock that looked like a bear watching television.

"It took him six months to forget about it, but, yeah, he's coming over later."

All eyes turned at the roar of an engine and a cloud of dust approaching the house.

"Here comes Larry and Albert," Amanda's father said excitedly, making his way down the steps to the lower level to meet them.

"I think your father wants to adopt those boys," Durango said with a laugh. Amanda smiled and nodded as a new Land Rover pulled up below, and Larry and Albert climbed out, their arms loaded with packages gift wrapped in baby paper.

"Guess what?" Albert shouted up, then proceeded to tell them before anyone could take a guess. "The CD went platinum!"

Amidst cheers and hugs and kisses, a sound came from the baby monitor, and instantly Durango and Amanda exchanged glances.

"I'll get him," said Durango.

Amanda's heart sang with delight as she watched her husband take long strides inside to get his son and thought she'd never known a more devoted father.

She stood there taking in the sight of the people she loved so much. The love in the air was palpable, the acceptance unconditional. She caught a glance flash between her mother and her father, one of many she'd noticed during this visit. It was hard to tell what those looks meant, and she didn't want to read too much into them, but it crossed her mind to wonder if there was any spark left between the two. She sincerely hoped there was. Only time would tell for sure, but right now, life was good in Monument Valley.

AUTHOR'S NOTE

My time as a Volunteer in Service to America (VISTA) on the Navajo Reservation in Monument Valley, Utah, was the inspiration for the events in this book. I lived in the same rooms and apartments in which Amanda took up residence, ate at the same restaurants mentioned, had my breath taken away by the same wondrous views of the desert, marveled at the same spectacular sunsets and sunrises, experienced the same wonder and terror of complete isolation, total silence, and billions and billions of stars in a jet-black sky. There does exist a gourd house. Twin Rocks is real, and so is Comb Ridge. Travelers on the highway will see The Three Sisters, The Mittens, and a rock formation that looks like a bear watching TV with a rabbit. Monument Valley High School is located exactly as depicted in this book, and I salute principal Pat Seltzer for her unfailing dedication to her students.

However, I did not intend this book to be a travel guide. For the sake of the story, I took some license with the actual layout and geography of the area as it relates to the existence and location of Durango's house, the Puebloan ruins, and the Yazzie family land. There really is a Wild Horse Mesa, but it is in San Luis, Colorado, not Monument Valley, Utah.

The artifact I call the charmstone in the story is an actual 1100-year-old stone pendant I personally uncovered while working on a University of Arizona–sponsored archaeological dig at an Anasazi site in Cortez, Colorado, a few months after completing my VISTA assignment.

    I plan to return to Monument Valley in another book where I'll reveal secrets about some of the people in this story.

ABOUT THE AUTHOR

C. C. Harrison lives in Anthem, Arizona. When she's not writing, reading, or working out at the gym, she can be found in the mountains of Colorado or some far-flung corner of the Southwest.